PAPARAZZI

A Becky White Thriller

Book 2

JO FENTON

BLOODHOUND
— B O O K S —

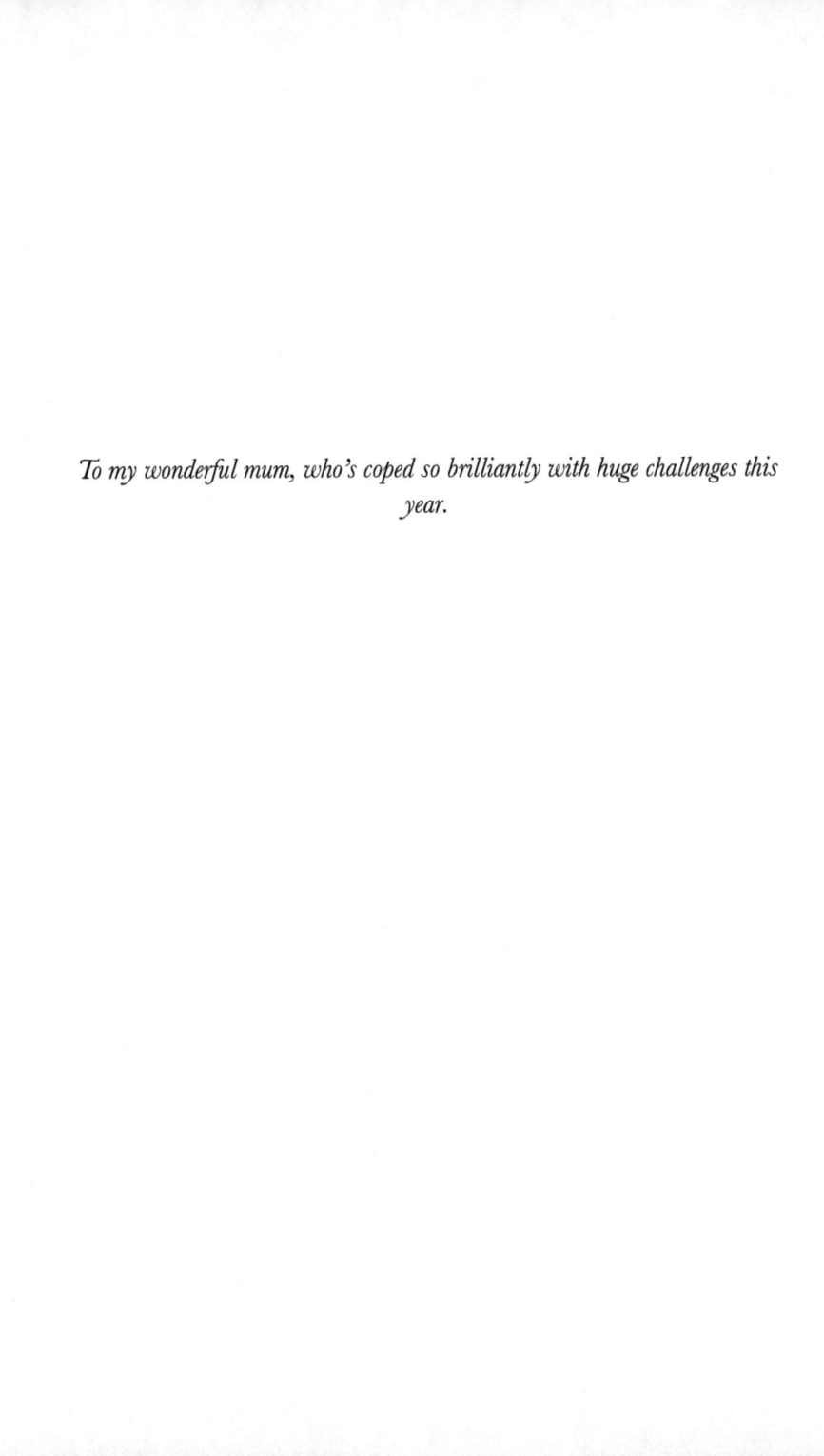

To my wonderful mum, who's coped so brilliantly with huge challenges this year.

Chapter One

As I watch from afar, I know this is the one.

I allow the camera to hang by its strap as I wipe clammy hands on my black jeans. The camera returns to its position, ready to snap the essential photos.

The music blares out in the club, and no one notices as I move around to capture the necessary angles. Once complete, I relax my grip and admire the view. The object is perfection; there is only one flaw. Possession is not yet in sight...

Chapter Two

There's a loud bang outside, and I drop the vase I'm drying. The flowers died three days ago. The vase lies in smithereens on the floor. Instead of clearing up the mess, I crouch down on the floor and clasp my trembling arms around my chest.

The doorbell rings. I can't move.

"Mum, are you getting that?" My youngest daughter Cheryl pokes her head around the kitchen door. "Blimey, what happened? Okay, stay there. I'll get the door."

The bell rings again, and I hear Cheryl fumbling with the latch.

"Mum, it's for you. You'll have to come to the door, sorry."

I take a deep breath. The bang must have been a car door. *Calm down, Becky, no gunshots. Not here.*

I stand up and walk towards the kitchen door, crunching glass under my trainers. In the hall, Cheryl still guards the door, but stands back when I arrive, to reveal a petite woman in a sodden grey jacket and trousers. She looks vaguely familiar.

"Becky! How are you doing, hen? Do you remember me?"

It's the Scottish accent that takes me back to when I was a student.

"Joanna! Oh my God, how are you?" I step back, realising that my unexpected visitor is dripping in the torrential, freezing rain. "Come inside and get warm and dry." I regret the words as soon as they've left my mouth. Manners before survival? That won't keep me alive for long.

Joanna picks up a huge black suitcase and brings it in. I stare at it in shock. Is she planning to stay?

"Thanks, hen. Sorry about the baggage. If you can't squeeze me in, I'll find a hotel…"

I hesitate. I should let her get that hotel, but I look at her more closely. She doesn't look well. We were close friends for a couple of years before life and distance got in the way, and we drifted, as people often do.

"Don't be daft. Anyway, my eldest is away at Uni. I'll make up her bed for you."

"I'll do it in a bit, Mum. You take your friend into the lounge by the fire. I'll sort out the kitchen and put the kettle on."

"You're a sweetie, Cheryl, thanks." I glance down at my hands. The trembling has eased off now. I take Joanna's coat from her, hanging it over the newel post at the bottom of the stairs. "Come in and make yourself comfortable."

Seated in the brown leather armchairs, as close to the gas fire as possible, we sit in silence for a moment. Thousands of questions race through my brain, but I focus my gaze on my visitor. She hasn't aged particularly well. I seem to recall she's a year or two older than I am, so fifty or thereabouts. She looks more like sixty; her hair is still black, but now streaked with grey. She's too thin, and lines cross her face, marring the beautiful features that I remember. There's a wariness in her expression too, though perhaps that's from her sudden intrusion on an acquaintance whom she's not seen for nearly thirty years.

"How did you find me?" I ask the most important question first, my heart hammering loudly as I wait for the crucial answer. I've done my best this year to wipe away any traces of my existence.

"With difficulty. You didn't make it easy, hen. You're not on Facebook or Twitter or LinkedIn. I found Dan, but he said he couldn't give me your contact details. I wasn't sure if he meant couldn't or wouldn't, but I sensed I wasn't going to have any success with him. I finally tracked down your brother, Ian, through your dad's business. I remember you telling me about them, and I was desperate. Ian took pity on me, but he did warn me it was for my use only." She looks faintly guilty, but it's not her fault. Ian was always a soft touch. I need to remind him of the importance of keeping my secrets.

"Okay. You've found me now. I'll explain properly one day, but you need to understand. Anonymity is crucial round here. We've changed the family name, returning to my maiden name. Perhaps that was a mistake, but then Ian wouldn't have differentiated whether you'd called me Becky White, or Becky Wiseman. I was never big on social media, but it was handy for keeping in touch with the likes of Dan and Sanj. I've lost touch with everyone else from Uni." I fall quiet, and silence reigns until Cheryl walks in with a tray of tea and biscuits.

"I forgot to ask, are you okay with tea?" she asks Joanna anxiously.

"Yes, sure. Thanks so much." Joanna smiles at her, and she retreats out of the room.

Bless her. She's not used to visitors other than her own or her sister's friends.

"How old is she? And how old is your eldest?" Joanna accepts the cup of tea I hand to her, but declines a biscuit.

"Cheryl's fourteen. Alison is just nineteen and is at

University in Nottingham. She wants to be a pharmacist like her dad. He's at work now, but he'll be back soon." I glance at the window where the rain continues to beat down. It's nearly dark, as expected for late January in Manchester.

Matt will be home at five, when he finishes his shift at the supermarket Pharmacy where he's providing cover for someone with norovirus. He works at the local hospital during the week, but is almost always on call for extra cover in the area – particularly at the moment. While I'm not working, we need to get money somehow. Uni's not cheap, and the girls always need clothes.

I rouse myself to ask Joanna, "Do you have kids?"

"One son. Will. Grown up now. He's twenty-six and has a little one of his own. Although he doesn't see his daughter very often. Her mum ran off with another man while she was pregnant with Chloë. Bitch."

"What about your husband?" I ask tentatively. I suspect all is not well, but if Joanna's going to stay here, she needs to be open about what's going on. There's a limit to the number of secrets that one house can hold.

"He ran off when I was diagnosed with breast cancer."

I can't hide the shock from my face. But it helps to explain the shortness of her hair and that pinched, unhealthy look.

"I'm okay now. All surgery, chemo and radiotherapy are done. But I had a falling-out with my landlord and needed to get away."

"What about your house? You had a house, didn't you, from your dad? Don't tell me the witch got it in the end?"

"My stepmother? God no. Do you know, I'd almost rather she had. Instead, I married the prick who fathered Will. I put up with him through his gambling and alcohol addictions, and his many affairs with blonde bimbos. The bastard gambled away all our money, until we had to sell the house to pay his debts, and to live. Six months after that, I got my diagnosis, and he buggered off." She grimaces. "At least the bastard got his comeuppance. I heard he's in prison now. Locked up for debt, and GBH – he beat up the bailiffs when they came round to his new girlfriend's house. Git!"

I'm speechless. I can't help feeling sorry for her. Impossible not to. But how long will she want to stay?

"What made you decide to come to Manchester and find me?"

"I want us to set up a detective agency together," she says with a grin. "You're the only detective I know."

My head fills with images, flashing and intense. They creep in any time of the day or night. A warehouse. Gunfire. A colleague dead on the ground.

I wipe my sweaty palms on my jeans and glance at Joanna.

"I can't do it."

Chapter Three

"What do you mean, you can't? Why not?" Joanna looks at me in shock.

"Why would you want to set up a detective agency? Last time I saw you, weren't you working as a teaching assistant or something?"

"I used to, but then I did a degree with the Open University, and got into lab work. I dabbled a bit with Forensic Science, but the head of the department near where I lived was a dick, and wouldn't employ me. I moved into medical research instead, and I did that for about fifteen years until I got diagnosed. Then, what with all the time off, and feeling so rough, then having to sell the house to pay off all the bastard's debts, well, the job didn't seem to hold any interest for me any more."

"But why a detective agency?" I dunk a biscuit into my tea, hoping Joanna doesn't notice my hand trembling again.

"I've always watched the crime dramas, and thought of you. It was something I've fancied doing for a long time, but having to leave home seemed a good trigger. I figured I'd look you up again, and we could get started. I changed my name after I kicked him out, so I'm now Joanna Knight. With you being Becky White, I thought we could be the White Knight Agency. What do you think?"

"I love the name. The idea sucks though." I take a deep breath. "I left the police last year. There was… an incident. I can't tell you about it just now, but detective work is not for me any more."

She opens her mouth as if to ask another question, but the latch clicks loudly from the front door.

"That'll be Matt," I say, glad for the interruption.

Seconds later, he walks in.

"It's disgusting out there. Why's there an enormous suitcase —?" He stops, and colour drains from his face as he looks at Joanna. His hand clutches his chest, and he turns from pale to grey as he drops to the floor.

"Oh my God. Get an ambulance," I shout at Joanna, who is standing there looking dumbstruck. "Matt, Matt, are you okay?" I crouch down at his side and check his pulse. It's beating erratically. Joanna snaps out of her reverie and takes out her phone. Matt is losing consciousness rapidly, and panic grips me.

By the time the ambulance arrives, my arms are aching from performing CPR, and my heart is beating loudly enough to drown out the emergency siren. The paramedics take charge immediately, and two shocks from the defibrillator bring my much-loved but infuriating husband back to life. He regains consciousness briefly, and I catch him glancing at Joanna with terror in his eyes. I've no idea what caused that reaction, but now is not the time to investigate.

Joanna looks at the floor, but then glances at me tentatively. "Maybe Cheryl can help me get some things together for you and your husband. We'll bring them to the hospital in a taxi shortly."

The female paramedic looks across from getting Matt strapped onto a stretcher.

"We're taking him to Fairfield Hospital. Even the Uber drivers should know where that is." She turns to me. "You can come in the ambulance with him."

I reluctantly hand my keys to Cheryl, who's hovering in the doorway.

"Will Dad be okay?" She looks terrified.

I give her a hug, and as much reassurance as I can manage, before leaving her, out of necessity, in the care of a woman I've not seen for thirty years and who appears to have been responsible for my husband's heart attack. If I could think of an alternative arrangement, I would, but we've only lived here for four months, and I don't know the neighbours well enough to ask for help.

Matt remains stable on the brief journey to the hospital. It's just as well it's short; the lack of suspension combined with the shock leaves me feeling nauseous, and I'm the one requesting a sick bowl before we arrive. I hold it in, but the paramedic is looking a bit anxious by the time we reach the hospital. Matt, on the other hand, is gaining a little colour in his face, although he still looks very unwell.

Although it's only early evening, A&E is full, and all the cubicles are occupied, except for the one at the very end. The paramedics wheel Matt in and transfer him to a trolley, and as soon as he's settled, I hold his hand. Now that I'm out of that rickety ambulance, my nausea subsides.

The paramedics leave as a nurse pops her head into the cubicle, informing me we'll be seen very soon. Matt's fully awake now, but there's fear in his eyes. I pretend not to associate this with my afternoon visitor, and instead hasten to reassure him of his safety now that he's in hospital.

"You're in the best place now. They can do marvellous things these days for heart attacks."

I'm rewarded by a slight receding of the haunted look. "Sorry, Becks. I had a hard day at work. I think I've been pushing myself too hard, and then…"

"It's my fault. If I could work properly, and bring in a bit more money, we'd have less stress and you wouldn't have to work so hard."

A young nurse interrupts, coming in briskly and performing observations, and taking blood with an efficiency that belies her apparent youth. I can't tell from her uniform what grade she is, and when a doctor follows her in a few moments later, he addresses her only as 'Ruth'.

Matt's had an ECG, bloods and an ultrasound scan, and is in bed on the Cardiology ward by the time Cheryl pokes her head around the door.

"Dad! Are you okay?"

"Yes. I will be anyway. They're admitting me for some procedure or other, which may or may not be done on Monday."

"You're medical, Dad. You ought to know what they're going to do to you." Cheryl rests her hip against the edge of the trolley and holds her dad's hand. I've long since retreated to the chair in the corner, unwilling to compete with nurse, doctor or daughter for my husband's attention.

"Well, yes, I suppose. They're going to put in a stent to open the artery they think is blocked. But I need to have other tests first so they can see what the damage is. For now, they've given me an injection to dissolve the clot that caused it." His voice quietens by the end of the sentence, and I leave my seat to stand at his other side.

"You're too exhausted to be answering all these questions, Matt. Shut your eyes and rest for a while. Cheryl, come and sit down for a bit. The porter will be here shortly to take Dad up to the ward."

"Okay, but…" She points vaguely toward the waiting area, and I hasten to interrupt.

"I know. We'll sort everything out when your dad's settled." Now is not the time to draw attention to Joanna's presence in the hospital.

Matt is sleeping on the ward, and his condition is stable, by the time a nurse comes along. Once we'd got to the ward, I sent Cheryl back to Joanna, so I'm sitting quietly when the nurse comes in. She beckons to me to leave Matt alone in the side ward.

"Will he be okay?" I ask as she pulls the door closed behind us. She guides me to the nurses' station, and hands me a leaflet.

"He should be fine now. He's on drugs to thin the blood, and there are lots of monitors and alarms that will alert us immediately if there's a problem. I think you should go home and rest. He's going to be in for a few days at least. That pamphlet tells you about our visiting times, and emergency contact details. We've got your number now, from the details you filled out in A&E, so please don't worry. We'll call you if there's a problem, but I think he'll sleep now until morning. You can phone after 8:30 tomorrow for an update."

She ushers me to the door leading back to the main corridor before I've had time to gather my thoughts, and she disappears without waiting for me to thank her. Not that she should have to wait, but being in hospital in that situation weirdly combines waiting around doing nothing, and flurries of intense activity from the hospital staff. There never seems to be the opportunity to ask questions, or to say something as simple as thank you.

In the corridor, I get my bearings. I assume Cheryl and

Joanna will be in A&E, so checking out the signposts on the wall, I head back to that part of the hospital.

I feel almost numb with all that's occurred, but I'm still conscious that the sight of Joanna triggered Matt's heart attack. Maybe it just altered the timing of an event that was waiting to happen, but either way, I'm shaking at the thought of seeing her again. Being in a hospital is not great either. I've not been here since... well, since that awful week. Now that the emergency is over, memories crowd in, and I'm relieved to see a sign for the ladies' loo. I rush in and throw up in one of the cubicles until there's nothing left.

I rest my head weakly against the edge of the cubicle as I try to summon the strength to stand up. I need to return to my youngest daughter. I will also need to contact my oldest at Uni. Unless Cheryl has sorted that. It's not her responsibility, though.

I finally stand up, but my legs feel as though they've been de-boned, and I have to lean against the wall for a moment. *Come on, Becky, pull yourself together.*

I splash water on my face from the basin before tottering out to the corridor and making my way the last few yards to the A&E waiting room.

Cheryl and Joanna are chatting as though they've known each other for years, and it's with mixed feelings that I interrupt.

"We can go home now. Your dad'll be in for a few days, but he seems settled now."

"You look awful, Mum. Are you okay?" Cheryl stands up and gives me a hug.

"I just need to get home."

"I'll order a taxi," says Joanna, heading to a Freephone box on the wall.

"Will she be staying with us?" My daughter gives me a

pleading look, and I suddenly realise that she doesn't want the responsibility of looking after me alone. Guilt floods through me. I should be looking after her, not the other way round. But I feel wiped out, and the thought of another adult in the house is a relief. Even if it is Joanna.

Chapter Four

We're home now. It's gone nine in the evening, and I just want to go to bed, but instead curl up on the sofa. Joanna makes herself useful in the kitchen, sorting out something to eat.

She's very good at finding her way around a strange kitchen. Is she trying to be helpful, or is it her way of assuaging guilt? Or of trying to get me to agree to the crazy idea of her detective agency? No way is that happening now. Why did Matt have a heart attack as soon as he laid eyes on her? Is she an old flame? Or a newer one? Has he been having an affair? Did Joanna know that he was my husband? Did she come here on purpose?

I put a lid on all the questions in my head as she brings me supper on a tray.

"Do you want me to leave?" she asks, setting the tray on the coffee table next to me. Her expression holds wariness and fatigue, rather than guilt. I can't quite believe she would knowingly have an affair with Matt, then turn up to invite me to go into partnership with her. The girl I was friends with thirty years ago was rebellious and had a wicked sense of humour, but she was never vindictive (except to her stepmother).

"Yes, probably. Do *you* think you should leave?"

"I know it looks bad, but I hardly know Matt. We met at a conference a few years ago and had a few drinks. That was all. I don't know why my appearance set off that reaction. I didn't even know we were connected through you until he walked in earlier this evening. I was surprised, but pleasantly, until he fell ill. Now I feel awful. I seem to have caused his attack, and I don't understand why." She looks embarrassed, but I've been trained to detect whether someone is being honest. I have a gut feeling that she's telling me the truth, but not quite the whole truth.

The door opens, saving me from answering. Cheryl comes in, holding a plate of pizza.

"I found this in the fridge, Mum. I think it's from yesterday. In case you don't fancy eggs."

"I'm fine with eggs on toast. Thanks. You have the pizza." I force a smile and turn to Joanna. "Do you want something to eat? It's nice of you to feed me, but you're a guest. You should eat something too."

"I had chocolate and crisps in the hospital. The vending machine was in front of us, and there wasn't much else to do."

"We did pig out a bit, didn't we? Do you want some pizza though? A bit of protein?" Cheryl offers the plate, and Joanna takes a small piece. "Shall we find a movie? It'll help us all take our minds off everything. I'm sure Dad's in the best place, and they'll look after him."

I love her practicality, optimism and kindness. Maybe I was like that once. Before life got in the way.

We settle down on the leather suite and let Cheryl choose a DVD.

Next morning, I'm up at seven, and itching to phone the hospital for an update. I slept badly, not used to the half-empty bed; and spent the night worrying about Matt, amongst other things.

I occupy the time to 8.30 by cleaning the kitchen cupboards. There's no sign of Cheryl or Joanna, but they'd stayed downstairs chatting about books and movies long after I went to bed. I think I heard them come upstairs at around 2am.

I'm about to call the hospital when my phone pings. It's a WhatsApp from my eldest daughter, Alison.

'How's Dad? I'm on the train home. Can you pick me up from the Met? I'll be there in about an hour.'

'Sure. Call me when you get to Crumpsall.'

We always do this. The time to get my coat on and drive to the tram station in Whitefield allows me to get there a minute or two ahead of her.

I'm going to have to throw Joanna out. She's sleeping in Alison's bed at this very moment. I push the thought aside. She can have another half hour to sleep. I have other priorities right now.

I key in the phone number on the leaflet the nurse gave me last night. The phone rings out for about a minute, and then finally it's answered by an elderly female.

"Hello, I'm Matthew White's wife. How is he?"

"I'll get the nurse who's looking after him. Just bear with me a moment."

A moment later, a male voice says, "Hi. Mrs White?"

"Yes."

"Great. Your husband is doing well. He'll be having scans and a stent put in this morning, but you can come and see him after two o'clock."

I thank him and disconnect, then immediately regret not asking to speak to Matt directly. I try his mobile, but it goes directly to voicemail. I decline the invitation to leave a message and send him a WhatsApp instead.

'Good luck for this morning. See you later. I love you. x'

It's now ten to nine, so I go to wake up Joanna. I knock on the bedroom door, and a sleepy voice calls out, "Come in."

"Hi. Sorry to wake you up, but my eldest girl is coming back from Uni this morning to see her dad. I'm afraid I'm going to need to get her bed ready for her."

"Sure. Am I okay to have a shower?"

I nod, and notice she's looking more alert.

"I'll find somewhere to stay tonight. Maybe there's a cheap hotel around here. Then tomorrow I'll start looking for somewhere to rent."

I leave her to get herself ready and go down to the kitchen to Google local hotels on my phone.

By the time we go to the hospital, Joanna has booked into the local Travelodge – a five-minute drive from home. I'm relieved to have her out of the house, but I strongly suspect I've not seen the back of her. I still don't know Matt's side of the story, and I don't really want to confront him while he's not yet recovered.

Alison's been quiet since I picked her up from the tram stop. She went straight to her freshly-made bed when she got home, with barely a hello to our guest. I refrain from telling her that the guest spent the night in her bed.

Now the three of us are alone in the car. She finally speaks.

"So, who's that woman?"

"That's Joanna. She's a really nice lady. An old friend of Mum's. She turned up yesterday, just before Dad got ill. I think she's going to live round here." Cheryl's description stirs up mixed emotions: a tinge of jealousy that Joanna wormed herself into my daughter's affections so easily, but also a recollection that Cheryl's character judgement is remarkably reliable for one so young. Maybe I'm the one who needs to learn to trust.

Alison is silenced again by her sister's enthusiastic approval. She remains quiet until we arrive at the hospital.

My heart pounds as we approach the cardiac ward. I clench my sweaty hands for a moment, but it doesn't help.

When we enter the ward, a tall male nurse, roughly in his thirties, catches my eye and comes over.

"Hi. Can I take your name?"

"I'm Becky White. Matthew's wife. Is he okay?"

"Yes. Are these your daughters?" He smiles, and I nod. "Girls, your dad is down the corridor, in Room Six. Do you want to go down and say hello, while I have a quick word with your mum?"

The girls head off towards their dad's room, while the nurse waffles for a few minutes, describing the treatment that Matt's undergone. It all seems to have gone smoothly, so I'm not sure why he had to banish the girls. Maybe he thought they were squeamish.

When I finally extract myself from the conversation, I follow the girls down to the other end of the ward. Cheryl's lively tones reach me before I get to the room.

"… and she says she met you in London a few years ago and that you had a few drinks with her. She had no idea that you and Mum were married."

I arrive in the room in time to see a strained look in Matt's eyes. But he forces a smile when he sees me.

"Cheryl, stop chattering and let Mum have a few minutes alone with Dad," Alison says. "Let's find somewhere to get a drink. I'd kill for a can of coke."

The girls leave me with Matt, and I sit on the chair next to his bed and take his hand. His face has more colour than yesterday, but he looks pale and tired.

"You look knackered. Have you had a hard morning?" I stroke the back of his hand with my thumb as I speak. I'm rewarded by a slight relaxing of the lines around his eyes.

We chat for a while about his treatment, and expectations for recovery, and by the time the girls come back he looks a lot brighter. Joanna's name is not mentioned again this visit.

Chapter Five

I leave the club at eleven, after the main band. The object is still in sight, and I take a few more photos outside, before walking to the office — a convenient half a mile away.

The cold air clears my head and allows me to think. Research is essential. The office is never completely empty, even so late on a Saturday night.

By the time I arrive at my desk, I have a strategy in place. I smile at the other late workers and place my bag on the floor. The office is organised to allow for privacy; it's difficult to see what others are working on without their permission. An arrangement that suits me well, particularly now. I turn on the powerful computer and search.

Information is more difficult to locate than I expected. I need help, but need to be careful. I return to Google with a different type of search.

Chapter Six

It's Friday morning – almost two weeks since Matt's heart attack, and he's recovering at home now, watching box sets on Netflix. Alison's back at Uni, and Cheryl is at school. A strange sort of normality has set in, albeit a different normality from a fortnight ago.

Matt gets sick pay, so we're not totally desperate for money, but nothing has been quite the same since I left the police. I took retirement, as I'd been in the force for over the required twenty years. But on only half-pay, with a daughter at university, money is a bit tight.

I've thought, at odd moments, about Joanna's suggestion. If I'm being totally honest with myself, I miss working. I don't think I could handle the danger any more, but maybe sitting at a desk doing research – that kind of detection would suit me fine. Joanna can do the dangerous stuff. That sounds mean, I know, but I'm still angry with her for appearing to trigger Matt's heart attack.

She said there was nothing to it – just a few drinks; a story that Matt has corroborated since he's been home. But then, Cheryl told him what Joanna had said. Now I'll never know what Matt would have said if he'd not heard her version of events first.

Could I work with her? We liaised all those years ago to help Dan. She was useful to bounce ideas around with, and had the handy ability to see things from unusual angles.

I put the kettle on, and make a cup of tea for Matt and coffee for myself. Setting his down on the coffee table in front of him, I look at him critically. He seems a lot better and has been making progress every day, but he gets tired easily, and even though he's watching TV I know he'll be going up for a nap after lunch.

"How are you feeling?"

"Not so bad. You should watch this, Becks. It's brilliant."

"What is it?"

"*The Marvellous Mrs Maisel*. It's hilarious, but it's very realistic too. Come and watch it with me. You've got nothing better to do."

Shit! Is that how he sees me? I'm turning into a bloody housewife. Not that I have anything against housewives; it was just never my thing.

"I need to remedy that. I'm just going to make a call. I'll leave you to watch in peace."

Joanna's number is in my phone still. I call her from the kitchen, with the door shut.

"Becky, hi. How are you doing? How's Matt?"

I can't help the hackles that go up as she mentions his name, but I suppress them for the moment.

"He's getting better; he's home now. How are you?" I inject friendliness into the inquiry, but it's an effort. Maybe this is a bad idea.

"I've been house-hunting. I just put a deposit on a little terraced property. It's about ten minutes' walk from you. They're doing the reference checks, but hopefully I can move in early next week."

"That's great. How long is the lease?"

"Six months to start off with, then they'll extend to a year if it suits both sides." There's a pause. "Becky, will you come and have a drink with me? I'd really like to speak to you properly." She sounds genuine and nervous.

The voice in my head that is pushing me in her direction gives me another nudge.

"Okay, sure. There's a pub near your hotel. The Paper Mill. We can get a sandwich or something there too." We arrange to meet at midday and end the call. I have an hour to get ready.

I don't tell Matt where I'm going, just that I'm meeting a friend for lunch. It's nearly true, even if I haven't yet decided if Joanna is still a friend.

"You look tired," she says, as I arrive at the table.

"Thanks. It's been a challenging week." I glance around the area, trying to look nonchalant, but my pulse is tumultuous. Apart from the hospital, I've avoided crowded areas since that day in the warehouse. Even shopping is difficult. Matt has been the regular supermarket shopper, with me managing brief trips to our local Co-op. I'm going to have to force myself to go to Tesco tomorrow, and I'm dreading it.

Most of the restaurant customers are parents with young kids having lunch; no doubt on the promise of going through to the soft play area if they're good.

Joanna stands up. "Do you want a drink?"

"I'll get them. What do you want?"

I swallow hard as I get to the bar. It shouldn't be difficult ordering the required two diet cokes, but my mouth is dry. There's no reason anyone here should know me as Becky

Wiseman, Detective Inspector from South Manchester. I'm just a stranger in a bar.

It's no actual surprise that I buy the cokes without incident, and I relax slightly as I sit down, positioning myself carefully with my back to the wall where I can survey the surrounding scene.

"Thanks. Cheers." Joanna holds up the drink, and I clink glasses with her. "You do it automatically, don't you?"

"What?"

"Observe. You're a natural detective. You can't help yourself."

"It's complicated. Not a story for today, and definitely not for here."

"Okay. Fair enough. So what do you think? I know you've been thinking about it. You wouldn't have phoned me otherwise."

"It's been difficult. I know you said nothing happened with Matt in London, but why would he have a heart attack on seeing you? It doesn't make sense."

"You're absolutely right. It makes no sense at all. But that's what happened." She looks down at the table and then glances around. There's no one remotely within earshot. "Look. I admit there's something else, but I'm bound by law not to tell a soul about it."

I stare at her. "Seriously?"

"Yeah, seriously. I swear to you on my life, and the life of my son, that I didn't have an affair, or a fling, or anything remotely inappropriate, with your husband. It's just this weird thing – a kind of work situation – that I'm not allowed to talk about."

"But why would seeing you cause Matt to have a heart attack?" I shake my head, totally confused by what she's said.

"Well, there was a bit of a mess, and it was my fault, and maybe Matt thought it had caught up with us, and that I was coming to warn him. But neither of us knew anything about the other's home life or anything. We were virtually strangers except for this… project thing. Please, Becky, believe me. You and I were best friends for over two years. I wouldn't lie to you."

"But you won't tell me the whole truth."

"I've already told you more than I should, and as much as I dare to." Her earnest expression finally convinces me, even if it doesn't solve the mystery. Matt's comment about me being a housewife still rankles, and I feel the need to do something about it. If trusting Joanna will give me that chance, perhaps I can give it a shot.

"Okay. Let's put it behind us. Why do you want to start up a detective agency?"

"I need to earn a living. I think it would be fascinating, and it could be fun."

"Fun?"

"Yeah. I'm not talking about taking on murder cases. Those are for the police. If anything like that happens (God forbid), we can liaise with your old pals. I assume you didn't cut off all contact?"

"I still have a few phone numbers in a book at home." And in my head. And a couple on my phone. Just their private numbers though. Finn (my best friend), and Wendy (my friend and mentor from all those years ago when I was a student). My insides lurch a few millimetres at the thought of Finn. I haven't spoken to him in over six months.

Joanna's speaking again, so I force myself to concentrate.

"Great. I think we should advertise discreetly. I've drawn up a few ideas." She fishes a folded piece of A4 paper out of her bag, and spreads it out in front of me. In the bottom right is a text box that catches my eye.

WHITE KNIGHT DETECTIVE AGENCY
Do you have a problem?

Do you need a white knight to come to your rescue?
Phone xxxxxx for details.

I point at it. "That looks quite good. Advertising isn't cheap though. Where were you thinking of putting it?"

"I think we can set up a Facebook page and Twitter account for free, and start growing those. And we can advertise cheaply in the local press." She writes down some figures for the advertising. They look affordable, even on my budget.

"Okay. We need to get something clear, though."

"What?" Joanna looks at me cautiously. "Obviously we split any proceeds fifty-fifty."

"I guess there are a couple of things. First, I'm going to be more of an indoor detective. I'm happy to do any amount of research on a computer. You'll meet the client initially, but I'll watch on CCTV. If I think it's safe for me to meet them, then I'll join you part-way through. If I don't appear, it's because I have a good reason."

"And the second thing?"

"Please stay away from Matt." I hold up my hand as she protests. "Look, I know you're innocent from your perspective. But for whatever reason, you increase his stress levels, and he needs to stay calm. So, please give him some space to recover."

"Sure. Both things are fine. We can use my mobile number for the time being, and I'll filter all the calls. Then I guess we'll see them when I get a house. I'm going to work part-time at Asda. They've agreed I can do twenty-five hours a week on the checkouts. It'll pay the rent until the clients flood in."

"That's sensible. I could do with finding something to do as well. But it would have to be something where I don't need to leave the house."

"Do students still need dissertations typing up these days?"

"I think they mostly write them straight on to the

computer. They couldn't afford me anyway." I give a tired smile. Suddenly, I feel exhausted. "I need to get home. I'll find something to bring in a few pennies while we wait for those clients. Are you going to put the ad in the paper?"

"Yeah, I'll sort it this afternoon. Leave it to me."

She grins. White Knight is open for business.

Chapter Seven

Back at home, Matt's upstairs having a nap. I make myself a coffee and sit in the kitchen thinking. How am I going to tell him about White Knight? Joanna's name hasn't been mentioned since he came out of hospital. How will he react? Common sense tries to assert itself. He's had a stent put in and he's taking medication to prevent another heart attack. He should be safe now, regardless of any stressful news. But then I recall the image of him clutching his chest, his face as grey as stone, as he looked at Joanna. The memory brings a wave of nausea. Maybe I'll see how he is later.

My phone pings. A text from Joanna.

'The ad's in. Going live tomorrow.'

'Wow. That was quick. Well done.'

'Thanks. The Knight owes me £30.'

'Sure. Make sure you log it. How're your accountancy skills?'

'So-so. Yours?'

'Rubbish. Sorry!'

Joanna sends me a couple of emojis in reply, showing she's okay with that and it's funny. We'll have to muddle through.

Matt's great with money, but I'm sure as hell not going to ask him.

I flick idly through the News channels on my phone, looking for anything that might be suitable fodder for us to investigate. There are a few missing persons, but the police are best placed to deal with those, unless anyone approaches us directly.

Popping upstairs to check on Matt, I see he's still asleep – snoring softly. I creep downstairs again and go into the lounge where he was sitting earlier. I'm about to turn on the TV, but there's a ping. Temptation is too strong for me, and I pick up his phone from the coffee table. A text is showing on the home screen.

'*RT: How are you doing? Shocked to hear the news. Take care. Don't worry about the drop. We'll sort it without you for now. KL is back from leave.*'

Who the hell are RT and KL? I put the phone down. The message has disappeared now. It flashed up only for a few seconds. I try a couple of obvious PIN options, but don't want to lock it with too many wrong attempts. It doesn't seem right that I shouldn't trust my husband, but recent events have eroded trust as well as confidence.

Feeling guilty, I put the mobile back on the table and turn on the TV, flicking through the channels and eventually locating an old episode of *Doctor Who*. It's one I've seen before, and I get a bit bored. I collect my phone from the kitchen and start surfing the net again. My eye is caught by a headline:

"*Manchester band, Troy's Tigers, have just been signed by EMI to do an album.*"

Below the headline: "*The band has been playing regularly at Band On The Wall in Swan Street. They were working in London on Saturday night and were unaware of the presence of the EMI scout. Lead singer, Troy Cassidy, says they are 'over the moon'...*"

I don't know why this catches my attention. I'm not

particularly into music other than classical, and the occasional bit of 80s pop. This article has given me goosebumps. I glance at the photo – taken by a P Ellsworth. Troy Cassidy is a good-looking guy of around thirty years old, with long wavy black hair and a hint of stubble.

I shiver. This has happened before. On several occasions in the past, I've seen something occur – an incident, or a news article, or I've heard a comment. The goosebumps and shivers have appeared, and within a few days, the subject of the article has been involved in a case that's landed on my desk. Not always the victim of a murder, but usually associated with a serious crime.

On an impulse, I share the article with Joanna, via WhatsApp, with a brief explanation of why it might be significant.

'Seriously?'

'Yeah. I know it's weird.'

'Not at all. I believe in premonitions and that sort of stuff. It's strange but credible. I'll see if I can find out anything more about them.'

'Great. Thanks. I'll look too. Different angles, different results. Who knows what we might turn up?'

I spend the next hour searching for anything I can find about Troy and the band. There are lots of musical references, with lists of gigs past and present, and of the songs. They have obscure titles and are mostly in the category of 'Heavy Rock with a Soul twist', whatever the hell that means.

I'm deciding whether to call the paper that published the article to see if there's any additional information, when I realise I have no idea why I'm searching, and whether I would know a significant clue if I fell over it.

Cheryl's arrival home from school puts a lid on my research for the time being, but after asking her about her day, I drop it casually into the conversation while I put the kettle on.

"Have you ever heard of a band called Troy's Tigers?"

"That's really weird," she says, getting her favourite mug out of the cupboard and adding a herbal tea bag.

"What's weird?"

"Mia was just mentioning them today. She saw them at Band On The Wall with her boyfriend the other week. She said they were amazing, and apparently they've just been signed with some huge record label. It's weird that you asked about them. You never follow music."

We sit down with our hot drinks.

"I found the article about it on the local news. It just caught my eye. The lead singer looks nice." I show her the picture.

"Wow. Yeah, he's hot. Bit young for you, Mum."

"Cheeky mare! I didn't mean it like that." It's nice to have a bit of banter with her, particularly after all the worry of the past week. But even before that, my mood has been too wobbly, and anxiety has been at the forefront of everything.

It's very odd. Between the text on Matt's phone, and worry about how I'm going to tell him I'm going into business with the woman who nearly killed him, I should feel awful. But for some strange reason, introducing Joanna and White Knight into my life has lifted my spirits. I guess I've missed being a detective.

Chapter Eight

"Alexa — turn up the music."

The sound of my favourite band fills the apartment. I open my laptop and load the photos I took last night. So beautiful. Such a vivid setting. The darkness of the club; the lit stage; and the audience. All so important to capture correctly.

The target is perfect. I get close, but not close enough. I need to meet, to touch, to know. Until then, I cannot be fulfilled.

The song ends, and another begins. The title, Death is Beauty, *is so apt. I shut my eyes and allow the melody to resonate through my body. Rapture fills me, and as the song reaches its peak, so do I.*

Chapter Nine

Joanna moved into her new house yesterday. I'm going after breakfast to help her unpack. She had a van bring her belongings down from Edinburgh.

I've been battling with the need to tell Matt, but he still seems so tired, it's hard to bring myself to say something that might upset him.

Cheryl's in school, and Matt is sitting at the kitchen table eating a healthy breakfast of poached eggs on wholemeal toast – made by my own fair hands. Yes, I'm trying to get him in a good mood. He's concentrating on the newspaper with a frown on his face. Not a very auspicious start. I sit down opposite him, with coffee and a banana. I wait a moment until he turns the page.

"Joanna and I are going into business together," I blurt out.

"Okay."

Okay? Is that all? It's taken me over a week to work up to this, and all he can say is 'Okay'!

"She moved into a house yesterday, quite near here. It's that estate at the back of the shops. I'm going round to help her get sorted out this morning."

He doesn't lift his eyes from the paper. "Good idea. It'll be helpful for you to get out of the house."

"Helpful to who?" That just slips out. I'm trying so hard not to be confrontational, but his lack of interest is infuriating.

He finally looks up.

"You need to get out more, Becky. You're looking tired and stressed. I know you've had a bad time of it with nightmares and flashbacks in the last six months, but maybe going into business is a good idea. It will stop you from—"

"Wallowing?" I'm not sure if he catches the dangerous note in my voice. He's in trouble if he carries on like this.

"That wasn't quite the word I was looking for. I was thinking more 'brooding'."

"Same thing, isn't it? And don't you want to know what sort of business?"

"Some sort of detective agency thing? Cheryl mentioned that Joanna wanted you to start one with her."

I gaze at him incredulously.

"You've known about this for how long? And you've not bothered to mention it?"

"You seemed reluctant to mention Joanna to me; I didn't want to upset you."

I take my coffee and manage to refrain from spilling the scalding liquid on his head as I walk past him into the lounge. I grit my teeth and slam the door shut behind me with my foot.

It's only as I sip my coffee in front of Breakfast TV that I wonder if there's another reason he wants me out of the house. I need to keep my comings and goings a bit unpredictable, and see if I can catch him talking to someone about 'a drop'.

Joanna's house is a pleasant two-bedroom semi, with a lounge at the front, and an eat-in kitchen at the back. There's even a downstairs loo. She seems excited as she shows me round.

"I thought we could interview any clients in the front room. I want to set up cameras to focus on the sofa and chairs, with a live feed into a laptop in the kitchen or the office upstairs. You'll be able to watch the feed and come in if you think it's appropriate."

"Sounds good. Will you inform the clients that they're being filmed? I think you have to these days."

"Yeah – I'll say it's saving me taking notes, as it's better to have things directly available if I need to recall something."

"Okay. You mentioned an office upstairs?"

"When we've not got clients in, I thought we could each work in a separate space. One of us in the kitchen, the other in the spare room. The lounge can be for conferences and interviewing."

"That's great. I'm impressed. We just need some furniture now." I look around the lounge. There's currently a couple of wooden dining chairs and a small glass nest of tables. The kitchen holds another two dining chairs and a matching pine dining table, big enough for four people. Apart from a double bed in Joanna's room, that's the full extent of the furniture. There are a few boxes dotted around the room, presumably containing personal items and ornaments. "Is this it?"

"Yeah. The bailiffs had a field day with us, thanks to my git of an ex. I had to give them cash to get them to leave what I've got here, and then I had to pay storage for it. But all these things were expensive when I first bought them, and I didn't want to have to replace them with rubbish. I've been back on Google, and there are a couple of furniture warehouses in Bury. They seem to sell stuff quite cheap. I did a lot of shifts at Asda in the last week while I was waiting for the keys to here, so I've got a bit of money for stuff. If I put it on my credit card, it should be fine." As she rambles on, she's fidgeting with the scissors.

"You're going to do yourself an injury with those. Put them down." I wait until she replaces them on top of a box. Diagnosing her anxiety as money-related, I do some quick thinking. "Why don't we just get the basics for now? A suite for in here, as this is where we'll be greeting clients; and maybe a desk for upstairs? Then we can go to B&Q and get the CCTV stuff. That can be my contribution, seeing as it's down to my paranoia that it's even needed."

"Okay, thanks." She relaxes visibly. "Let's get this lot unpacked, then we'll go shopping." She finishes with a grin, and I have to repress a shudder, as I don't want to dampen her enthusiasm. Shopping, particularly in anything resembling a warehouse, brings me out in a panic.

I take a few deep breaths, trying to quell the anxiety that is rising just at the thought.

The reality of shopping is even worse than the thought of it. Just driving into Bury, we have three near-crashes. By the time I park up next to the shop – on a side road half a mile from the town centre – I'm shaking like a jelly. Joanna untangles her fingers from the handle on the door. Her knuckles are almost as white as her face.

"I didn't mean to scare you. Sorry." I give a wry smile and try to control my shaking hands. "I don't always drive this badly."

"We could have got a cab, Becky." She looks at me. "Are you okay to come into the shop?"

I inhale deeply and exhale slowly. It calms me a fraction, but my pulse is still doing double time.

"Sure. Come on. Let's go."

Once inside, I try to view the scene impartially. The area is filled with sofas, chairs, dining sets and other paraphernalia, with a sign at the foot of a staircase stating that beds are upstairs. Compared to the warehouse where it all happened, this is completely different. In fact, apart from the high ceilings and faintly damp air, this could hardly qualify as a warehouse. My heart rate slows to near normality as I re-engage with the scene – a new definition of the place as 'shop' helps. It also helps that it's empty apart from myself, Joanna, and a tall, dark-haired and moustached chap who's drinking a cup of tea. He approaches us.

"Can I help you, ladies?"

"We're looking for a suite. Probably a sofa and an armchair. Cheap, cheerful and comfy." Joanna smiles sweetly at him, and I'm reminded of the charm she can turn on when she wants something. Seeing her use it now, I realise how much she's got round me since she's been in Manchester. Despite everything, she always seems to get her own way, and she succeeds before anyone's had time to realise they've been played. On the plus side, it's a useful skill in a detective.

Half an hour later, Joanna has ordered an olive-green suite (2-seater settee and 2 armchairs). The wallpaper in her lounge has an olive-green leaf pattern, so it should match nicely. They don't seem to sell desks, and the sales chap suggests IKEA or Argos.

When we get back to the car, I give her a choice of ordering from Amazon, or going to IKEA without me. I don't think I could handle another warehouse right now.

"I'm sure Amazon will be fine. You seem a bit calmer now. Are you happy to drive?"

"Sure. Let's get back and see what we can find online." My driving is now normal, and we return to Joanna's house without incident. I'm turning the engine off when her phone rings.

"I don't recognise the number," she says, pressing the green *Connect* button. "Hello, White Knight Detective Agency?"

I sense her excitement as she listens to the person on the other end of the call.

"Yes, of course. Would three-thirty tomorrow afternoon be convenient? Great." She gives out the address and some basic directions. "Wonderful. See you soon then."

She ends the call and turns to me, her face lighting up. "We've got our first client."

Chapter Ten

Because Joanna bought it from an independent store, the furniture should arrive tomorrow morning. So our client, whose name is apparently Penny Moore, will have something to sit on.

Joanna makes me an omelette in one of the frying pans we extracted from a box this morning, and we eat it at the small table in the kitchen, using plates and cutlery that we also rescued earlier.

"Are you up to B&Q this afternoon?" she asks.

I sigh and agree. It's another shop in a warehouse-type building. Six months ago, I wouldn't have flinched; now, the idea of going into any area remotely resembling that place reduces me to a quivering wreck. However, with the client coming tomorrow, we really don't have time to wait around for Amazon orders.

I give myself a good talking-to before we get back in the car, and manage a better trip than the morning expedition. We then spend three hours battling with the newly-bought CCTV, the receiver and the various wires. The instructions that came with the kit are worse than useless, and it's only thanks to the multitude of YouTube videos that we're able to set up a system that works.

I arrive home at six, exhausted and too tired to cook. Cheryl orders pizza for all of us from an app on her phone, and I fall into bed shortly after eating, too shattered even to discuss the day's events with Matt, or to wonder what he's been doing.

It's only the next morning that my curiosity returns.

"What did you do yesterday while I was out?" I hand him a mug of coffee, place another on the table, and sit down opposite him.

"Just rested mostly. Obeying doctor's orders. I did a bit of reading. Watched daytime TV. Nothing unusual. Well, not unusual since I got out of hospital." He's gazing at me – perhaps a bit too steadily, as if trying not to look shifty. "How did your day go?"

Experience tells me he won't tell me anything if pressed. I must be more devious. I launch into an explanation of my day.

"Why didn't you call me to sort out the tech stuff? You know I'm better at that than you."

"Last time you saw Joanna, you nearly died. I'm sure you can understand my reluctance. Especially as you won't tell me why."

Matt reaches across the table and takes my hand. "You know I'd tell you if I could. I've not had an affair or anything so sordid. It's complicated though."

"You're making no sense. What's going on?" But I leave my hand in his, enjoying for a brief moment the comfort of physical contact.

He looks thoughtful, then speaks. "Joanna and I got involved in a government project to do with some pharmaceuticals. It was, and still is, very secret, and I can't tell you about it. Seeing her here that day, I thought something had gone wrong. There could be very serious implications if it had, and that was why I was so distressed."

Now I pull my hand away and stare at him. I can't believe he's told me as much as this. I guess he cares that I suspected him of infidelity.

"How the hell could you get involved in a top secret project?"

"I got approached, Becky. It was two years ago. Your job in the police made a difference because they could vet you properly. It got complicated after... Well, you know when I mean. With you not in the force anymore, they wanted me to stop working on it. I think they were a bit suspicious of the circumstances in which you left." He pauses. "They're not always decent people. In fact, they rarely are. I regret having got involved, and I've already said far too much. Forget it, love, please."

"How can I forget something like that?" I decide to make a confession. "Also, when you were asleep the other day, I noticed a message come in on your phone. It said something about a 'drop'. What was that about? And who are RT and KL?" I get a suspicious look for my pains. "I only glanced at it because it pinged, and that message popped up on the home screen." Even to my own ears I sound ridiculously defensive now, but he relaxes.

"It's nothing for you to worry about. I was supposed to help with a new job, but they got someone else on to it. KL is just another operative. RT is the guy in charge. Put it out of your mind and focus on your new case. You've got a client coming today. Prepare yourself for that."

His expression is set again. I've already learned much more than I expected, and I need time to take it all in.

I get to Joanna's at 11am. It's earlier than planned, but even after an hour's walk in the woods to clear my head, I don't feel ready to return home and pretend nothing has happened.

Joanna welcomes me in.

"Thanks for coming so early. I had a bit of a lie-in this morning and have just had breakfast. Do you want some coffee? The delivery men will be here shortly."

I accept the offer, and we sit in the kitchen sipping our drinks in silence for a few minutes.

"Something's up? What is it?" she asks me, as the quietness becomes heavy.

"Matt told me you and he had got involved in some government project, top secret thing. I kind of dragged it out of him."

"Wow, well done. I suppose he didn't really have a choice. It was that or let you continue to think we'd had a fling." She narrows her gaze at me. "What exactly did he tell you?"

I repeat the conversation as accurately as I can.

"Okay. Well, I'm glad that's out of the way. I'm sure you want to know more details, but it's not safe right now. Believe me, we'll let you know as soon as we can."

"So, are you and Matt still working together?"

"Not really. The project finished about six months ago. At least, Matt was taken off it then, and I resigned last month, as I needed to move, and leave my job. It closed my avenues of research, and therefore of usefulness. But I wanted to continue to use those skills, hence the detective agency. I'm pleased we can be open about it now, but only between ourselves. I'm still highly bound to secrecy, and I've probably endangered us all by telling you as much. Except I don't think they know yet where I am. I hope not. My married name isn't really Knight, but I chose it because I thought 'the White Knight' agency sounded cool."

"It does sound cool. But surely, if these are professionals

they'll have been able to track you down by now. And how did you set up bank accounts and get a job with a changed name?"

"It may have been foolish, but I changed it by deed poll as soon as I left the project. So yeah, I had to tell people like the HMRC, and get my driving licence and passport amended, but I don't think they'd think anyone would be so stupid as to do it officially."

I take a deep breath and try not to show impatience. I can see she's done everything in good faith, but I reckon Matt would have a fit if he knew.

"Okay. When I was in the police, I would always do the basic checks first. Mostly nothing would show up, but every so often, a criminal would be very daring or perhaps a bit naïve, not realising what we could access. In those cases, it made it really easy to catch them."

"You're saying I'm naïve?" She looks hurt. Shit.

"I'm sorry. I don't want to offend you. But I think any operative worth their salt will have tracked you down by now. On the other hand, if you've nothing to hide, why worry?"

"I've not really got anything to hide. It's just that I don't like people keeping tabs on me, and once you've worked with them at all, they kind of never let you go."

"I can see that, but changing your name and stuff makes it looks as though you're hiding from them. Why don't you make contact? You can say that you're trying to avoid your ex, who's being a pain, and that you wanted to make a new start. Let them know where they can contact you if they need you, and thank them for everything they've ever done for you."

Joanna wraps her hands around her mug and sits back in the chair, looking thoughtful.

"Maybe. Yeah, I could do. I suppose looking at it from their point of view, it would seem as though I've done a runner because I wanted to avoid them. They'd think I've done something wrong."

"It does look like that." I give her a quick, nervous glance. "So, how well do you know Matt?"

"We met about half a dozen times. Usually in London, but twice further North – Newcastle, Carlisle. I never got to know him though. He was just another operative. Someone I worked with remotely on a project. We discussed the project when we met." She hesitates.

"Carry on."

"The only thing is that we had to meet in hotel rooms, to make sure the discussions were private. There'd be this thing, where one of us would book the room, then when we arrived, we'd always ask for a different room, and it would usually be the third or fourth room they offered. We had to be sure we hadn't been set up. If our enemies had known we were meeting there, they might have bugged the room or something. So we avoided it by changing rooms. Nothing ever happened between us. I didn't fancy him anyway, but he made it clear that he was happily married and the hotel rooms were a necessary evil. I was fine with that. I had enough complications going on in my life. And obviously if I'd known who he was, the question of marital status wouldn't even have arisen."

Clearly the question did arise, but Matt's alleged response sounds very like the sort of thing he'd say – upfront and before it became an issue – so I do believe Joanna.

"Fine. I think it's time we prepare for our first client. What do we know about her so far?"

Joanna gets out an A5 notebook and opens it to the first page. "Penny Moore works for a press agency – primarily taking photos of celebrities."

"Do we know anything else about her?" I ask, but any response is delayed by the doorbell. Joanna jumps up and goes to the door, and we spend the next several minutes directing the delivery driver and his mate to get the sofa and chairs through the front door, which suddenly seems much narrower.

Eventually we're alone again. The suite is arranged appropriately in the lounge, with the plastic covers safely stowed in the bin. It has that lovely new smell, and I breathe deeply.

"You daft woman," says Joanna. "Why don't you sit down, and test it out? We've never sat on it without the plastic. It might be awful."

I give her a look as if to say *It wouldn't dare be awful*, but sit down as instructed. The soft fabric has just the right amount of support, allowing my legs and bottom to melt into it. I feel my muscles relax.

"This might be a bit too comfy. We'll never get rid of the clients."

"No, it's good." She settles herself into the armchair. "It will encourage them to talk." She flashes me an evil grin.

"Maybe. Anyway, you never answered my question. What else do we know about Penny?"

"Not as much as I'd like. Bloody data protection laws. I kept hitting a wall. I might have to teach myself to hack?"

"How easy it to teach yourself something like that?"

"The kids seem to do it all the time. My son's not a bad hacker."

"Where is he?"

"He lives in Edinburgh, to be as close to his daughter as he can be – he has joint custody - but he's a software engineer, and can work from home. If we give him some warning, he could come down here for a week and stay with me. I spoke to him last night, and he wants to see me settled in, so that could work out well."

"Okay. Alternatively, and perhaps more legally, I still have friends in the police who could check things out for me." My thoughts return to Wendy and Finn. I've avoided contacting them for the last few months, and I wonder if they'd be pleased to hear from me now – just because I want something.

My phone pings. I glance at it, and it blurs before my eyes. I blink hard and try to slow my suddenly rapid breathing.

'Becks. How r u doing? Don't hide from me. BF'

BF stands for Big Finn (he's six foot three), or Best Friend. He once joked that he's happy with either.

"Oh my God, that's really spooky. That was my best pal from the force. Can I just answer this?"

Joanna nods, and I type out a quick message.

'Great to hear from you. Fancy meeting up?'

'Obvs! Lunch tomoz? Village hotel near u? 12:30?' His texting is more like that of my youngest daughter than a grown man. In anyone else it would drive me mad, but I smile and type back *'Sure'* and add a smiley emoji. We had a conversation about messaging once a long time ago, but his comment still sticks in my mind: "Just because I don't put kisses in my messages to you, Becks, it doesn't mean I don't care. Quite the opposite in fact. I wouldn't want the wrong person to pick it up and get the wrong idea."

He meant Matt and the kids, but it would have only been partly the wrong idea. Finn and I have never had an affair (I don't count a few drunken snogs at Christmas parties), but he's held a special place in my heart for the last twenty-five years, and if we'd ever both been single at the same time… Well, who knows? It obviously wasn't meant to be, but he still makes my insides go all gooey.

Joanna doesn't need to know any of this, although she's clearly curious.

"Best pal, huh? Male?"

"Yes, why?"

"You're smiling as you type." Her knowing smile immediately irritates me.

"He was my partner at work for a long time. We had each other's backs. He's a close friend, that's all."

"It's fine. You don't need to justify anything to me. But if you've got a soft spot for someone, cut Matt some slack, particularly when he's not done anything to earn your anger or jealousy."

"I'm neither angry nor jealous. And it's two-thirty. Don't you think we should check out the equipment, to make sure all the angles are correct?"

She agrees, but with a glint in her eye. I have a horrible feeling she's not forgotten the subject.

We spend the next twenty minutes adjusting camera angles and playing back film of a cuddly elephant sitting on the sofa. The elephant is the size of a ten-year-old child or thereabouts, and apparently watches over Joanna while she's asleep in her bedroom. I find that a bit strange, but I'm happy to make use of Elinor Elephant to get the CCTV set up correctly.

At ten to three, Joanna returns Elinor to her dressing table, and returns downstairs to pace the kitchen. I make myself another coffee and obey instructions to raid the cupboard for biscuits; and settle myself at the table with the laptop to view the live images of the now empty sofa.

"Shit." I bang my hand against my forehead.

"What's up?"

"We forgot about speakers," I say, frustrated with myself.

"We've got a few minutes; we could test them out now?"

"We didn't buy any. I'm going to have to listen at the door, or just come in really early on."

"Play it by ear – if you don't mind the pun. I'll try to take notes while she's talking. That's the doorbell. Shut this door for now and listen as well as you can."

Chapter Eleven

As I watch on the laptop, with my ear as close to the door as I can manage, the guest settles herself in the seat indicated by Joanna. I can see her perfectly. The image is quite good. I'm looking at a young woman in her mid to late twenties, with short blonde hair and a pixie-shaped face. Joanna introduces herself, and then the prospective client speaks. I can hardly hear her. Damn. She's got one of those soft, indistinct voices. I watch her again for a few seconds. She's a complete stranger and doesn't set off any alarm bells in my head. I leave the camera running on record, so we can watch back later, and open the door to the lounge.

"Hi, sorry I'm a few minutes late. I'm Becky, Joanna's business partner." I hold my hand out, and Penny shakes it. She has a limp, damp and pathetic sort of shake that leaves me wanting to clean my hand on my trousers. I control the temptation and smile at her instead.

"It's okay. It's nice to meet you." Her smile is shy, and doesn't reach her eyes, but I put this down to her obvious nervousness.

I sit down in the free armchair, and nod to Joanna in the other chair, to lead the conversation.

"So, Penny, how did you find us, and why?"

"You were in the paper, advertised as white knights who could rescue a damsel in distress. I need a white knight."

"Why don't you tell us the problem?" I can see Joanna controlling her irritation, by the way she speaks slowly and carefully – totally unlike her usual rapid communication.

"Okay." Penny's voice is still so quiet that I have to lean forward to hear her properly.

"Can you speak up a bit please? I think my ears are a bit blocked." I know they're not, but I feel the need to make an excuse.

"Sure." There's an increase of about half a decibel. "I go to this nightclub for work. Well, it's a kind of club. You might have heard of it; Band On The Wall. It's in Manchester, near Ancoats."

"I know it. I used to go there when I was younger than you. Probably before you were born. In the days when people could smoke in clubs and bars, and the air was thick with smoke – usually a mixture of tobacco and weed. I've not been there for a few years though." I know some of my ex-colleagues have been for work reasons, and a few of them socially. They said it's changed.

"It's not like that now. It's nice. Anyway, I'm a photographer for a local press agency, and I go to take photos of the bands. A bit like the paparazzi." She chuckles, and I warm to her by half a degree. "There's this one band that's on quite a lot, but whenever I'm at their gigs, I feel like someone's watching me. It freaks me out, and I wondered if you'd be able to help."

"How many times has this happened?" I ask.

"At least three, going back over the last three months. They play there about once a month."

"Can you tell me about the first time?" Joanna chips in.

"It would have been about the middle of November, on the Friday night. They like Fridays."

"Sorry," I interrupt. "What's the band's name?"

"Troy's Tigers."

Joanna raises an eyebrow, and I have to stifle a grin. I guess she agrees with me that it sounds like a group of primary school kids.

"Sorry for interrupting. Carry on."

"Yeah okay. As I said, it was November. I'd taken a good lot of photos and was walking home when I heard footsteps. I turned around, but couldn't see anyone. The hairs on the back of my neck were standing on end though."

She seems to need a prod to carry on.

"So what happened?"

"When?"

I take a slow deep breath; patience is clearly going to be needed for this case.

"That night. Did you get home safely? Did you see who was following you?"

"No, I didn't. I got a taxi home, just in case. My moped is in and out of the garage for repairs. There's an intermittent fault, and it keeps breaking down. I wondered if someone has tampered with it."

"That was sensible to get a taxi," says Joanna, apparently having controlled her own impatience. "We can check out the moped with the garage if you give us the details. For now, though, when was the next time you were followed?"

I try to pay attention as Penny describes the subsequent events in her soft tones, but I find myself watching her instead. There's a soft sheen of sweat on her forehead, not warranted by Joanna's central heating. As she talks, her eyes dart between the two of us. There are lots of reasons she might be nervous. Few people have cause to visit a private detective, and she seems very young. This appears to be a simple case of a stalker; probably an ex-boyfriend, or some admirer she's picked up at the gig. She's pretty and slim, both factors that are likely to provide wide appeal.

I suppress a surge of envy. My middle-aged spread no longer attracts such attention, having gone beyond that description – I'm now bordering on chubby. A lack of exercise combined with comfort eating since the events last summer have been bad for my health in far too many areas.

Joanna and I had rehearsed the questions yesterday after she made the appointment, so I let her follow the plan, and focus my observations on Penny's body language. My business partner is surprisingly good at this, and is gradually putting the client at ease. Using a technique I learned from a valued colleague, I separate out the different senses, and work out what each one is telling me.

Penny's eyes are doing less darting now, focussing mostly on Joanna with the occasional glance at me. Her voice has become stronger too; she's now talking in almost normal tones – still a bit softer than most people, but definitely more audible. Whilst her eyes are on Joanna, I take a discreet sniff. There's a hint of perfume. Perhaps she was expecting someone more romantic than us. Maybe '*White Knight*' conjured up the idea of more masculine assistance. The perfume itself is one I recognise – a brand preferred by my own elder daughter. Touch is always harder, as I'm not about to make contact, but I already have done once, and recall clearly that limp, nervous handshake. Taste will have to wait, and is far less important. I don't care whether she prefers tea or coffee, or is vegetarian or carnivore.

I turn my attention to Joanna for a moment. She's doing a superb job at interviewing the client and taking notes at the same time. Note-taking was never one of my strong points. I always relied on recordings for the details, and on my senses to fill in those gaps where gut instinct is required. My police training focussed on the facts, but years of experience taught me to follow my instincts until the facts turned up. My instincts only betrayed me once. Trust hasn't yet returned.

Joanna ties up the end of the interview neatly, explaining the fees and the next steps, before seeing Penny out into the pouring rain. I glance out of the window, and watch as she extracts a black umbrella from her handbag, and opens it up. She walks hurriedly in the direction of the bus stop, but only in the manner of someone wanting to escape the foul weather. She doesn't appear to think her stalker may be in the vicinity.

Chapter Twelve

I stand entranced as the music flows around me. The audience is intent, focussed on the band playing so brilliantly.

But I have eyes for just one: a person I am desperate to know better, to know intimately, and to possess. Only when this occurs can I become fulfilled.

Until that moment, I will need to satisfy my craving with images. I raise my camera and focus the lens, but a rush of longing defeats me. After only two shots, I lower the expensive equipment, and gaze with naked eyes at the object of my desire.

It won't be long now. I've begun my quest.

Chapter Thirteen

The morning after our first client meeting, I pull up outside Joanna's house in the car. I'm about to turn the engine off, but I sense that something is wrong. I release the handbrake and drive off, do one lap around the block, and then ease the car into a space outside the next-door house but one. I sit in my car for a moment, surveying the street through the heavy rain. It's nearly 11am, and most people will be out at work by now. There are a few cars dotted around, parked on the edge of the road. My gaze rests on each and I locate my first source of unease. There's a spotless black Audi, parked just a bit further down the road. It's not totally out of place on this street, but it's newer and more expensive than most of the other cars. It wasn't here yesterday, or the day before.

Obviously there could be many innocent reasons for its presence, but my body is telling me otherwise. Goosebumps, shivers and nausea have always been signs for me – even before the warehouse, although if I'd paid them more attention that day, it could have all turned out differently. Here and now, it's important that I don't make the same mistake, but I'm now a private individual with no reason to get attacked. So why don't I get out of the car?

I take some deep breaths. Who's likely to visit Joanna? As far as I know, the only person who knows her whereabouts is her son. But then, any investigator worth his salt would have tracked down her location by now. I know from my years as a police detective that it's quite difficult to hide from the authorities. I'm hiding, but from criminals, not from the police. Joanna has no chance against whichever secret service she was working for. It's almost certain that her visitor is from that source. So I have nothing to hide. I do another quick survey of the surrounding area, to make sure I've not missed anything, but nothing else seems awry.

Feeling a bit more rational, but still with a frantically thumping heartbeat, I force myself to get out of the car. The rain has let up a bit, so if anyone was to ask, I could use that as an excuse for not getting out immediately. I walk with steady dignity up to the front door and ring the bell.

A full minute elapses, during which raised voices reach me, but too muffled to make out exact words. Then Joanna answers the door. She looks white and strained. A man is standing behind her, a couple of feet back. He's of medium height, medium build, maybe in his forties. He's clean-shaven and has no significant features. An ideal candidate for secret service work.

"Mrs Wiseman?" His voice is also unremarkable, but the tone is sharp and formal.

"Mrs White now, but yes, I was Mrs Wiseman."

"Come in and shut the door behind you." I obey, and follow him and Joanna into the lounge. He sits on the armchair that Joanna occupied yesterday. She sits on the sofa, and I take the other chair.

"Matthew told us you changed your name to protect your identity after you left the police force last summer."

"Yes." There's no point in asking how he knows Matt.

"So how do you know Joanna?"

"Surely your research of Matt and Joanna must have found me as a mutual connection – even if neither of them were aware of it?"

"The operative who found your husband and your friend missed the connection. So perhaps you could answer my question. How do you know Joanna?"

"We met whilst I was at university, through a mutual friend. We stayed in touch afterwards but drifted after a couple of years. It was before the days of Facebook, where it obviously became much easier to stay in touch with old friends."

"Such a strange coincidence." He stares at each of us. If he's hoping to evoke further information with this strategy, he's dealing with the wrong women. We both remain silent and impassive for a few moments.

Joanna is the first to break, but only to ask if anyone would like a cup of tea. To my surprise, the visitor nods.

"Thanks. Milk and no sugar for me."

I smile reassuringly at her. "In that case, please can I have a coffee?"

"Sure," she says, giving me a weak grin. She shuts the kitchen door behind her, and a second later, I hear the faintest whir starting up. I hide it with a cough.

"Sorry – tickly throat. It's this awful weather."

"It is grim. Your friend was wise to absent herself for a few minutes. I need to ask you something else."

"Go ahead. I have a few questions of my own too."

"I'm sure you do, Mrs White. First, though, can you tell me how you found out about my existence, and what you know about me?"

"Matt told me briefly that he'd got involved in some government project, and that was how he met Joanna. He said it was top secret, and he couldn't tell me any more. But he was under extreme pressure to tell me even that. When he first saw Joanna in my company, he had a heart attack. I'm sure you can imagine how that looks to a wife. In order to save our marriage, he needed to reveal something of the truth. I was in the police force. I'm no stranger to secrecy."

"Of course. And what about Joanna? What did she tell you?"

"When I told her what Matt had said, she corroborated his story, and then revealed that she was running away from her ex-husband's messes, and that she'd forgotten to advise you of the fact. I suggested she rectify that as soon as possible, so I assume that's why you're here."

"Interesting." He resumes his staring tactic.

"Do you have a name? Perhaps not your own, but something by which we can address you?"

"Very funny." He doesn't even smile. "I usually go by the name Roger Taylor. I'm a big Queen fan."

"Me too." I hold out my hand, and he shakes it grudgingly. "Nice to meet you, Roger. I'm Becky."

"I know, but thank you for permission to use that name."

Joanna apparently considers that's a good point to enter, as the door opens and she emerges with a tray of drinks and biscuits. Putting the tray on the coffee table, she hands Roger his tea, and me the coffee, before taking a mug of pale green liquid.

"I prefer green tea these days," she says, sitting down. "It's healthier." As she takes a handful of chocolate fingers at the same time, I'm mildly sceptical, but Mr Taylor appears to accept the statement at face value. It's not terribly important, after all.

"Joanna, Becky has just been telling me that you were about to rectify your omission."

"Yes, it was on my list for this morning, actually. I was just about to look through my papers to identify the best contact, when you turned up. Quite a coincidence, but you've saved me a job. Thanks."

"As I'm sure Becky has told you, you can't go off and leave us wondering where you are. We've spent more time and resources than we can afford in tracking you down. I'm sure that wasn't your intention; however, there are penalties."

"What penalties?" She sits up straighter and spills tea on the new sofa. "Damn, I hope that comes out."

"That won't stain. It's the same colour as the fabric." I smile at her, then turn to Roger. "The circumstances were unusual. Joanna needed to get away from her ex-husband's contacts. She had more pressing things to think about than you, particularly as you'd been leaving her alone since she left her job."

"So she told you more about us than your husband had done?"

"I told you, she'd explained that she's not involved any more." I glare at him and set my mug down hard on the coffee table. "I have no idea what this is all about, what either of them have been working on, or why the hell you're involved. And frankly, I'm surprised it was worth you revealing yourself to me. Was it necessary, or was it only because I showed up this morning?"

"It is necessary, and you saved me the job of showing up at your home. Matt had asked me to avoid that if possible. But he did help me to find Joanna. He didn't realise we'd lost touch with her, and mentioned that he was surprised when she'd showed up at your house. It was easy after that. But now that you're aware of our existence, it's imperative to bring you in to some degree."

"I get that, but I'm still waiting for you to tell me something."

His brief pause is breached by a mobile phone ring tone; ironically, *Skyfall*, one of the more recent James Bond theme tunes. He answers it with a brief 'Yes'. There follows a series of yes and no responses, during which Joanna and I exchange frustrated glances. A moment later, with the call ended, he puts his phone back in his left inside jacket pocket.

"I'm afraid I have to go, as I'm needed elsewhere. Becky, I just need you to sign this. When I get home I'll scan it and email you a copy." He extracts a plain white envelope from his right inside jacket pocket and hands it to me. I open it and read. It's a brief statement confirming that I am bound by the Official Secrets Act and will reveal nothing under any circumstances.

"I don't know anything to reveal." I shake my head, frustrated by the lack of information.

"You know enough. You'll learn more in the days ahead, as I believe your skills and knowledge will be useful to us. Meanwhile, continue with your current case. It has no bearing on our present work, but it should prove a useful exercise for you to renew your skills."

He hands me a pen, and I sign. My chest tightens. I feel as though he's backed me into a corner, and I have no choice, but Joanna smiles at me, and nods. I hand back the pen and the signed document, and Roger leaves without another word.

Chapter Fourteen

With Roger gone, we return to the lounge, and settle back into the seats we occupied before. I turn to Joanna.

"Right, so I've now signed the Official Secrets Act. Can you tell me what's going on?"

"It's not for me to say. I think you probably know enough. Anyway, I don't think Roger cares about the past. I have a feeling he wants you on his team for the future."

"Fantastic. I'm just about getting my head around becoming a private detective. I don't think I can handle the idea of being a spy." Bile rises in my throat.

"No one's asking you to be a spy, Becky. But sometimes there are activities a civilian can handle best, and Roger and his team like to have people on the ground to help. I guess in our new roles as White Knights, we might be able to investigate a few things for him."

"What did he say to you before I arrived?"

"He was having a bit of a go at me for running away without telling him where I was. I'm pleased you turned up when you did. He just kept going on about it before then."

"So what makes you think he wants us to investigate stuff for him?" I rest back in my chair, curiosity overcoming fear for the moment.

"He handed me this before he left." She shows me a torn piece of newspaper. It's got an advert on it – recruitment for a lab technician. It's obviously at the top of the page, as the name of the newspaper is on it, and yesterday's date.

"Is he suggesting you apply for it?"

"I reckon so. It's not far from here, and it's got to be more interesting than Asda. If the pay is okay, I might be able to buy myself a cheap car. Roger might part with a few hundred quid in advance if I ask nicely."

My phone buzzes, and I glance at it. "Shit, is that the time?"

"Why?" Joanna looks at her watch. "I make it just gone twelve-thirty."

"I should have been meeting someone at half past. I'd better just message to say I'm running late." I tap a quick apology into my phone and click *Send*.

Finn will be waiting for me.

I park outside the pub, tucking the car as obscurely as possible between two large SUVs and with my rear bumper against a hedge. Opening the sun visor, I check my face in the mirror. I look a wreck. I'm already late, so an extra minute won't make much difference. A quick attack with a hairbrush and lipstick, and the worst is hidden. Hopefully Finn won't look too closely. I get out of the car and head inside.

He's sitting at a table near the back of the pub – a fact which he informed me of by text. I find him easily and get a few seconds of observation before he lowers his newspaper. In the six months since I last saw him, he's gained a few grey hairs, and lost weight. He looks tired.

"Becks!" He folds his paper quickly, throws it on the table, and gets up. I'm enfolded in a hug tight enough to crack ribs. "God, I've missed you, girl," he whispers against my ear.

I cling on for a moment, then pull away, a little too conscious that we're in a public place. I sit down and pick up a menu, using it to shield my hot face.

I notice he takes his time to sit down and watches me intently while he does so. It's been too long since we met and spoke, and there's too much history for us to pick up and carry on as though nothing had happened. I feel as tongue-tied as a teenager on a first date. Actually, I think Cheryl would make a better job of this meeting than I'm doing right now. The thought of my youngest daughter calms me. I'm part of a close family unit. I'm not on a date. Finn's an old friend and colleague – nothing more, despite my physical reaction to him.

I take a deep breath and lower the menu so I can read it. Middle-aged eyesight demands the use of varifocals, but I hate the things, and can never find the right place to look through for reading. More often than not, I just take the damn things off to read. This time I manage to find the sweet spot on the lenses so keep the glasses on my face. They hide some lines anyway – a good thing right now.

"What do you recommend?" I ask.

"I don't know. I've not been here for a while – not since last summer."

I can feel his gaze on me, intent and determined, and I flush, although I keep focussing on the menu.

"You know what, I'm not that hungry. I think I'll just have a coffee." My insides are churning.

"I'll get it. I think I'll just have a coffee as well." He takes the menu out of my hands and goes to the bar. I feel a little bereft with nothing left to hide behind, and my pulse races once more. I've not seen him since the warehouse. There's so much to say, and so much that shouldn't be said. I don't know where to start. I take some more deep breaths and try to clear my mind. A moment of meditation whilst he's at the bar should help.

Back home three hours later, I manage a perfunctory hello to Matt, and head upstairs to run myself a bath. I need some space to think about the events of today. I set my Kindle next to the bath, in case I reach the point of wanting to escape from my thoughts. There's a lot to take in, and I'm not sure I'm ready to handle it all yet. I trail my Echo Dot into the bathroom and tell Alexa to play Take That.

Settled in amongst the bubbles and hot water, I try to make sense of all I've heard. Roger is relatively easy, and I dismiss thoughts of him for the moment. He's clearly going to be a part of my life in the future, and I think Joanna's right about him wanting to use the agency.

Finn is the one who drags my thoughts back. I try to block the memories of him holding me: the long hug which said so many things, and yet maybe nothing at all. Okay, maybe I don't try very hard. I'll allow myself to dwell on it for just a moment. I shut my eyes and hold on tight for several breaths.

Right, Becky, get a grip. He's just a friend. You're happily married.

The problem is that it's easier to dwell on the chemistry between me and Finn than to think about our conversation today. I don't want to remember what happened in that warehouse, and he'd made me describe it to him in detail. I'm not ready yet. Why would he do that? He said it was to help me, but there was something in his eyes, and maybe a hardness in his tone... If I hadn't known him so well, I'd never have spotted it, but we worked together as partners for over ten years. Something is not right, but if I try to analyse it, I'll have to face the details of that damned awful day again. I've been through it once already today, and that was more than enough.

I give in to my weakness and pick up my Kindle so I can escape into someone else's world.

Chapter Fifteen

Friday morning, I get a text from Joanna. I've just finished breakfast, and I take my coffee into the lounge before looking at my phone properly.

"Troy and his band are playing tonight at BOTW. We should go. Suss it all out. See if we can find Penny's stalker."

I take a moment to realise BOTW is Band On The Wall. Meanwhile, panic fills me at the thought of going to such a crowded place. Any kind of gig has been out of bounds for me for many months. The noise alone would totally freak me out.

"Can't do it. You go. Fill me in tomorrow."

"No way. You don't get out of it this easily. Penny said there's a separate area with a bar. They do pizza. Sit in there and eat and drink. I'll bring people out to you to interview."

Shit. That woman has got an argument for everything. Can I do this?

I text Alison. I'm fairly sure she's been to Band On The Wall in the last couple of years.

"Hey Ali, got a couple of minutes to chat?"

A minute later my mobile rings.

"Hi Mum, I'm just between lectures. I've got five minutes. How's Dad?"

"He's doing fine. How are you?" I have a sip of coffee.

"All good. You called? Not like you to call on a Friday morning. What's up?"

"Have you been to Band On The Wall recently?"

"Yeah – I went in the summer holidays. Cool vibe. Depends a bit on the bands though. Why?"

"You know I told you I'm doing this private investigator thing with Joanna?"

"Yeah. Go on."

"We've got a case, and she wants me to go there to follow up on a lead."

"What's wrong with that? Mum, I'm going to have to go in a minute. I'm standing outside the lecture theatre, and I can see Prof coming down the corridor. Just go along, it'll be fine. There's this breakout area with a bar and food. Just sit there and chat to people. It's not too loud there. Got to go. Love you."

"Love you too." I end the call and return to my texts. Joanna has sent me three messages in the last few minutes whilst I was talking to Alison.

"*Becks?*" "*Becky, will you come along? Please!*" "*Hey, Becky, where are you? I'm freaking out here. Are you okay?*"

I click on the *Call* button.

"Why the hell are you freaking out?" If anyone should freak out here, it's me. Better left unsaid though.

"Thank God you're okay. I thought I'd sent you into some crazy panic."

"I just phoned Alison for a bit of info on Band On The Wall. She endorsed what you said about the separate area."

"So will you come along then tonight? Are you allowed out on Friday nights?"

"We're not religious. We like to have a Friday night

dinner as a family, but it's no big deal if I miss a week. I suppose I can come along. But I'm not going inside. Not while the band's playing. It will be way too noisy for me." I take a large gulp of now lukewarm coffee. "How do we get there?"

We spend the next few minutes arguing the relative merits of bus, tram and taxi, before I bravely offer to drive.

"I won't be drinking, will I? We can park in one of the nearby streets, or I think there's a car park not too far away." I'm breathing fast now, trying to block out the realisation that we'll be less than a mile from the warehouse where everything happened.

"Becky, give me five minutes, hen. I'll call you back."

I spend the next few minutes using the loo, then raiding the tin for chocolate digestives. I'm halfway through my third biscuit when my mobile rings.

"Hi." I know I sound antsy, but my nerves are on the edge of a cliff now.

"Relax. It's all sorted. I told Penny we were coming tonight. She said she'll pay for a taxi both ways. She's ordered an Uber for us. Picking me up first at half past seven, then I'll come and get you. Do you want to pop around here after lunch and we'll plan strategy?"

I agree and disconnect. I'm actually relieved I'll be seeing her this afternoon. Otherwise there are far too many hours to sit and stew.

It's shortly after 8pm when we arrive at the club. I've been close to hyperventilating in the taxi, and despite Joanna's anxious reassurances, I feel nauseous by the time we arrive. I wipe my damp palms on a tissue from the pocket of my jeans as we leave the cab. They're the only jeans I could find that still fit me, but they look okay with a pretty, flowery top that hides a multitude of flabby bits.

My business partner throws me a concerned look over her shoulder as she opens the door. I follow her in, curiosity temporarily overcoming my nerves.

The place has a trendy vibe, with a bar at the far end, opposite the door, and a hatch behind which cool-looking ticket sellers are seated. Tables and chairs occupy most of this area, and the glorious smell of pizza hits my nostrils on entry. Surprisingly, this settles my nausea rather than exacerbating it.

About half the tables are occupied, so I grab a free one, facing the door through to the gig area. I settle my thick coat on the chair next to me and dig in my purse for some money.

"I'll keep the table. Do you want to grab some food and drink?" I hand the money over to Joanna.

"Sure. What are you drinking?" I settle on a white wine and ask for any veggie pizza. I'm not veggie, but have a mild aversion to meat on pizza.

While Joanna's at the bar, a pretty girl with a camera slung around her neck emerges from the internal door. I take a few seconds to place her. She looks much more confident than at Joanna's house.

"Becky. Thanks for coming tonight. Troy's not on until later – about 10ish – so I don't know if... if the person we're expecting will turn up before then."

"Hi Penny. How are you?"

"Okay, thanks. No spine tingles yet, so I reckon they're not here. It always seems to be when Troy's on, so I'm sure they'll turn up."

"Have a seat. Do you want a drink?" I ask, but she shakes her head.

"I prefer not to drink while I'm working. Increases the percentage of blurred photos." She grins, and I'm surprised by the difference compared to the shy, quiet girl I met last week.

"Anyway, I'd better get back in there. Other bands to photograph. See you soon."

I wave to her and then smile at Joanna, as she unloads paper plates loaded with pizza.

"I'll just go back for the drinks." She gives a curious glance in the direction of the door, following Penny's departure. "Then we'll talk."

A minute later, I'm sipping wine. Joanna's seated, facing me.

"Was that Penny? I almost didn't recognise her. She looks very different."

"It's just posture. She seems much more confident here. I guess she's in her comfort zone, but if I was being stalked in a particular place, I'd be a gibbering wreck. I don't get it."

I look around the room. There are a few people at the bar, but most are going through now into the other area, where the first band are now in full swing. Screens overhead show the band and the audience, and the music is audible out here too, but not blaring.

"When you go in there, I think you should keep an eye on her too."

"Obviously. I'll go inside shortly. I want to get a kind of baseline. Do you know what I mean?"

"Of course. Compare a non-Troy band with what happens when Troy and his lot come on. That makes perfect sense. If you meet anyone interesting, send them out to me. Or monitor them and we can interview them in the interval."

Joanna goes inside shortly afterwards, and I retreat to a chair where I can have my back to the wall. Not being able to see potential enemies behind me is a source of extreme stress. My new seat is roughly level with the old one, in that I still have an excellent view of the door through to the gig, and I now have a slightly better view of the screen showing the band and the audience.

I try to find Joanna on the screen, but the picture is hazy, and I soon give up. I settle for surveying the few people left eating pizza near me. A group of four – older adults in their forties or thereabouts – are making a lot of noise and clearly enjoying themselves. They show no desire to move, and I suspect they're waiting for one of the later bands to come on – perhaps even Troy.

I'm more curious about a young man sitting alone near the window. He's alternating between checking his phone and looking compulsively out into the street. He looks at his watch a few times, and appears to be getting ready to leave when a stunningly pretty girl walks in. They kiss, a long and intimate embrace. I glance away, feeling as though I'm intruding. A moment later, they head in to the main area, and I lose interest.

Time passes. I switch to drinking diet coke. I need to keep alert, and preferably awake, as it's unlikely that we'll be home much before midnight tonight. For someone who's usually asleep by ten, that's late.

Joanna comes out to get me when the first band finishes, and I cautiously follow her in to the main band area. It's not as awful as I expected. The area near the stage is busy, but at the back, near the bar, there's plenty of space to stand and watch without getting trampled or feeling squashed. A set of stairs up to a VIP area is blocked off, so I fold my heavy winter coat and place it on the bottom stair so I don't have to keep carrying it. No one challenges me, and I relax a bit.

On stage, there's minimal action, with instruments being moved. A stage hand replaces one drum kit with another and strategically arranges the microphones.

"Is Troy on next?" I ask Joanna.

"No. It's some band I've never heard of. It's interesting sussing out the place though." She turns and raises an eyebrow as Penny approaches. "Not great for keeping low key if you want us to dig out some information for you."

"Sor-ry," says Penny in sarcastic tones. "I was going to introduce my colleague, Nigel. He's a fellow-photographer for the same paper as me. Is that a problem?"

A young man at her side grins awkwardly. "Hi. Hope I'm not intruding."

"It's fine. Nice to meet you, Nigel." I hold out my hand, and he shakes it in a surprisingly firm grip. I cast him a second glance. "Do you want a drink?"

"Thanks, that would be great." He names a beer that I've never heard of.

"You'd better come to the bar with me. Joanna, Penny, what can I get you?" With a round of drinks orders vaguely in my head, I lead the way to the bar at the back of the main area, but Nigel puts a hand on my arm.

"You're better off at the main bar outside. They don't do my beer in here. It's really limited. Come on. I'll give you a hand, anyway."

There's a small queue at the main bar, and I make small talk with Penny's colleague until we get served.

"Why don't you take these to a table? We'll stay out here and have a chat. I'll just run in with the drinks for Penny and your friend. Back in a sec."

He arouses my curiosity. Why would this young chap want to talk to an old fogey like me when he's got Penny in tow? And a fair number of attractive young women are dotted around inside the club. I take his beer and my coke to the table I left a short while ago, and resume my seat facing the door. Old habits die hard.

A minute later, Nigel is sitting opposite me, taking a gulp of beer.

"Thanks," he says. "So it sounds like a helluva cliché, but what's a girl like you doing in a place like this?"

I laugh. "Sussing it out. My fifteen-year-old daughter wants to come here one night. I'd heard that her favourite band were on tonight, so I said I'd come along and check it out and see if it's safe."

"You don't look old enough to have a fifteen-year-old daughter. How do you know Penny?"

"Friend of a friend. I believe you work together?" I'm keen to get the conversation on to a more suitable track. I'm the one that should ask the questions. Also, I'm a bit freaked out by the idea of this spotty youth flirting with me. He looks about the same age as Alison.

"I've been a photographer in this industry for about ten years," he says, answering my unspoken question. He must be older than I thought. Still too young to be flirting with me though. "I'm Penny's boss, but we work on similar projects. I heard she was worried about getting home safely after being here, so I came with her tonight. Her usual transport is playing up."

"That's nice of you. Are you into the band that's coming on?"

"Yeah, I love music. It's great getting to photograph the musicians. We try to get a lot of natural shots, particularly when they're performing. Then you can portray the atmosphere to the fans that couldn't make it this time." He grins, enthusiasm shining from his face. "What do you do? Sorry, it's awful. I didn't catch your name."

"Rebecca." I'd already agreed with Joanna, that I would be as incognito as possible tonight. Obviously I couldn't stop Penny calling me Becky earlier, but if people I meet now think I'm Rebecca mostly, it will reduce any chances of my past coming back to bite me. As for his first question… I really don't want to answer that. "Hey, look. The next band's on. Shall we go back in?"

"I'm not in a rush. Penny can sort out their photos.

They're no big deal. I'd rather wait out here chatting to you until Troy and his lot come on. So, what were you saying you do?"

Bugger! Why can't he leave me alone? I pin on a false smile.

"Mostly just a housewife. Looking after my husband and the kids. Shopping, cooking, cleaning. Same old, same old. Have you got a family?"

"I live by myself, in a flat not too far from here. If you ever fancied getting away from the boredom of housewifery for a bit, I could show you a good time."

"I'm too old for you." I stand up and drain my glass. "Time to go back in. I need to keep my friend company." I head for the door into the bar area, but a hand on my wrist stops me halfway there. I turn round. "Excuse me?"

"Come on, Rebecca. You and me. We could do a quick getaway to my flat and be back in time for Troy."

"Don't you get it? I'm not interested." I look pointedly at where he's holding my wrist. He grips more tightly for a second, then, appearing to see something or someone behind me, releases me. I turn to see Joanna standing there with a tall, attractive man. I recognise him from the newspaper article, and from research done on the internet prior to this evening's outing.

"Nigel, Penny wants you." Joanna gestures behind her and waits until Nigel is the other side of the door. "Becky, this is Troy. I've told him why we're here tonight."

I hold out my right hand to shake, and notice red marks from where Nigel has just been mauling it. Troy looks keenly at my wrist, then at my face, then at the door through which Nigel just departed.

"Nice to meet you, Becky. Sorry to see that prick was hassling you. I reckon I know him from somewhere, but no idea where. Anyway, I think we should speak privately, but maybe not here, and not tonight. Joanna's just given me her card. Can I come to see you both tomorrow?"

"Sure. What time?" That brief tangle with Nigel has left me feeling weak, and I don't really want to stay any longer than necessary.

"Probably about two, but I'll call late morning and confirm the time. I'm gonna have to go now. On stage soon, and I gotta prep. Cheers. See you tomorrow." He's gone with a quick wave.

Joanna turns to me. "Are you okay?" She puts an arm round my shoulders. "Come on. Let's go inside and grab our coats. I think we can go now."

"Before Troy's on? Won't he be upset if we don't stay? And won't Penny be angry? She wants to check out possible stalkers."

"We'll talk later. It's fine. Come on."

Ten minutes later, we're in a black cab on the way home. It's ten o'clock – a lot earlier than I thought we'd be leaving.

"I thought we were getting an Uber?"

Joanna grins. "Troy sorted this out for us. He said he wanted us to get home safely, and this is a driver he often uses. He's nice."

"Why's he coming to see us tomorrow?"

"He's had threats that his family will be hurt. There's no other information and they're not asking for anything. He said he'll tell us more tomorrow."

"How did he know about us?" I lean against the leather seat back, feeling exhausted and confused.

"Penny pointed him out. He came out to speak to the sound and lighting guys whilst the other band was on. I went over to him when he'd finished and handed him my card, telling him I'd like a chat. To be honest, it surprised me when he looked at the card, but even more so when he manoeuvred me into a corner, asked my name, and said he might have need of our services. He asked to meet you, then we came out to find you being manhandled by that pimply idiot."

"He was coming on to me and wouldn't take no for an answer. Do you think it was safe leaving Penny with him?"

"Yes, because Penny left just before we did. She told me she had a headache and was leaving. While I was waiting to speak to Troy, she asked me to tell Nigel that she was going home."

"But you sent him in to see her. Had she already gone?"

"She was putting her stuff away. I figured she could deliver her own message."

"Bloody hell, Joanna. We had a duty of care. We should have made sure she got away before he knew. I don't trust that guy at all. What if he's the one who's been stalking her?"

"Shit. I didn't think of that. But wouldn't she have recognised him if he was the stalker?"

"I don't know. Maybe he disguised himself. Can you try to call her?"

Joanna digs out her mobile. I look out of the window. We're halfway up Cheetham Hill. It's not too late to turn around if we have to.

There's a moment's tension as the phone rings out, then a breathless voice answers. Joanna hits the speaker button.

"Joanna?"

"Yes, are you okay?"

"I think I was followed again. I was going to get a taxi, but there were loads of people around, and I thought the fresh air might help my head."

"Are you safe now?"

"Yeah, I'm home. I've locked and bolted all the doors and windows. I'll be fine. I'll call you tomorrow."

Joanna looks at me as she ends the call. "Oh my God. I can't believe we let that happen."

"At least she's okay for now. What we need to do tomorrow is ask Troy if he saw Nigel in the audience taking photos."

Chapter Sixteen

Standing in the shadows, I watch the house in silence. It's nearly eleven o'clock, and she'll be alone in that house tonight.

I was here earlier, unseen by anyone, and observed as a little girl hopped into a car, waving to her mum and saying "See you tomorrow". Sorry, kiddo, but you won't be seeing your mum tomorrow, or ever again.

The street is quiet. It's a leafy suburban road in one of the posher parts of Manchester.

I clutch my weapon of choice, a steel blade, currently sheathed in what looks like an umbrella. It's time to go inside…

Chapter Seventeen

It's quite early on Saturday morning, and I'm sitting in the kitchen nursing my third cup of coffee when Cheryl pokes her head around the door.

"Morning, Mum. Have you got time for a chat?"

"Of course, love. Are you okay?" Focussing properly on my daughter and dismissing all other thoughts from my head, I see a pale face, and rings around her eyes. She's obviously not okay.

"Kind of." She stops. "Do you want another coffee? I think I need one."

I decline, and try to control my anxiety as she moves around the kitchen, banging into the edge of the fridge-freezer, and dropping the tub of sweetener on to the floor. Luckily, it's plastic with a secure lid.

"Sit down. I'll make your drink." I get up and finish the job easily. "Why don't you come and sit in the lounge? It's a bit cosier, and we're less likely to be disturbed. Dad will be down for breakfast soon."

She's settled down on the sofa next to me before she starts talking.

"There are a couple of girls at school," she starts abruptly. "I couldn't work out what they were doing at first, but it looks like they've identified a few people who they don't like, and they've been spreading rumours. They've divided the year. It's like a bad American high school. There are the popular kids, and the rest."

"Should I ask which category you're in?" Cheryl is beautiful and clever, but shy and sensitive. A perfect target for jealous bullies.

"I would have probably got away with it, but they were saying awful things about Danielle. Obviously I stuck up for her – I'm not going to let anyone slag off one of my friends – and it was clearly a load of rubbish. So now, I've been added to the target list. And it's horrible." She drains her mug and puts it on the coffee table.

"So what did they say about Danielle, and what are they saying about you?"

"They said she's been sleeping around. She had a photo on Facebook from her birthday party last month, and they've Photoshopped it and sent it round the school. It looks like they've swapped her body with someone who was posing topless, and it's really horrible."

"Do you know if it was definitely these girls who've played with and posted these images?"

"It's difficult to trace, but it was one of them that first approached me about being on their side against Dan. When I refused, I got a Facebook message from her, warning me I'd be next if I didn't get my act together."

"May I see?"

She pulls out her phone and shows me a screenshot. The name is obscured, but the message is clear.

'Do what we want, bitch. Get your shit together or you'll be next.'

"Charming. Do you have the original message? And the photo of Danielle?"

"Why?"

"Because," I put my arm around her, "this is not only nasty, it's illegal. I still have some friends in the police who could investigate and give these girls an official warning. I imagine their parents would be very concerned about the possibility of a criminal record for their daughters."

"Probably, but would they know it was me that told on them?"

"There's no need for them to know that. Would you mind if I ask Finn to come round and have a look at your phone? He'll be very discreet, and it would mean I don't have to pry."

"I've not got any secrets from you, Mum. But I'd rather it wasn't Finn. He's a man, and I don't want that picture of Dan to be seen by anyone who might lech over it."

"Finn's not like that."

"I know, but he's still a man. How about Wendy?"

"I'll call her and see if she's free. Meanwhile, I don't think there's a fifteen-year-old in existence who has no secrets from her mum." I squeeze her shoulders to let her know I'm teasing.

"Well, I might not tell you about every single boy I fancy, but there's nothing on my phone about that."

"You'd be surprised. Twenty minutes with your phone, and I'd know your whole search history and everyone you'd checked out on Facebook and Instagram for the last five years."

"Maybe I'd better keep it hidden then." She giggles, then turns to look at me, and her expression becomes serious again, and perhaps a bit scared. "Please ask Wendy, Mum. I want this to stop, and I know it sounds selfish, but it would be great if it could stop before they Photoshop me."

"Of course. Can I make some suggestions to protect yourself?" I wait for her to agree. "Great. Block everyone from your accounts who isn't a close friend, and make all your settings private, so that these girls or their pals can't access any of your photos. Ask your friends to do the same, or to delete any photos they have of you. That's a reasonable first step."

"Okay, thanks. Would you be able to ask Wendy to contact the school as well please? That way it hasn't come from me. She can have had anonymous reports of this happening, and it would be reasonable for her to contact the head."

"Of course."

"I think I'll go back to bed for a bit. I'm exhausted. You will call Wendy, won't you?"

"I'll call her now. Get some more sleep, love." I kiss her forehead.

When she's gone, I scroll through the numbers on my phone to find Wendy. I've not spoken to her for seven months now, but perhaps it's time to break the silence.

It's lovely speaking to my old friend and mentor. We're on the phone for ages discussing what each has been up to for the last seven months. I tell her about Matt's illness and my new venture into private investigations. She tells me about lecturing at Manchester University and her trip to Australia to see her eldest son. It's almost an hour before we finally arrange that she'll come round after dinner this evening for a drink and to speak to Cheryl. My phone beeps several times whilst we're on the call, but I'm too busy catching up to check on it. But when I disconnect and check my messages, I see eight WhatsApp messages and five missed calls from Joanna. The messages just say to call her, each one become increasingly urgent and rude. I'm about to call back when Cheryl comes in. She's looking a lot better, but still tired.

"Did you get some more sleep?" I ask.

"Yes, thanks. Was that Wendy on the phone?"

"She's coming round this evening to chat to you. Is that okay?"

"That's great. Thanks, Mum. And I've blocked everyone from my accounts that isn't a proper friend, so hopefully I'm not too late doing that."

"Good girl. Yes, let's hope you were quick enough. If not, we'll deal with it. So don't worry too much, but better to prevent than have to cure."

"God, yeah! I'd hate to go through what Dan's had to deal with."

"It's funny hearing you talk about Dan. You always used to call her Danni, and that was fine, but my best friend at Uni was called Dan."

"I know. We went to his wedding at the beginning of last year. He married that gorgeous guy that looked like he'd stepped off the front cover of GQ or something."

"Gray Monton. Yes, he was a bit of a dish. Dan's still in good shape though."

"Mum! Dan's nearly fifty. Gray can't be a day over thirty-five."

"He was forty last month. I sent him a card on MoonPig. Such a sweetie as well. Very suited to Dan." My phone pings again.

'Where the f*** r u?'

"Sorry, love. I'm going to have to call Joanna. We'll chat later, okay?"

She smiles and leaves the lounge.

I don't bother replying to Joanna's message; I just click on her number to return a call.

"Where the bloody hell have you been?" She doesn't bother with hello.

"I was on a call with an ex-colleague. I'll tell you more about it later. What's the matter?"

"Troy's been in touch. His wife's dead. She's been murdered."

Chapter Eighteen

I pick Joanna up five minutes later, and we drive to the address she got from Troy. It's in Didsbury – a four-bedroom detached house on a quiet road. At least, it looks as though it's usually quiet. This morning it's heaving with police and forensic teams, methodically working the area. The road is sealed off with police tape, and we park on the next street up, walking a couple of hundred yards to join the onlookers and gathering press teams. Finn is standing in the road at the end of what must be Troy's drive. He's talking to his Sergeant; a pretty girl whose name I remember after a minute or two of racking my brains. Molly. She joined GMP just before everything kicked off and I left, so I didn't know her well. I'm hoping she won't remember me.

Joanna and I loiter at the barrier of the tape, and after a moment or two, Finn comes over. Molly heads in another direction, towards the house.

"Becky, what are you doing here? How do you know about this? What do you know?"

"Troy is a… client. He was due to visit us today, but he called Joanna to tell her his wife had been killed."

He frowns and then glances at my business partner. "You must be Joanna. I'm Finn. I've been assigned to this case as Inspector. I used to work with Becky."

My breath catches in my throat at the cold impersonality of his tone.

"Nice to meet you, Finn." Joanna holds out her hand to him and he shakes it. "Any chance of coming through? Troy really wants to see us." She shows him her phone, presumably with the message she showed me earlier.

'*Please come. I need your help.*' His address follows.

Finn speaks into his own phone for a moment, turning his back to us and walking away as he does so. Joanna gives me a look, as if to say, 'Is he letting us in or not?' I shrug. He needs to check. He may be in charge of the case, but he can't just let us in on our say-so. I'll explain this to her sometime, but not now. Not while we're surrounded by press and curious neighbours.

Eventually, Finn returns and beckons us through. With a quick glance at each other, Joanna and I duck under the tape. It's a bit too high to climb over.

Molly comes over. "What's going on?" she says. "We can't have just any old body swarming through here."

"Do you remember, Becky, my old partner?" I cringe as Finn introduces me. So much for keeping a low profile.

"Oh yeah. You left after—"

"Becky's working on private cases now, with her partner, Joanna." Finn interrupts. "They were engaged by Troy, but we don't know why yet."

"He's pretty devastated," says Molly. She sounds hostile, and I guess she sees me as a threat.

"He wants to see them. Away from the press though. Where do you suggest?"

"My car is the other side of the cordon. Away from this

lot." She points to the hungry media folk pressing in as close to the tape as they can get.

"Hey!" Troy is standing near a bush, just out of sight of the photographers. He looks grey and ill. We move towards him, but Molly stops us.

"Troy, come this way. You can all sit in my car." She hands over a set of keys to Joanna. "Go chat in there."

Joanna takes off her coat and gives it to our client to shield his face as we emerge into the road. But we're only in their sights for a minute as we turn away from them towards Molly's car.

I sit in the front passenger seat, but turn towards the back where Joanna is sitting next to Troy. He slumps forwards with his head in his hands, and his body shakes with sobs. My partner rests her hand on his back, providing a bit of comfort through his utter devastation. I allow him a few minutes, but when I see Molly heading towards us, I realise our time with him is limited. I hold up my hand to her, to delay the inevitable. To my relief, she nods and turns away.

I turn again to face the back seat.

"Troy," I say gently, "I'm so sorry. We want to help, but we've not got a lot of time to talk here. Are you able to tell us what happened?"

He sits up, his face even greyer than before. His red-rimmed eyes are stark against the rest of his face, making him look like a haunted demon.

"I got home late last night. The gig went well, and I went for a few drinks afterwards with the rest of the band. Oh God." His head returns to his hands.

"I'm sure that wouldn't have made any difference, Troy," says Joanna.

"Maybe not. They said she'd been gone a couple of hours by the time I got home."

"What time was that?" I ask.

"Ten to one. I went into the kitchen to get some water, and…" His breath comes quickly, and he struggles to speak.

"Hush, it's okay. Take a minute." Joanna soothes, but he turns to her, anger in his eyes.

"It'll never be okay again. Not ever. What the hell do I tell my daughter?"

"A family liaison worker will help with that sort of thing. Have they sent one to you yet? Where is your daughter?"

"She's with Linda's parents, Olivia and Mike. Emma usually goes there on a Friday night if I'm at a gig. Linda often goes out with a couple of her girl-friends but last night she said she'd have an early night, as she was a bit tired. I phoned her parents last night after I called the police."

I give a brief thought to his in-laws, and how they must have taken the news that their daughter had been murdered. Will they have told their grandchild anything yet? I glance at my watch. It's almost midday.

"Have you heard from the family liaison officer yet?" I ask.

"Yeah. Some woman popped in, then said she was going round to see Olivia and Mike, and she'd see me later."

"Do you remember her name?" It's not that important, and I can ask Finn later, but I'd like to know if it's someone I can work with.

"Isabel? Annabelle? Something like that." He runs a hand through straggly hair. "Does it matter?"

"I just want to make sure you and your family are being well looked after. Was she a tall lady? Late forties?"

"I didn't really notice. Yeah maybe."

"DC Janice Rose?"

"Yeah. Could have been."

"She's lovely. She'll do her best for you and your family. You can trust her." I worked with her many times over the years. Janice is a couple of years younger than me and joined the force at around the same time, but she's never been ambitious. She always just wanted to help people, and has the incredible inner strength to make family liaison work her vocation.

A nervous flutter in my chest reminds me I must be careful. I can't afford to get too far drawn in. I need to keep a healthy distance from ex-police colleagues, and this isn't the way to do it. Getting involved in a murder case was not part of the plan.

"Sorry. Carry on if you can, about what happened. You said you'd gone into the kitchen." I hoped I'd distracted him sufficiently for him to carry on now, but I know it will be difficult.

"Linda was on the floor near the sink. Someone had stabbed her, like, loads of times. It was the worst thing I've ever seen, and my poor... Oh God, my poor Linda. She hadn't stood a chance." He balls his fists into his eyes. Joanna rests a hand on his shoulder in silence, interrupted only by a tap on the window. Molly opens the back door.

"You've had long enough now," she says to me and Joanna. "Mr Cassidy, my colleague is going to take you round to your in-laws where your daughter is waiting for you. I'm sure these ladies will resume their discussion with you some other time."

Obeying the Sergeant's signal, we all get out of the car. Molly takes Troy to another car, parked a little further down the road. Joanna and I, sharing a quick glance, head over to Finn, where he's consulting with the head of the forensic team, another old friend.

Finn looks up and gives a half-smile. Somewhere between friendly and resigned.

"Alec, you remember Becky, don't you?"

"Of course I do. Becks, my dear, I'd give you a hug, but I'm all geared up here." He points at his chest to show his full protective suit − worn to prevent him depositing anything inappropriate in the crime scene.

"Sure, the hug can wait. It's good to see you, Alec. How's Deb? And the baby?"

"All well. How are you? It's lovely to see you again too. We were worried about you. You disappeared after everything happened, and no one knew where you'd gone."

"It took a while for me to pull myself together. And there are a few people I want to avoid, so I changed a few things. Get Finn to send me your number again, and I'll put it in my new phone. I'll call you one evening if that's okay."

"That would be great. Who's your friend?"

I introduce Joanna. There's no need for us to stay much longer. I know I can pump Alec and Janice for all the information I need, and my body is beginning to betray me. I've been in this crime scene for too long and seen too many familiar faces for one day. I have to leave.

"Sorry, guys, we need to be going. I don't want to keep you from your work any longer. We just had to speak to our client, but that's done now. I'll call you both in the week if that's okay."

They agree, and Joanna and I head towards my car. I know this area fairly well, as it was part of my patch, so I lead her round the back to avoid the press, who are still hovering at the edge of the tape.

When we get in the car, I put the radio on. I'm suddenly exhausted. It's been a long time since I had to deal with a crime scene in any form, and I'd almost forgotten the intensity of action and emotion. The radio is a good option, as it defers significant conversation. I notice Joanna glancing at me as she puts her seatbelt on, but she refrains from comment. We accomplish the drive home in a companionable lack of conversation – just the occasional discussion if a song comes on that we both like. That lasts until the News comes on. I turn the volume up.

"...*and Manchester musician Troy Cassidy is distraught today after finding his wife murdered in their home. The police are investigating, and there are no suspects at this time."*

"Standard News report really," says Joanna. "It doesn't tell us anything we didn't already know."

"True. The question is, do we leave this to the police, or try to investigate ourselves?" My mouth is dry. I know this is not our job, but I need to know Joanna's reaction.

"Murder is very much in the police domain. We might help, but I think we should concentrate on Penny."

"What if they're connected?" I slam on the brakes as a youth walks out in front of the car without looking. "Bloody idiot. Do they not teach kids to cross roads these days?"

"He's too busy looking at his phone. He's not even noticed that you had to do an emergency stop to avoid hitting him."

"You're bloody right." I pull over and wind down my window. "Hey you!" I bellow. I see from the corner of my eye that Joanna puts her hands over her ears. The lad doesn't look up from his phone. "I'm going to get out and give him what for." I click the seatbelt release button at my side.

Joanna puts her hand on my arm. "Don't, Becky. It's not worth it. This is not a safe area. He's probably got a knife."

"How do you know about the area?" I ask.

"A bit of research, combined with common sense. It just looks run-down. Small terraced houses. Graffiti. Junk in front yards. Come on. Belt up. Lock the doors, and let's get back to mine for a coffee. Or maybe something stronger."

Chapter Nineteen

We stop en route for a drive-through McDonald's and take it back to Joanna's for lunch. Settled in the kitchen, we have a few mouthfuls to settle the worst of the hunger pangs, before I resume our earlier conversation.

"So, we focus on Penny then?"

"Yes, but I think we should have another chat with the police. Do you think your friend Finn would want to meet up with us?"

"He's going to be dead busy, but I can ask." I take out my phone and tap out a message.

A minute passes, during which we continue eating. Then my phone vibrates.

"Hi Finn, are you okay? How's it going?"

"As well as expected. Janice is with Troy and his daughter and in-laws, so they're being looked after, and she'll get back to us if they say anything that might be useful."

"Great. We were just wondering if there's anything Joanna and I could help with? Maybe something a bit out of your usual sphere?"

"What do you have in mind?" His tone is dry, revealing his scepticism.

"We're working on it. Will you have any time to join us later, and we can discuss it?"

"Yeah, why not? When I get off duty, and who knows what time that'll be. I'll aim for around eight though. Are you at yours?"

"No, at Joanna's." I give him the address. "Message me when you leave. I'll go home for a while in between."

"I'll bring food for me, but don't wait to eat. You know what it can be like."

"Sure. We'll eat first, and maybe have some chocolate when you arrive, to stop us dipping into your dinner. See you tonight." I end the call.

"So what do we have in mind?" I ask Joanna.

"That's a damn good question, hen. It's half past two now. That gives five and a half hours to come up with something that won't make Finn feel like we're wasting his time. You know him better than I do. What would he accept?"

"Something between a basic premise and a full-blown plan. The closer to the latter, the happier he'll be." I grin. "At the moment, I'll settle for a workable premise!"

We spend the next hour tossing ideas around before we come up with something that might work. Another hour to fill in a few details, and although we're a long way from the thorough plan that Finn would prefer, we've got a decent proposal for him.

I return home to have dinner with my family. It's been a long day, and I need a few hours' rest before meeting up with Finn.

"Mum, what time is Wendy coming?" Cheryl asks as I step through the door. "You've been out for ages."

A stream of swear words appears in my brain, as if in a cartoon bubble. I'm ashamed to admit, even to myself, that with everything else that's happened today I'd completely forgotten about my daughter's troubles. I pull myself together to check my phone. Wendy sent a quick WhatsApp after our call this morning, confirming that she'd be with us around 7pm.

"I'd better get dinner going. Wendy will be here in about an hour and a half." I delve through the kitchen cupboards.

"What are we having?"

"Do you fancy Spag Bol?" It's one of Cheryl's favourites, and there's mince in the fridge.

"Sure."

"Any developments today?" I ask.

"A couple of my friends messaged to say they'd heard I'd been blocking certain people. They wanted to know why, and whether they were on my hit list."

"Did you tell them?"

"I just said that I was tightening up security, and that they were safe, but they might want to consider who their real friends are, and block those who didn't meet that standard."

"Ouch. That's a bit harsh, love. Were they okay? And who are we referring to here?"

"I don't think you know them, Mum. It's just a couple of girls I chat to in Chemistry. They're my lab partners. They're nice. I called them afterwards to explain a bit more, cos I realised that message sounded a bit horrible."

"Okay, good. You're not aiming to alienate your real friends here." I get the vegetables out of the fridge. I'd quite like to have eaten and washed up by the time Wendy arrives. "Where's your dad?"

"He's in the study on his laptop. He had a call from someone earlier and disappeared in there. That was about two hours ago. He's not emerged since."

"Can you check on him, please?"

She nods and leaves me to ponder on the apparently mysterious call. I wonder if it's the elusive Roger Taylor.

I'm frying mince and onions by the time Cheryl returns with Matt.

"Everything okay?" I glance round. Cheryl's white, and Matt looks stressed. He's not supposed to get stressed. He's still recuperating.

"Hey, what happened?"

"I was talking to Roger on the phone. There's been a bit of an issue. We've been back and forth for the last couple of hours. Chezz overheard me."

"What did you hear, love?" I add tinned tomatoes to the pan, but watch discreetly as she rubs tears from her cheeks.

"Dad said something about dealers and terrorists, and that 'all hell was going to break loose if this gets out'." She turns to Matt. "What's going on? You're a pharmacist, and you're off sick."

There's a moment's silence. A pregnant pause, as it's sometimes called, and I know why. It's as if we're all awaiting the birth of something earth-shattering.

"It's nothing for anyone to worry about. Just forget you heard it please, Cheryl."

The contractions dissipate. Birth is postponed.

"How can I forget that, Dad? What are you involved in?"

"I sometimes do some work for a government organisation, particularly related to drug delivery logistics. Sometimes controlled drugs go astray and get into the wrong hands. I just give some advice from time to time."

Okay, so the baby popped out after all. I suppose it was important for Cheryl to know, and Matt's explanation makes it sound quite innocent really.

"Are we all safe here? Is Ali safe?" Cheryl goes over to her dad, and he puts his arms around her and gives a hug.

"I would never do anything to endanger you, or your sister, or your mum. I just need you to keep shtum about this though. Don't discuss it with your friends, or with Wendy when she gets here. Government bodies don't always talk to each other, so a senior police officer wouldn't know about this, and it's not appropriate to tell her, okay?"

Cheryl agrees, and I send her to wash her face and hands before dinner. I wait until she's gone from the room.

"Did Roger say anything about me?"

"Not today, but we've already discussed you. He'll want your help when he's ready. And you'll know soon enough when that is."

"You know I went to that gig last night?"

"Yes. I meant to ask, how did it go?"

"It was okay." No need to go into details just now. "But that lead singer of the top band from last night got home to find his wife dead."

"Oh my God. How awful. Was she ill?"

I take a minute to connect the dots.

"No. Bloody hell, no. She'd been murdered. That's why I've been out all day. Joanna and I seem to have got ourselves involved. We're meeting with Finn after eight, when he's finished work."

He glances at the clock. "In that case you'd better get dishing up, if we've got to eat before Wendy gets here."

Wendy arrives on the dot of seven, just as I've finished loading the dishwasher. I open the door to her, and we hug. It's been far too long since I've seen her. She's been my friend and mentor since I was eighteen, and seeing her now reminds me how much I've missed her these last few months.

"Come on, Missus," she says, stepping back. "You and I

will catch up properly next week over a bottle or two of wine. How does that sound?"

"Fantastic." I smile at her. "For now, though, Cheryl's in the lounge. Why don't you go and find her, and I'll get the kettle on?"

By the time I join them, armed with tea and Jaffa Cakes, Wendy's scrolling through Cheryl's phone and frowning.

"Everything okay?" Watching her look through the photos half-triggers a thought, but it drifts away before I can catch it.

"These girls seem to be more tech-savvy than I'd like. What they've done with these images looks quite professional. I had to look closely to see the signs that the photo was fake." Wendy takes a mug of tea and puts it on the coffee table. "Thanks. Would you ladies mind if I contacted your school head? I won't mention any names. I can just say that it's been brought to my attention through a police investigation that illegal activities have occurred in the realm of cyber-bullying. Would that be okay?"

Cheryl nods. "I think so, as long as they can't pin anything on me. I don't want them to have any excuse to target me."

"I just want to come into the school for an assembly or something and talk about cyber-bullying, how it can be traced to the perpetrators, and the lengthy penalties attached. A very general warning, with a request that all bullying activities must stop immediately, otherwise further investigations will ensue, and the guilty parties will find themselves with a criminal record, and possibly imprisonment in a juvenile detention centre."

"Do you think that would help, Cheryl?" I ask.

"I'm sure it would be a start. Those stupid bitches might think twice if they think it could affect their careers. Do you think you could persuade the head to send a letter home to all the parents about the penalties related to cyber-bullying? It would horrify a lot of the mums and dads."

"And others wouldn't believe their little darlings could possibly be involved. It's worth a shot though. Wendy, do you think that's reasonable?"

"I'll ask if a letter home to all the parents could be part of the remedy for this. As you say, Becky, many of them won't believe it of their kids, but others might decide to take more of an interest in their teenagers' online activities."

With a plan of action agreed, Wendy reviews my daughter's new security processes, and approves them. By the time she leaves, it's almost eight. My phone pings as I watch her get into her car. Finn has sent me a WhatsApp.

"*Just left work. Picking up grub. See you at Joanna's in twenty minutes.*"

I check on Cheryl before I leave. She's in her bedroom playing games on her iPad.

"Are you okay? You've had quite a day." I drop a kiss on her forehead.

"I'm fine thanks, Mum. Are you off out again?" She lifts her eyes briefly from the game. "You look nice."

"Thanks." I hope she doesn't see me blush in the dim light in her room. "Yes, back to Joanna's to meet with a police officer in charge of a case that we've got involved in."

"Is it to do with Troy Cassidy? I heard it on the radio this afternoon."

"I'm afraid so, yes."

"Good luck. I hope you find the killer. Can you imagine if it was just some jealous girl wanting him for herself?"

"That's certainly a line of enquiry, Chezz. Thanks."

"I can't imagine being that obsessive with anyone, but you see it on films and in books all the time."

"You might be right. Anyway, I have to go. I'll see you in the morning if I'm back too late tonight."

I pop my head into the study on the way out. "Matt, you

need to rest. Let Roger sort it out for now. You can do some more tomorrow."

"I'll finish shortly. I just need to check out a couple of routes that might have been used." He turns and looks at me. "Take it easy yourself, Becks. You're looking tired."

Outside in the car, I check my appearance in the mirror. Maybe I'm a little flushed, but I think that's more of a sign of who I'm meeting, rather than of tiredness. Perhaps the silk blouse is a bit of overkill for a meeting with Joanna and 'a police officer', but my pulse is saying otherwise.

I start the engine. The lights come on automatically, and I catch a movement in the bushes. Did I lock up properly? Is my family safe? I tap a quick message into my phone, asking Cheryl and Matt to both check that they've locked all the doors and windows, and mention a possible prowler outside. I let them think I'm talking about burglars, but my thumping heart is now a result of remembering Troy's wife. Would the murderer be after my family too?

By the time I get to Joanna's, a few moments later, I'm a quivering jelly, and it's not because of Finn. I have a good look round, surveying the area before I get out of the car. I don't think there's anyone here, but if someone was on foot, they wouldn't have been able to keep up with me. Unless they're part of a gang. I've been responsible for the breakup and imprisonment of a lot of gangs in my career. There are far too many people who could have a vendetta against me.

For now, though, I'm reassured that there's no one lurking in the street. All the same, I make a very quick dash from car to house. Joanna opens the door.

"Bloody hell, Becky, are you okay? Come in. Finn's not here yet."

"I think... there was someone... outside my house." I take a few deep breaths as I stumble into her lounge and collapse on the sofa. Joanna goes into the kitchen and emerges with a glass of water. She sits on the sofa next to me and puts her hand on my shoulder.

"Have a swig of this, hen, and get your breath back." She looks as if she's going to say something else, but then the doorbell rings. "That'll be Finn." She stands up, but I grab her wrist.

"Can you check it's him before you open the door?"

"Of course. I got one of those door cameras installed after Mr Taylor turned up unannounced. It doubles as CCTV as well, so if we get any unwanted visitors, we can follow up afterwards."

The doorbell rings again, and Joanna checks her phone. She shows me the live feed. Finn is standing at the door, looking impatient and holding a pizza box. I nod, and she goes to the door.

"Come in. Do you want me to plate that up for you, or will you eat out of the box?"

"The box is fine, thanks. Becky, how are you doing?" He grins at me, but sits on an armchair. I try not to feel disappointed at the lack of physical contact. This is a business meeting after all.

Joanna does the hostess bit, making sure we're all provided with drinks, and that she and I have a good supply of chocolate biscuits. But once we're all sitting down, the room goes quiet: that awkward silence where everyone is hoping another person will start the conversation.

Finn's the first to break it. "So how are you planning to help with this investigation? Becky knows only too well that murder is a police matter."

I glance at Joanna and she nods.

"We know that, Finn, but we're already working on a case that links into this in a strange way." I explain about Penny. "So we've got some lines of enquiry. Penny asked us to find out about Troy's fans, in case one of them is her stalker."

"It seems a bit unlikely." Finn finishes chewing the mouthful of pizza he took a moment ago. "Sorry. Yeah, why would the stalker of a female photographer want to kill a popstar's wife?"

"We don't know yet, but we could pursue that unlikely angle, while you focus on the more obvious channels."

"I'm not really used to working with civilians, and I can't get my head around your status yet, Becks. You left us in July. Why should we work with you now?"

"Because you know me, and you should trust me. I thought you did. But if there's no trust, perhaps Joanna and I should do our own thing and not bother to liaise with you." Joanna goes to the kitchen and shuts the door behind her. The tension in the room is palpable, as Finn stares at me for a long moment.

"You don't need me to tell you that withholding information is also a crime."

"Seriously?" I glare at him. "What are you playing at? Do you want us to help or not? If the answer's no, we'll just get on with our case. But I think Troy was beginning to trust us, and he might speak more openly about his past to us than to you."

"What do you know about his past?" Finn still sounds suspicious.

"So far, only what's on the internet. Troy's been a musician since he left school, but when he was seventeen he had a run-in with the police about drugs. I don't think he's going to be too trusting with you and Molly poking around."

"Back to bloody trust again. Why should I trust you when you left me?" There's a peculiar expression on his face, and I shiver.

"What do you mean? I didn't leave you. I left the force, after they bloody abandoned me in that sodding warehouse with Rachel dead at my feet. No sodding support for my own injuries, whether physical or mental. Just *'If you can't work through it, you'd better leave'* from the big man himself. Arsehole." I fight back tears as pain and fury compete for supremacy. I can't believe Finn's accusing me of abandoning him.

"I'm sorry. I didn't realise they'd treated you like that. Was that Quentin?" Finn lowers his voice, as he seems to realise he was out of order.

"Who else!" The Chief Inspector, our boss, Douglas Quentin, was a first-class git, with the sensitivity of an iron bar. He was an ambitious, ruthless taskmaster who really didn't like women, but saw them as a necessary evil to keep his statistics within acceptable bounds. He was a significant factor in my resignation.

"You're right, Becks. I do trust you. I was just angry and hurt when you left and then didn't get in touch for six months." He puts his pizza box on the floor and comes to sit next to me on the sofa. Pulling me into a hug, he whispers in my ear, "Are we friends again now?"

I hug him back. We hugged briefly in the pub the other day, but I could sense that he wasn't at ease with me. A tightness eases in my chest.

"Sure, and I'm sorry about not getting in touch for such a long time. I was very freaked out by what happened, and cut off all my friends from work until Joanna talked some sense into me."

The door opens and Joanna comes in from the kitchen.

"All sorted now?" She grins at both of us and picks the empty box up from the floor. "So what's the verdict on this case? Can we help, or are we relegated to mere 'civilians'?"

Finn releases me from the hug, although as he sits back he drapes an arm across the sofa behind me.

"It'll have to be unofficial. My boss is a…" He struggles to provide a suitable epithet.

"Git? Prick? Misogynistic old fart?" I offer as solutions. I know exactly who he's talking about, and they're all true.

"Yep! So, if he hears I'm accepting help from outside the

team, I'll get lynched. I think I'll be eating a load of pizza in this living room if that's okay. Just gained a new friend. Totally not work-related."

"And I suggest not mentioning that I'm here at all. If Molly asks about us, we're working on our own case. She might say something."

"Yeah. Molly's a stirrer, and an ambitious bitch. She licks Quentin's arse whenever she gets a chance. Dumping me in it would give her the greatest pleasure."

"Well, that's sorted then. Finn is coming round here to see me, having taken a fancy for my company when I turned up at the crime scene today. If he also happens to be in your company, Becky, I'm happy to cover to Molly or anyone else who might ask."

"He'll only be in my company for work reasons, of course, so there's no need to cover with Matt." Joanna gives me a sharp look. "I wouldn't cover with Matt anyway. You're allowed to have male friends, I presume?"

"Yes, of course. And Finn and I have been friends for ages. If I'm meeting Finn, Matt will be told, regardless of whether or not it's for work."

"I'd better go. I'm going to let you two make your own enquiries about Troy, but be discreet. Speaking to him whilst Janice is there would be a bad plan."

"Who's Janice?" asks Joanna.

"Do you remember, she's the family liaison officer?"

"Oh yeah. Sure, we won't drop you in it, Finn. We know how to be discreet. You know Becky, and secrecy is my middle name."

Back out in my car, with my headlights on, my earlier fears come back to me. I'm fairly sure there's no one hanging around outside, but what if they're at my house? I type a quick message into my phone, and Matt responds almost immediately.

'*I'll open the garage and put the light on. Drive straight in. You'll be fine. Didn't see anyone when I looked out earlier. They might have gone.*'

With his reassurance, I drive home, but I can't help looking around as I approach my house. I don't see anyone, but my heart is beating fast as I drive into the garage and turn off the engine. Matt's at the internal door waiting for me and slips past the car to close the garage as soon as it's safe.

Once inside the house, I glance out of the kitchen window to the front. I'm in the dark so I can see out more clearly. A car is moving along the road, slowly and with its lights off. It's too dark to identify it properly, but it appears to be a standard hatchback. Absolutely no use as a clue.

Chapter Twenty

Sunday is a frustrating day. Troy failed to reply to a message from Joanna. Finn later phoned me to say the distraught widower was under sedation and unable to help anyone. My ex-partner sounded as frustrated as we felt. Possibly more so. Finn's neck is on the line if he doesn't solve this.

But I do get through to Penny.

"Hi, how are you?" I check my watch. We've been trying to call most of the day, and it's now nearly six. Joanna's in her own house preparing for her son who's due to arrive tomorrow.

"I'm in shock." But Penny sounds almost as though she's enjoying the excitement. "I heard on the news about Troy's wife. I can't believe I only saw him on Friday and everything was fine."

"You're a photographer, Penny. Did you see anything that night that was suspicious?"

"I was having enough problems of my own, to be honest. I was freaked out by the time I got home, and I just wanted a drink and bed. Any finer nuances of the evening were swallowed up."

"I understand. I'm so sorry we abandoned you."

"It's fine. Nigel was being a dick. He gets like that sometimes. A bit... well... He doesn't always get social signals. I know he seems okay most of the time, but I think he's got Asperger's."

"I have several friends with Asperger's and none of them would behave like that." I try to keep the irritation from my voice. Nigel had been downright aggressive, and I don't think blaming it on a condition is appropriate. But Penny's a client. I need to remain civil. Time to change the subject. "Did you get any sleep on Friday night? You must have been very stressed out."

"I got a few hours. It's happened a few times now." There's a hesitation on the end of the line. "It's strange, but I get the feeling there's a connection with what happened to Troy's wife. What if my stalker got annoyed after I eluded him and took it out on Troy instead? Don't forget, they've never followed me after any other gig. It's only when he's on. Maybe you need to check out his life a bit more closely."

"We're exploring several possibilities. So, are there any fans you see at every gig?"

"It's not my job to check out the fans. Only to photograph the bands and capture the atmosphere." The tenuous thought returns from last night when Wendy was looking through Cheryl's photos, and I suddenly know what I should do next.

"Do you have any photos of the audience at different gigs?"

"Just Troy's you mean?" She doesn't wait for an answer. "I suppose I can have a look through some photos over the last couple of months and see if I can spot anyone."

"Why don't you just send over all the photos from Troy's gigs, and Joanna and I will go through them? It's our job after all."

"Sure," she says. We say our goodbyes, but a minute later, a text pings on my phone.

'*Internet's down. I'll send them over tomorrow from the office.*'

It's been a while since I had any internet problems, but I don't know her provider, so I can't easily check. I take it at face value for now, but call Joanna to update her.

"Thanks, Becky. But you'll have to go through the photos when you get them. Will's arriving this evening now. He said he had some news for me, but didn't want to tell me until he gets here. I've got a feeling we'll need to talk a lot while he's here."

"How long is he staying? I'd like to meet him, if it won't cause any problems."

"I think he's planning on a week, but let's see what the news is when he gets here."

"Of course. I'm going to spend some time with my family today, I think. I've been neglecting them lately." My mind wanders for a moment, recalling that Cheryl now knows a bit about her dad's undercover activities. With all the other issues she's having right now, I definitely need to make some time for her.

After ending the call, I invite Cheryl to come with me to get bagels. It's eleven o'clock, and most teenagers her age would still be asleep this time on a Sunday morning, but she's in her room doing homework. I look at her as she turns around to speak to me. She looks pale and tired.

"I ought to get this finished, Mum. It's got to be in tomorrow."

"Will you have some time this afternoon? I thought you, Dad and I could take a ride out somewhere, and maybe go for a walk. Your dad should exercise more after his heart attack. It's been four weeks now, and he's barely moved from the house."

"The cardiac rehab nurse came round last week and said he should be walking for twenty to thirty minutes a day by now." She looks at her watch. "You get the bagels, Mum. I'll have finished this in time for lunch, so maybe we can go afterwards? How about Blackpool?"

"That's a good idea." I suppress the thought of some of the criminals I've put away who operated out of Blackpool. But I don't have a distinctive appearance, and although it's February, it's a lovely day. The prom should be busy enough for me to blend into the background. I've become very paranoid. The fresh air is surely just what I need.

Even leaving the house to get the car out of the garage sets my heartbeat rising. It's broad daylight, and there are plenty of people out on the estate making the most of the unusually good February weather, washing cars and tidying their gardens.

I take a deep breath and open the garage door. I have to get past this.

Despite my apprehensions, we have a pleasant and uneventful afternoon, including a wander around the shops, and a play in the amusement arcade. Our walk along the prom hardly affects Matt, who banters cheerfully with Cheryl about football. I'm not desperately into it, but raise sufficient interest in the league positions to join in the discussion. We complete the outing with fish and chips at Harry Ramsden's.

It's six-thirty and getting dark by the time we get back to the car. Everyone is rosy-cheeked with the sea breeze and exercise, but I know that reality is lurking under the surface. The radio keeps us going until we get to the M6, with the last half-hour of the charts playing on Capital. But the News again mentions the murder of Troy's wife, although just briefly, to state that there have been no arrests yet.

"You're working on that case, aren't you, Becks?" says Matt.

"Not officially, but we're helping Finn, or at least, hoping to. It's early days yet." The undercurrent is getting closer to the surface, but I'm not sure how or when it will erupt. "Our client is actually a press photographer, who's been photographing Troy's band. At this stage we don't know if there's a connection."

"Maybe Dad can help. He seems to be an old hand at investigating." Cheryl's tone is bitter.

So here it is. The elephant in the car has woken up. Time to take notice.

"Don't be angry with him, Chezz. I only found out last week. If someone is helping the government with secret work, they can't exactly be discussing it with their family. We shouldn't be discussing it now, either."

"We're not. No one's telling me a damn thing here."

"There's nothing to tell, love." Matt turns his head to talk to her from the passenger seat. I carry on concentrating on the motorway. It's an unlit stretch, and I need to focus. "I did some work to help with some pharmacy stuff a couple of years ago, and now and then it bobs up and I have to help again. That's how I met Joanna. She was working on the same project. When she turned up at our house those few weeks ago, I thought something had come back to bite me. It stressed me out, and the hassle that I'd been dealing with at work had been building up. It all crashed in on me."

"So are you still doing it, Dad? Can't you quit? You've been ill."

"There are some jobs you can't quit from. If you want the truth, I'd never have started if I'd known. But you and your mum are not in any danger. Not from my work. And neither is Ali."

"I've got enough trouble at school without this."

"Wendy's going to help with that, though, isn't she?" I decide it's time to intervene. Cheryl's sounding hysterical, and it's not like her.

"Yes, but it's not fair. Why is everything going wrong just now?"

"I don't think it's as bad as it was last summer. We're all well now, and there's no immediate threat to any of us." I'm lying, but it's my job to protect Cheryl – and just now, it's better for her not to worry. I catch Matt give me a funny look. He knows me too well, and he saw what state I was in last night.

My phone rings, but I don't want to answer it in the car. My car media system is not sophisticated enough to show who's calling, and my phone is in my handbag, so I can't check. I ignore the call, hoping I can call back. It rings again two minutes later.

"You should answer it, Mum." As Cheryl says it, the sign for Rivington Services appears. Half a mile to go.

I pull in to the Services, drive into the car park and turn off the engine. I take my phone out of my bag and check the screen for the missed call details. Joanna. Twice.

"Dad and I can get some chocolate while you call back. Come on, Dad."

Matt rests his hand briefly on my shoulder before he gets out of the car. I wait until they're halfway across the car park. I'm not sure why, but I have a bad feeling about this call. I get a grip of my fears and press *Connect* on the screen.

"Becky? Are you okay?"

"Yes, are you? Is Will there?"

"Yeah, he's here. He came to tell me that his dad's out of prison and wants to kill me."

Chapter Twenty-One

Despite the fresh air and exercise, I didn't sleep well. After finally dozing off sometime around 4am, I wake up at quarter past seven. I promised to take Cheryl into school today. She's nervous about what will happen this week, and worrying if Wendy will be in time to prevent repercussions.

I'm nervous too. Obviously I'm worried about her, but I've spent half the night gnawing at my other fears: Joanna's ex, Troy, Penny, and my own stalker fears. I still don't know if they're justified, or if I'm being paranoid.

The drive into school is quiet except for the radio – and the interminable, inane banter of the morning presenters. I tolerate it for the music, but as soon as Cheryl's out of the car (with a brief interchange wishing her luck), I switch to one of my CDs: the soundtrack of *Evita*. I feel stress flowing out of my shoulders almost immediately, and focus for the brief journey home purely on the road ahead and the story of Eva Peron.

At home, I toy with the temptation to go back to bed and get another couple of hours' sleep, but my phone vibrates. I check it and notice an email has come in from Penny.

'*These are the photos I found. I've zipped them to make it easier to*

*send, but there's no password on the file. There's nothing particularly
private about them. See if you can find anyone in the crowds that could be
relevant. I had a quick look, but didn't notice anyone. Thanks.'*

Curiosity wins out against sleep, and I put the kettle on to
make myself a strong coffee before turning on the laptop. I
leave the study to Matt in case he has any more interactions
with Roger today, and take my coffee and laptop, and a spiral-
bound notebook and pen, into the lounge.

The photos are easy enough to extract from the zip file,
and I have a quick skim through first. Penny has sent me thirty-
eight pictures, and the initial surf through is sufficient for me to
see that she's only sent the audience ones. The reason for this
could be purely convenience for me. It's bulky to send lots of
photos, even by zip file, and some email servers have limits on
the size of file that can be attached, although it's easy enough
these days to send files and folders through file-sharing apps.
She might also have tried to save me time, by removing the
photos that are just of Troy and his band.

I examine my increasing irritation. Am I annoyed because I
wanted to get the full picture (pardon the pun), or is there
something else? Is Penny hiding something on purpose?

Nearly thirty years in the police force taught me that
everyone has secrets. People hide information for the most
trivial and mundane of reasons. Often nothing to do with the
crime or investigation, and they muddy the waters just because
they don't want to reveal their sordid and unimportant
thoughts. I spent many years chasing red herrings until I
developed some intuition about which were important, even if
only to shed some light on the bigger picture. That same
instinct is telling me I need to see the pictures that Penny hasn't
sent.

But for the moment, I settle down to view in more detail
the photos she's sent me. She labelled the folder *Band On The
Wall, Troy, September to January.* Each photo is named with the

date and a number. The pictures would have originally been numbered sequentially, but I only have a few from each date – another clue that she's only provided some of the images.

All the photos were taken inside the club, in the gig area. I recognise the walls and layout from my visit, even though I was only in that room for a short time. I scribble a few observations in the notebook:

- *dark-haired girl – mid twenties – tall and slim – every gig*
- *short, balding guy – maybe early thirties – every gig except October*
- *short fair-haired girl with wavy bob – appears to be alone – all gigs*

There are a few other people who crop up at more than one gig, but never more than two gigs each, and they all seem to be part of a group – whether three or four friends, or a larger group or party. None of them ring any alarm bells.

I isolate the photos with my three 'persons of interest' (I'm reluctant to call them suspects at this stage). Each photo needs some editing to make the relevant person the only face in the picture. Online face-matching software provides me with names. The entire process takes over three hours, and when Matt brings me a tuna sandwich at quarter past twelve, I'm just about ready to turn off the laptop.

I eat quickly, keen to tell Joanna of my developments, but then I remember that she has her own problems today. I slow down and force myself to chew my food.

"That's better." Matt's watching me across the table as he eats his own sandwich. "You'll make yourself ill if you keep downing your food like that. Why don't you talk to me about it?"

"About what?" I stall for time. I know exactly what he's asking me, but I'm not used to discussing my cases with him.

"Come on, Becks. I know you. We've been married long enough for me to see when you're stressing about things. And Cheryl's not here now, so you wouldn't be upsetting her if she overheard."

"There's so much going on at the moment. It's hard to get my head around it all, but this morning I whittled down some of Troy's fans into three… call them super-fans. They were at all, or nearly all, his Manchester gigs for the last few months, and they may be of some use in identifying either Penny's stalker or even Troy's wife's killer – although that's probably a bit of a stretch."

"Have you talked to Joanna about it yet?"

"No, that's the problem. I told you last night about her ex coming out of prison."

"Yeah – I got the feeling there was something you weren't telling me about that."

"I didn't want to worry Cheryl any further, but Joanna's ex apparently wants to find her and kill her."

"Shit! That's… I don't know what to say. Anything would be pretty inadequate. But I think she needs to talk to Roger. He might help."

"I guess that's not a bad idea." I finish my lunch and make the call.

"Joanna?"

"Hi Becky." Her voice sounds as if she either has a cold or has been crying.

"Are you okay? Is Will still with you?"

"I'm fine, and yes, Will's still here."

"Would it be okay if I come round? I'd like to meet him, and also, I think we have a lot to discuss."

"Sure. I want you to meet him. You need to hear the full story for yourself. Come round about two o'clock. We're just having lunch."

"Thanks. See you then." I end the call.

"Do you want me to come with you?" Matt asks. He looks concerned.

"Maybe not this time. Perhaps tomorrow. But if you want to help, you can check out the local press and the internet to see if there's any information about prisoner releases in Edinburgh."

"Do you know his name?"

"Shit, no. Not yet anyway. I'll message you discreetly as soon as I know it. Meanwhile, it might take you a while to find out how to get the information, so you can work on that."

"Do you want me to contact Roger?"

"I think that should come from Joanna, but if she wants you to do it, I'll let you know."

Half an hour later, I pull up outside Joanna's house. Parked in front of me is a silver Audi with the latest registration plate. I've not seen it before, and I reckon it's Will's car. Nice car for a divorcee with maintenance payments to keep up. My curiosity about my friend's son rises several notches.

I get out of the car and knock on the door. The man who lets me in is instantly recognisable as Joanna's son, having the same-shaped eyes, albeit green instead of brown, and similar features. He's taller than I would have expected though. Joanna's petite at five foot one; her son tops six foot at a rough guess. More important is the delightful smile that greets me.

"Becky!" He holds out a hand to me once I've stepped inside. "Lovely to meet you. I've heard so much about you." The skin around his eyes crinkles as he grins at me, and I can't help but warm to him.

"That's a nice car outside. Is that yours?"

"What, the Audi? I wish. My car blew up last week. It was the final straw after a long line of mechanical faults, but I needed to come and see Mum, so I hired this for the trip – it was only two hundred and fifty for the week. I need to get myself a new car when I get back, but I'll check out some lease deals. This is a gorgeous drive though." His enthusiasm is infectious, and I laugh as I follow him into the lounge.

Joanna emerges from the kitchen with a plate of chocolate biscuits – the posh type that comes from the expensive tins. I figure she's splashed out for her visitor.

"I see you've met Will. Sorry I couldn't come to the door." She hangs her head as though embarrassed.

I take the plate from her, and put it on the coffee table, then wrap my arms around her slight frame. She breaks down in sobs immediately. I hold her, rubbing her back gently, and murmuring soothing nothings into her ear. "Shh, it's okay, don't worry, it's all going to be fine." All probably untrue, but appropriate while she's mid-meltdown.

"I'll put the kettle on," says Will, and disappears quickly into the kitchen.

After a few minutes, Joanna sniffs and moves back. I let her go, but reach into my handbag, which is still over my shoulder. A minute's delving results in the locating of a packet of tissues. I hand them to my friend, who's now sitting on the sofa, and I plonk myself in the place next to her. I think she needs to be within huggable reach.

"Do you want to talk about it?" I ask.

"When Will comes back." Her voice sounds even thicker than it did when I called. She blows her nose. "First, though, I just want to say, although I'm shit-scared, I feel better with him here, and now that you've turned up as well, I guess it makes me feel a bit safer."

"Matt wants to help too. And he suggested talking to Roger. I don't know what you think about that, but maybe it's something to discuss."

"Definitely happy for Matt to help – I trust him. Not sure about Roger yet."

Will comes in, carrying a tray with a teapot, three mugs, a jug of milk, a jar of coffee, some sugar sachets and a packet of tea bags.

"I didn't know what everyone would want. The teapot just has boiling water, so everyone can help themselves."

"Great idea. Thanks Will."

I make Joanna a cup of tea and add sugar.

"You know I don't take sugar."

"You need it right now. Frankly, if I had some brandy to add, I'd give you that too. For now, sweet tea and biscuits will have to suffice." I hand her the mug. "Drink it!"

She obeys, which scares me more than anything else. I'm not used to seeing her upset. She's usually the calm one, helping me to keep it together.

I make myself a coffee, and after a quick question to Will, make him one too.

"Okay. Will, this is your shout. Please tell me what's happened, and, well, pretty much everything I need to know."

Chapter Twenty-Two

There have been developments. A woman is dead. And it's because of me. I felt a surge of energy as I stuck the knife in for the first time. A thrill as she screamed. But then panic struck. I'd stabbed so many times, and it was only when I was sure she was dead that I noticed the blood on my clothes. Thank God for a cloudy night – pitch black away from the street lamps.

Urgent measures were needed. I removed my shoes, before returning home unseen. I then stripped, bagging my clothes carefully in a compostable bag. The cleansing shower was exhilarating. I will incorporate this in any future activities. It will become part of my ritual.

Dressed in clean dark clothes, a short walk to the bins behind my flat enabled me to bury the evidence deep. Bin collection is in two days. I pray that no one will come looking before then.

Chapter Twenty-Three

"I don't know how much you know, Becky?" says Will.

"I remember that your dad was in prison for beating up a bailiff at his girlfriend's house after walking out on your mum when she had cancer. That's about it though."

"Yeah. Dad was a right bastard. I wish I could say he had a good side, but he was a crap father as well as being a shitty husband to Mum."

"In what way, if you don't mind me asking?"

Joanna takes her tea and goes to the stairs. "I'm going for a lie down, Will, tell Becky everything she wants to know."

There's a moment silence until constraint is released by the sound of the bedroom door closing.

"Sorry. It's hard for Mum to hear all this. She feels like she's failed as a mother. She hasn't, of course. Mum's great, and she always protected me, even when it meant her getting hit instead."

I don't ask why Joanna stayed with her abusive husband. I've interviewed a lot of abuse victims over the years, and the reasons become obvious after a while. The abusers (and women can be culprits and victims) gradually remove all confidence from their prey, depriving them of the ability to leave. I met so many women and men over the years who'd plucked up the courage to leave but were terrified that they wouldn't cope alone.

"Your mum did well to escape then."

"Yeah, well. It's not often that cancer is a godsend, but Dad couldn't cope with illness unless he'd inflicted it. Cancer was well out of his comfort zone. He packed his bags and left. The only downside was it was after he'd gambled away Mum's inheritance, and it left Mum penniless and ill. She came to live with me for a while, but it was just after my marriage breakdown. I don't think I looked after her as well as I should have done. As soon as they gave Mum the all-clear, she left to come down here and find you."

"So when did your dad walk out, and when did he go to prison? I'm just trying to get a sense of the timelines."

"He left Mum about eighteen months ago, and six months later he was sentenced for assaulting the bailiff that came round to his new girlfriend's house. I'd hazard a guess that the old git gambled away her savings and wages as well."

"It sounds probable, doesn't it?"

"Dad had a pattern. I mean, I don't really remember him ever being nice to Mum, but I guess he must have been at one time. But then, by the time I came along, he'd be going to the bookies every afternoon, and placing bets on the horses. If he won, everything would be great. He'd treat us to fish and chips, and play games and watch TV with us in the evenings…" Will tails off, lost in the past.

I give him a moment, but then prompt him. "And when he lost?"

"When he lost, he'd get roaring drunk. Sometimes at the pub; other times he'd come home, raid Mum's purse and grab some booze from the off-licence. Either way, a few drinks in, he'd start having a go at Mum. Criticising her for everything –

the house wasn't clean enough, she wasn't making any effort with her appearance, all sorts of shit. Then if she answered back, he'd start hitting her. Mum worked full-time and looked after me. I mean, this went on from as long as I can remember. I guess back to when I started at school, so I'd have been about five. But then it carried on, throughout primary school, and secondary school, and college. He'd hit me too if Mum wasn't around, but I learnt fast to stay out of his way. The problem was, Mum didn't have any family to go to. There felt like no escape. I don't know how she survived it. But his violence was always within boundaries, even when he was really pissed. He'd go from being sober enough to know just how hard he was hitting, to falling asleep when the alcohol levels got too high. I guess that little trick saved our lives. He probably realised he couldn't explain away a dead wife and kid."

"I'm sorry, Will. That sounds like a hellish way to grow up."

"It was bloody awful. I left home at sixteen, as soon as I could get out of there, but I rang Mum most days. I had to check she was okay. I was twenty-five when she told me she had cancer. In all the years of living with Dad, I've never been so terrified in my life. I thought I was going to lose her."

"Your mum's a survivor. She's the strongest woman I know. You can be very proud of her." I remind myself that I need to ask Joanna about when she got involved with Roger. I can't quite get my head around the timings. "So tell me about your dad, and prison. When did he get out, and how did you find out?"

"That's an easy one. He got out on Friday. And he was at my flat yesterday, threatening to kill me if I didn't tell him where Mum was."

"You're still alive, so did you tell him?"

"The prick threatened me from outside my front door. I was inside with the chain on. I stood well back and threatened to call the police if he didn't back off. He'd have been back inside faster than a computer can add two and two. He left, but not until he said he'd kill Mum if he found her."

"Did he give a reason?"

"Not a coherent one. He blethered on about Mum tipping off the bailiffs, but it's a pile of crap. I think there's something else going on his head. He muttered about working with drugs, and that he needed to sort everything out, or 'those bastards inside'd be after him'. I don't know what he meant. As soon as he'd gone, I called Mum and arranged to come here. I didn't want to tell her why until I got here. I sorted the hire car. I mean, I was supposed to come on Monday anyway. Mum said she needed some help with something on the computer. Computers are my job. I'm a security geek. I set up anti-hacking, anti-virus, anti-phishing, all sorts of defences that people might need."

"I guess you can hack them too?"

"Of course. Can't beat the hackers if you can't play them at their own game."

"I can see that would be important. Can you hack the prison service records?" I take a mouthful of lukewarm coffee.

"Possibly. What help would that be?"

"I just wondered if you could find out why your dad was let out so soon, and what his parole conditions are? Maybe reporting his threats could land him straight back inside."

"I don't need to check anything to know that. The speed he skedaddled when I threatened him with the police told me all I needed to know on that front."

"So why didn't you report him?" I drain the coffee mug and put it down. I watch Will flush.

"He's my dad. However much of a prick he is, and however scary, it doesn't feel right shopping him straight away."

"Not even if it's putting your mum at risk?"

"He doesn't know where Mum is, or have a clue she's even left Scotland."

"Maybe, but there are ways people like your dad can get information. It only needs one corrupt official or a clever ex-con that your dad's in touch with. You're not the only one who can hack."

"I suppose. I'll think about it. I don't want to put Mum in danger."

"Don't leave it too long, otherwise they'll be asking you why you didn't report it immediately."

My phone pings. Joanna's just forwarded me a message:

'*Troy: Sedation is wearing off. Can't bear this. Need to find the bastard who killed my wife. Help me.*'

I call her. It's easier than messaging back and forth.

"How are you feeling?"

"Okay. It'd be good to have something to do."

"Can you arrange to meet Troy somewhere? Away from Molly and Janice? We can't exactly interview him at his own house."

Will touches my arm.

"Hang on a sec." I turn to Will. "What?"

"Why can't you interview this Troy in his own house?"

"Because the police will be hanging about, and although we've got support from the Inspector, the Sergeant on the case hates me. Your mum and I need to be discreet."

"Ask this guy to download Skype onto his phone, and you and Mum can interview him that way. It means no one needs to go outside, so surely safer for everyone. Also, we can set it up so it records the call." He puts his hand out for the phone, and I hand it to him. "Mum, did you hear what I just said?" I don't hear the answer, but I assume she said no, as he repeats the suggestion. "Why don't you come back down, and we can discuss it properly?" He disconnects the call and hands my phone back to me.

While we wait for Joanna to come downstairs, I go into the kitchen and put the kettle on. I reckon we could all do with another hot drink. A short while later, I return to the lounge to find Will instructing his mum on what to say to Troy. I let them get on with it and sit patiently with my coffee and biscuits.

Five minutes later, Joanna announces, "Troy's joining us on Skype. He says his house is empty except for him, so he can speak freely."

"Surely he's not back in his own house yet? It must still be a crime scene."

"I don't know. He didn't say."

"I guess we'll find out in a few minutes. Will, how do we set up Skype so Joanna and I can both talk to Troy?"

At Joanna's suggestion, we move into the kitchen and sit at the table. Will opens his mum's laptop and lets her type in the password before pressing a few buttons at lightning speed. Two minutes later, and we're ready to go. Troy's exhausted face fills the screen.

Joanna and I turn to each other for a moment. This will not be an easy interview.

Chapter Twenty-Four

"Hi Troy, how are you doing?" I don't wait for an answer, before continuing. "Can you hear us okay? And see us?"

"Yeah. Thanks for doing this. I really wanted to talk to you without the cops hanging around."

"Sure. Where are you?" I ask.

"Staying with my mum and dad in Withington. It's only a couple of miles from the in-laws, so I can see my baby every day, but she's better off staying with them for the moment."

"You said you're alone in the house?" Joanna joins in. Perhaps she realises how accusatory she sounds, as she tempers it with, "Not that it matters. As long as the police aren't around."

"Mum and Dad are out shopping. Once they saw I'd woken up and wasn't about to end it all, they reckoned it was safe to leave me."

"Let's take advantage of it then and ask some questions."

"You don't need to ask anything. I'll tell you everything." Troy sounds exhausted but determined. I'm curious to see where he'll start. It's so much easier when you're being questioned, and there's a structure to the interview, but if he wants to play it this way, it's fine with me. I glance at Joanna. She's sitting up straight on the kitchen chair, looking into the webcam. Her face is serious but calm. I look back at the screen and see we're both in a thumbnail-sized image at the top. Troy's face fills the screen.

"Go ahead then, Troy."

"Where do you want me to start?" He's finally realised it's not that easy just talking. Joanna takes pity on him.

"You told us on Saturday about how you found her, so let's go back a bit further, and tell us about your band and how you got started?"

"Oh, okay. I reckon I've always wanted to be in a band. I messed about with bands even when I was in primary school. But I met Harry, Gaz and Zach at college. We were all studying music and hit it off straightaway. It helped that Gaz is a drummer, Harry plays guitar, and Zach does keyboards and a bit of sax. It makes for a cool sound. We all write music and I guess it started from there. We rehearsed, then started doing gigs. First ones were pretty crap, but we got better and started working more on our own stuff; sussing out what went down best, and what we enjoyed performing. We've been doing Band On The Wall for a few years now, as well as other places. We travel around doing student gigs a lot. Then a few weeks ago, down in London, this producer turned up at one of our gigs. We didn't know he was there until he came up to us at the end and offered us a recording contract. We were made up." His face sobers. "Then this happened, and I don't give a shit about the deal anymore. I'd ditch it in a flash if it would bring Linda back."

On the screen, I see Joanna's expression soften, and she says, "It's probably got nothing to do with the record deal, Troy. This might have happened anyway. Can you tell us how you and Linda met?"

"Yeah, it was kind of crazy and romantic. I was twenty when I got appendicitis. Like, sudden and horrible pain, although afterwards I realised I'd been feeling a bit dodgy for a few days. But anyway, I doubled over in rehearsal and the boys got an ambulance. I don't remember much else until I woke up in hospital, minus an appendix, but with an angel standing next to me at the side of the bed. Doesn't that sound corny?"

I smile. "It sounds sweet. Carry on."

"Yeah. Well, there was this beautiful girl standing there looking at me with concern on her face, and when I was fully awake, she asked me if I was okay. She had the loveliest, most musical voice I've ever heard, and the sweetest smile. I think I fell in love there and then. Anyway, she was my nurse for the next few days while I was in hospital. I reckon I stayed in a couple of days longer than I needed to, just to be close to her, but she always had a special smile for me, and stayed to chat as often as she could. She gave me her number on the day I left, but I still got Harry to drive me to the hospital in time for the end of her shift. I waited for her at the entrance, and I didn't even ask her out. I just said, 'Linda, you're the most amazing girl I've ever met. Will you marry me?'"

"Wow. What did she say? You'd been her patient for three or four days, right?" says Joanna.

"Five, but I take your point. She suggested we get to know each other a bit better first, but she liked the idea – I could see it in her face. So we did date for a while. A short while. After three weeks, she agreed that this was the real deal, and we got married a month later. That was five years ago." His voice thickens, and moisture fills his eyes. "I honestly believed we'd be together forever. Whoever did this deserves to die so horribly. My poor Linda must have been so scared at the end, and she was always so brave. I want to kill the bastard that did this."

Joanna gives me a barely perceptible nod, and I take over the questioning.

"Did you or she have any enemies you knew of?"

"She just made friends with everyone, she was such a lovely person. No one could have hated her enough to do this."

"Unfortunately, there are some horrible people around who detest loveliness. Beauty, sweetness and kindness can inspire intense jealousy and hatred. If you know of any issues that Linda might have had, maybe at work, then please let us know. Even if you can't think of them just now. What about you? Did you have any enemies, or anyone that was perhaps jealous of you?"

"There were a few other bands that got a bit narky on social media when we got our deal, but nothing to make me think they'd kill. And even if they did, they'd most likely want to kill me rather than... Oh God, why the fuck would anyone want to kill Linda?"

"That's what we need to find out, Troy. How about your fans? Would anyone want you enough to want to get rid of your wife?"

"That's bloody ridiculous."

"Do you have any – I don't know what you'd call them – super-fans? Is that the right word?"

"Probably, and yeah, I've got a few. Maybe three that I can think of."

"If I show you some photos, would you be able to identify them?" I've spotted a *Share* button on the screen.

"I can try."

"Okay, thanks. Give us a minute."

I have the photos of the fans on my phone, and I email them to Joanna, with a request that she opens them on her laptop. A few clicks later, and we're sharing the photos over Skype. The first one we show is of the man. I found a name from face-matching software, but it's not reliable, and I'm keen to see if Troy recognises him or the two girls I half-identified.

"So, Troy, have you any idea who this guy might be?"

We can still see him in a thumbnail at the top of the screen. He stares for a moment, presumably at the picture.

"I recognise him. He's been at most of our Manchester gigs, and he's come up to us afterwards a fair few times. Says he wants to be in a band. I'm trying to remember his name. Sean? Dick? No, shit. What was it? Dean! Yeah, that was it. Dean. I don't think I ever knew his surname, but he gave me his number once in case we ever needed a new band member. Not likely, and even if we did, we wouldn't choose him. Girls like the band members to be young and hot. You can see from the picture, he doesn't quite meet those criteria. He was a bit of a slimeball as well. Probably harmless, but a bit creepy."

"Do you still have his number?"

"I'll have a look. It might be in my phone. I'll text you afterwards if I've got it."

"How about this one?" I show the next picture: the tall, dark-haired girl. She looks about the same age as Troy, who I now know is twenty-five.

He gives a wry grin. "Yeah, I recognise her. She's tried several times to give me her number, and a fair few times to get me to go out with her. I've told her I'm happily married, but she doesn't seem to take no for an answer." Shock and horror show on his face, as the awful possibility crosses his mind. "No, she couldn't. Surely not." But doubt is there too.

"What's her name?" I ask gently.

"Sarah. I don't know her last name, but I've got her number too."

I refrain from asking him why he's got the number of a girl he was trying to reject. Maybe he was trying to be nice, but it could easily have raised her hopes – perhaps catastrophically.

"Finally, what do you know about the girl in this photo?"

He identifies my final potential suspect as Gemma Harris, a photography student, who's done some portraits of him and the boys.

"She's a nice girl; really into the band, but in a good way. She wouldn't harm a fly, I'm sure."

"Actually, I've just got one more photo to show you." I bring up a photo of Penny, one that Joanna took at the gig we attended – I can't believe it was only three days ago.

"Yeah, I know Penny. She's a press photographer. Turns up to a lot of our gigs. I think she's a bit of a secret fan, but she tries not to let on. I don't know her that well, and I've not got her number, so you might need to contact the newspaper if you need to speak to her."

"No, that's fine, thanks. We've got her number already. I just wanted to know how well you knew her."

"Yeah, well, I don't really know her that much. She seems okay. There's that bloke that hangs around with her sometimes, Nigel, who's a bit of a prick. In fact, didn't I see him hassling you on Friday?"

"Yes, and he is a prick. How well do you know him? Was he still at the gig after Penny left on Friday?"

"Sorry, I don't remember seeing him. I was trying to work out where I know him from, but he seems to be vaguely connected in my head with… oh my God… with Linda. I can't think about it now." He looks away from the screen. "I think Mum and Dad are back. I'd better see them. Thanks for letting me talk. I'm sure I've told you more than I've said to the police. That stupid cow with the red hair never seems to ask the right questions. Let me know if you find out anything."

Joanna laughs. "Sure. Speak soon."

"Of course. Thanks, Troy. Take care." I wave, and turn Skype off.

A couple of minutes later my phone pings three times.

Each one is a contact sent via WhatsApp. Gemma Harris, Sarah Fan, and Dean Fan. Joanna looks across the table at the messages.

"I guess Fan is a designation rather than a surname."

"It must be. Troy said he didn't know their full names." I dial the first number.

Two hours, a tuna sandwich and three cups of coffee later, we all head to Will's car. It's now four o'clock, and the traffic will be building up.

"It seems a shame not to use it, and I might as well ferry you around while I'm here. Also, being in a hire car will lend some additional anonymity."

"Thanks, Will. And it's nice not having to drive."

"No worries. You'd better get in the front though. If Mum navigates, we'll end up the opposite end of the country to where we need to be."

I sit in the front, but defend my friend. "To be fair, she's navigated very well so far. We've not been lost yet."

"Thanks. I am here you know, while you talk about me. Who do you want to see first? I'm sure Becky can program the satnav as well as I can."

I turn my head and grin at her. "What would we all do without satnav? I think we should start with Gemma. She seems to know Troy and the band best, and is also the least likely suspect. Also, she lives furthest away, so we can start with her and work back in this direction."

"Where do they all live?" asks Will.

I consult the addresses I've typed into my phone. "Gemma's in Stockport. Sarah's not that far from her, in Parrs Wood, towards Didsbury. Dean lives in Chorlton."

"Where does Troy live?" He doesn't wait for an answer before adding, "Becky, can you type Gemma's address in to the satnav please, so we can get started?"

I start typing and leave Joanna to reply to his first question.

"Troy's wife was murdered in Didsbury, less than a mile from Sarah, four miles from Gemma, and about four miles in a different direction from Dean."

I sit back and fasten my seat belt, as Will starts the car. He spends the first few minutes of the journey swooning over the smooth ride, quiet engine and general beauty of the car, but then we discuss the three suspects we're about to see. We'd gleaned little from the phone conversations, other than an agreement for us to visit. Actually, the order of visiting works out well with the requests from the suspects. Gemma has no lectures on a Monday afternoon, so is home anyway. Sarah and Dean both requested visits after six to give them time to get home after work.

I've warned Matt that I'll be back late, so he can sort out dinner for himself and Cheryl.

Between the rush hour traffic and a loss of GPS signal getting lost in Stockport, it's almost five by the time we pull up outside Gemma's house.

"Big house for a student, isn't it?" Joanna says as she gets out of the car.

"Most likely a house-share. I reckon she's just got a room."

Will's probably right, but I refrain from making assumptions at this stage. It's a pleasant road, with lots of trees and grass verges. The houses are large semi-detached properties, dating from probably the 1950s or 60s.

"Do you want me to stay in the car? In case you want to make a quick getaway?" Will's sense of humour is infectious, and I can't help grinning.

"Probably won't be necessary, but it might be a bit daunting having all three of us descending on her. Are you sure you don't mind?"

"Not at all. I can do a bit of research on the area while I'm waiting. Including where's the nearest McDonald's!"

"Perfect. We'll see you in a bit then."

The girl who opens the door is instantly recognisable from the photos. She's about Joanna's height, but a bit plumper than she looked in the club. Maybe it's because of the baggy navy sweatshirt and jogging bottoms. Not a flattering look. Her hair is fastened back with Kirby grips, and she looks about twelve.

"Hi, come in," she says, opening the door wide and heading indoors, obviously expecting us to follow her."

"Don't you want to check who we are first?" Joanna halts in front of me, just inside the front door.

Gemma turns around, looking surprised. "Aren't you the detectives?"

"Yes. The White Knight Detective Agency." I give Joanna a gentle nudge in the back, and she shakes her head slightly before following Gemma into a messy kitchen. There's a table and four chairs, and a skinny girl cooking something aromatic on the hob.

"Give me a couple of minutes, Gem. This is nearly done, and I'll be out of your way. Pip and Jade are out tonight, so you can entertain your guests in peace." She gives us curious looks before dishing up a professional-looking curry and rice onto a plate. "I've made too much as usual, so you can have some later." Unfortunately, this is directed at Gemma, and not at us, as my mouth is watering from the smell. I glance at Joanna, who takes out her phone and types a message. I hope she's asking Will to research local curry houses. In obedience to a signal from Gemma, we sit down at the table.

When we have the kitchen to ourselves, Gemma puts some cans on the table, and sits opposite us.

"Help yourself to a drink. I've only diet coke, or caffeine-free diet coke; or you can have water if you like."

I help myself to the caffeine-free can and thank our host. Joanna declines a drink.

"Thanks for agreeing to see us. Do you live here permanently, or just in term-time?"

"It's a student house. We're all third-years and have lived here for a year and a half now. They're a friendly bunch, and we're all good mates."

I see an opportunity and throw in a casual question that could clear her immediately. "Were you all here on Friday night?"

"Of course not. Why would we be in on a Friday night? Anyway, Troy was on at Band On The Wall on Friday so we all went there. After Troy, we stayed on for the late-night comedy act. We left about 1am. Jade wanted to go to clubbing after that, but the rest of us'd had enough, so we went home. Got back here about 1:45 cos it seemed to take forever finding a taxi." She shakes her head. "Can't believe that poor Troy got home that night to find his wife dead. It's so awful."

"Had you met his wife?"

"No, I don't think so. I've been to his house though. I did a photoshoot with him and the band about a month ago. It's part of my final year project, and they were all really lovely about it. He's got a nice house, and I got some great photos."

"Would you mind showing us?" I have nothing specific in mind, but I'd like to see more of his house. Without official authority, I can't access the house. This might be a wonderful opportunity to get some useful information.

Gemma leaves the kitchen and returns a couple of minutes later with a slim, silver-coloured laptop. She opens it up and presses a few buttons before turning it towards us. The photos are a mixture of black and white (arty and cool, but not terribly helpful) and colour.

"These are all digital, aren't they?" I ask, as a sudden thought crosses my mind.

"Of course. One or two people on my course still use film, but I much prefer digital. It gives the photographer so much flexibility."

"So could you make all these black and white photos into colour?"

"I could but they look better in monochrome."

I raise my eyebrow at Joanna, and she nods. "We're investigating Troy's wife's murder, and it would be really helpful to the case to examine these photos, but only really in colour."

"Shouldn't murder investigations be confined to the police?"

"The investigation overlaps with another case we're working on, so we're unofficially helping the Inspector on the case. It's a bit hush-hush to be honest." I give Gemma the most disarming smile I can manage. "The Sergeant doesn't like me very much, so it's a bit complicated. She can't know I'm working on this, but the DI said he could use our help."

"I see what you mean – definitely complicated. My dad's in the police force down in Exeter, where I'm from, and he said the office politics are crazy. He moans about it all the time. It's a bit of a relief to be up here out of the way actually."

"I can imagine. So would you be able to help us with these photos?"

"I guess so. Give me your email address and I'll send them over to you – probably tomorrow or Wednesday as it'll take me a while to get them optimised. I hope you don't mind, but there'll be a little copyright watermark in the bottom right-hand corner. I'll make it as small as I can, and if I think there's something important in that part of the photo, I'll move it to the other side. Is that okay?"

"That sounds great. Thanks, Gemma."

Joanna stands up. "Yes, thanks a lot. This will be great. We need to be going now, but really appreciate your help."

Back in the car a couple of minutes later, Will's sitting there perusing a menu.

"There's an Indian takeaway on the main road. I popped

over to grab a menu. I think we should order, then go to see Sarah. We can come back and pick the food up afterwards."

After a bit of haggling, I convince him to hang on, and we'll order from the local Indian near his mum's house. "We'll enjoy it more sitting at a table after we've finished work."

"Now that's settled," says Joanna, "let's get to Sarah's and find out what she's got to say."

Chapter Twenty-Five

Sarah may have said she lived in Parrs Wood, but the satnav leads us to a block of apartments a short distance from Levenshulme station. It's pleasant and modern, with a tree-lined lawn, dotted with a few wooden benches. There's off-road parking, and Will volunteers once again to remain in the car.

The tall girl who lets us into the flat is immaculately made-up and wearing a red pencil skirt and black silk blouse. Her dark hair is in a ponytail.

"Hi. You're here about Troy? You'd better come in." Although she's polite, there's a hint of hostility in the air. I glance at Joanna and roll my eyes at her as we follow our host through a dark hallway into a modern, minimalist lounge. "Sit on the sofa." She points to a black leather 2-seater and takes a seat herself on a matching armchair directly opposite. Unlike our previous interviewee, she doesn't offer us a drink. A peculiar smell is drifting around us – quite hard to describe, although there's possibly chamomile, lavender and rosemary in the mix.

"Thanks for agreeing to meet us this evening," I begin, in a conciliatory tone. We'll get a lot more from her if she thinks we're friendly. "I hope you've not had to rush from work?"

"No, I got back half an hour ago. But I've not eaten yet, and dinner will be ready soon."

"We won't keep you long. It smells great though. What are you having?" asks Joanna. She's a great liar.

"Lentil stew. I grow my own herbs and spices and use them in my cooking. I'm a bit of a health freak." She says all this without a hint of a smile, and I realise we're not going to warm her up at all. Time to dive straight in.

"So I believe you've met Troy a few times?"

"More than that. He came back here several times after gigs."

"In what capacity?"

She glares at me. "What do you think? He liked to brush my hair." She sneers. "We slept together. You must be crap detectives if I have to spell it out for you."

"We'd rather you told us in your own words." Joanna's still trying to be friendly. "How long had you two been having an affair?"

"I wouldn't say it was an affair exactly. He's said he wanted to leave his wife for me, but couldn't because of their little girl, so we had to be very discreet." She reaches behind her head and removes a band from her hair. Shaking out an enviable mane of dark brown wavy hair, she adds, "He was in love with me."

"Were you in love with him?" My suspicion is growing that this is a load of bullshit.

"I held out for a while, particularly when one of the other band members let slip that Troy was married. But he's a charming guy. And he's pretty hot in bed."

"So you had reason to hate his wife?"

"He'd have tired of her after a while. There was no rush. I wouldn't have killed the silly bitch anyway."

A buzzer in the kitchen calls an early halt to the interview.

"Just one quick question before we go, if you don't mind." I take a photo of Penny out of my handbag and show it to her. "Do you know this girl?"

"I don't know her name. I recognise her face though." She pauses, staring at the photo. "Hang on, is she a photographer? I think I've seen her hanging around Troy and the band taking photos."

"Okay, thanks." We take our leave, wishing her a pleasant evening (which she doesn't deserve).

Back at the car, Will asks us how it went.

"She's a bloody lying bitch, but I don't think she's Penny's stalker," says Joanna.

"I agree. And I'm pretty sure she's not been having an affair with Troy. It sounds like she was making it all up – a figment of an overactive imagination."

"Yeah definitely. She's clearly obsessed with him. Do you think that's sufficient motive for her to kill Linda? She was pretty horrible about her." Joanna puts her seatbelt on. "Anyway, let's get out of here. One more to see this evening."

As Will drives to our next destination, we discuss the chances of obsession leading to murder.

"Surely it's mostly a device for crime fiction?" says Will.

"You'd be surprised. Nearly thirty years in the police force, and I saw a lot of obsession, and yes, it's often a motive. Obsession with power, money, hatred, jealousy, revenge – they're all very real, and powerful, reasons for harming someone. Having said that, I can't say I'm convinced that Sarah would have done it. As we've said, a lot of her story was pure invention, but I didn't get a genuine sense of what the girl was really like."

"Yeah, you're right, hen. She wasn't a nice girl, but I couldn't get a sense of what she was about. Gemma, on the other hand, was really sweet."

"So far, they've both been how we'd have expected from Troy's descriptions."

"So, sorry for asking, I don't mean to be rude…"

"But you're going to be anyway. Carry on, Will, ask what you like." I grin at him, but he's watching the road, and he doesn't notice.

"Okay. Do you think your perceptions have been coloured by Troy's comments, or is it just that you're both great judges of character?"

"We're excellent at character assessment of course," says Joanna. I turn around to look at her, and she winks at me. "Seriously though, I suppose that's a point, but if Troy reckoned Sarah was constantly badgering him to go out with her, it's not an unreasonable reaction for her to pretend they were having an affair."

"Come off it, Mum. Of course it is. Why not just deny fancying him in the first place? It's a lot more sensible. Especially when his wife's just been bumped off."

"You've heard the phrase about a woman scorned, Will."

"Yeah. Hell hath no fury like a woman scorned. All the more reason she did it, and why she should try to cover it up by pretending never to have liked him."

I frown, thinking it over. "So, by that logic, she can't have done it, otherwise why would she be so stupid as to pretend to be having an affair, even if she doesn't admit to the terminology?"

"Perhaps she's so obsessed with him she believes in her own story and is oblivious to the fact that she could be a suspect?" says Joanna.

"Only an innocent person could be oblivious. The murderer must either know they're a suspect, or believe themselves to be safe. But whichever it is, they're not in cloud-cuckoo-land about the concept."

"So, does that rule Sarah out?" Will glances at the satnav

and applies the brakes sharply as he turns left down a side road.

"You concentrate on driving. Becky, what do you think? I'm inclined to think that exonerates Sarah, even though I didn't like her."

"I'd say it puts her lower down the list." I glance round as Will parks at the side of the road behind a white van. "Are we here?"

"Yeah. I reckon it's that house." He points at a scruffy terrace, set slightly back from the road by an overgrown patch of grass and an uneven path. The house, lit up by a street lamp and the moon, looks to need a decorator, and probably some building work.

"Do you want to take the lead this time, Joanna?"

"No, you're fine. You're the expert."

"Thanks." I get out of the car and pull my coat round me. The temperature feels like it's dropped five degrees since we left Sarah's twenty minutes ago.

I let Joanna ring the bell as she gets there first. There's no sound. We wait for a minute, but still nothing.

"Do you reckon the bell's broken?" I use the knocker, but it's heavy, and falls back against the door with more of a dull thud than a rousing knock.

"Let me." Joanna grins at me, removes an umbrella from her handbag, and thumps it several times against the wood.

"Hang on, I'm coming," shouts a muffled voice from inside. A minute later, the door opens. "Why didn't you use the bell?" The owner of the voice is a short, balding man dressed in a dirty grey sweater and baggy jeans. He looks about thirty-five. "Who are you anyway?"

"White Knight Detective Agency, and your bell doesn't work. Are you Dean?" Joanna smiles pleasantly at him. I'm about to do the same, but a whiff of either boiled cabbage or serious BO hits my nostrils, and I try not to gag.

"Yes, I'm Dean. Dean Bennett." Do you want to come in?"

"No, it's okay. We can ask you some questions here for now." I reckon I'll need to give myself a really awful cold if I need to come back. I try to breathe shallowly as I take a discreet step backward. Unfortunately, although cold, it's a still night. A bit of a breeze might have helped.

"I believe you know Troy Cassidy?"

"Yes, a bit. Once, he offered me a chance to play with the band, but after a couple of rehearsals, he said it wouldn't work out. He was all right about it – just said I wasn't the right fit. He's always friendly when I see him at gigs."

"Did you ever meet his wife?"

"That poor girl that got herself killed? No, I never met her. I think she was working both times when I went there for rehearsals."

"So you knew where they lived?"

"Yes, of course. Is that it now?"

"Not quite. Where were you on Friday night?"

"Here, in my front lounge, watching telly."

"Was anyone with you?"

"No. I live by myself. I thought about going to the pub, but I was tired and couldn't be arsed. I watched *Breaking Bad* on Netflix." He scowls. "Sorry I don't have an alibi, but I'm not a killer, so it didn't occur to me I'd need one."

"I totally understand. Thank you. Just one more thing." I take the photo of Penny from my bag. "Do you recognise this girl?"

"I don't think so," he says, after staring at the picture for a minute. "Her face is vaguely familiar, but I couldn't tell you where from." He shakes his head. "No, not got a clue. Who is she?"

"It's not important. She's a photographer. I just wondered if you'd seen her at any of Troy's gigs."

"I don't really pay any attention to young girls. Now if

you've finished, and you really won't come inside, can I go? I'm bloody freezing here."

"Sure. Thanks for your time, and sorry for keeping you." I put the photo back in my bag, glance at Joanna and turn to go.

"Hey," Dean calls after us. "There was a lot of conflict in the band. Maybe one of them did her in."

"Thanks." I nod. I don't trust him, but I've not discounted the band members either yet.

The journey back to Joanna's house is much quieter. We're all tired and hungry, and I'm getting anxious now about Cheryl. I've not heard from her yet, although she's been back from school for hours. It's nearly seven now. After we've been in the car for ten minutes, I take out my phone and type in a WhatsApp.

'R u ok?'

There's a moment's pause. Will puts the radio on to fill the silence in the car.

'When r u coming home?' Cheryl's message only partially answers my question. If she wants me home, I guess she's not totally okay.

"How far away are we?" I ask Will.

"About half an hour. Plus takeaway collection. Maybe forty minutes."

"Can you drop me back at my car before the takeaway please? I think I need to get home."

"Sure."

"Is everything okay?" Joanna touches my shoulder, and I turn to look at her. She looks worried, but I think the trip out has been good for her.

"I think so. Cheryl's got some stuff going on at school. She wants me to get home."

"Course. Why don't we drop you straight home, then you can call Will when you need to collect your car, and he'll pick you up?"

I agree, and thank them, then type back in my phone. '*Back in about 30 mins. See you soon. If you can get Dad to order or cook pizza, I'll be eternally grateful.*' I forget sometimes to use text-speak when I'm messaging her.

'*k.*' There's no other response, so I guess she's too stressed to worry about my perfect grammar. Hopefully she'll pass on the message about pizza. I don't feel ready to deal with her problems on an empty stomach.

Chapter Twenty-Six

Jumping out of the car as it stops in front of my house, I notice there's a rustle in the bushes. My pulse rate picks up a few notches, but Will is watching me as I put my keys in the door. I unlock it and step inside before turning to wave goodbye. As the car moves away, I shut the door quickly and lock and bolt it from the inside.

I take a deep breath as I hang up my coat in the hall cupboard, and the scrumptious aroma of garlic bread assails my nostrils.

"Mum! You've been out for ages. Are you okay?" Cheryl appears in the hall, and I wrap my arms around her. She responds by hugging me back fiercely, and I feel her sobbing against my shoulder.

"I'm sorry, darling. I've had a busy day with the investigation. Why don't we sit down, and you can tell me what's happened?"

There's a sniff and a hiccup from my daughter, as she extracts herself from the hug. She wipes her sleeve across her eyes, but pops into the downstairs loo to get some tissue for her nose. She's still in there sorting herself out when Matt emerges from the kitchen holding a takeaway box.

"Garlic bread. Fourteen inches. You're going to have to help us eat it, Becks."

"Did you get any pizza?"

"Obviously. Nine-inch veggie for you – no olives, but with pineapple."

"Perfect. What are you and Chezz having?"

"Sharing a fourteen-inch cheese feast. Oh, and some chips. And there's Phish Food ice cream in the freezer." Matt gives me a sheepish look. "I might have gone a bit overboard. Sorry." He lowers his voice. "She's had a shitty day at school. She needed a treat. You look like you need one too."

"It's been intense. Don't worry about the food. It will hopefully provide lunch and dinner for tomorrow as well, otherwise we'll all end up in hospital having heart surgery. We might need to work on improving the nutrition in this house, but that's something we can worry about tomorrow or Wednesday. Let's take this in the lounge and eat, and you and Cheryl can tell me what's happened."

Cheryl appears at this point, with a red nose and red-rimmed eyes. "I need to eat."

We settle in the lounge with *Big Bang Theory* playing on TV, as we guzzle an extremely unhealthy but tasty feast. I'm desperate to ask my daughter about what's happened today, but she seems a bit calmer now she's eating, and I don't want to upset her again. Instead, I fill them in on the case so far. They're interested, but that elephant is lurking again, possibly lured by the smell of pizza. Now we've eaten, it's time to address Nellie directly.

"So, Cheryl, you've had a bit of a respite, but there's no point you going to bed without discussing this. You'll only stew all night. What happened today?"

"I guess you're right, Mum. But we've not had ice cream yet."

"That can be your reward for telling us everything now. Come on, love. You'll feel better."

"Okay. Wendy did her bit, and must have contacted the head first thing this morning, cos we had a 'special assembly' straight after lunch." Cheryl makes inverted commas in the air with her fingers. "The whole school was made to attend, and Wendy stood there talking about cyber-crime and bullying."

"Did she keep quiet about your involvement?" asks Matt.

"Yeah of course. She said her team are always on the lookout for this sort of thing, and will soon have the names of the people who posted these images." She has a mouthful of lemonade, swallows hard, and takes a deep breath. "It was after she'd gone that things got weird."

"In what way?"

"At afternoon break. Elaine and Karen apparently called all the girls over to them. I was with Dan, and didn't know, cos obviously she was excluded, but at the end of break, Elaine cornered me, and said, 'It had to be you. No one else would tell on us, and you've refused to stop being pals with Fat Danni.'. I said, 'Stop calling her that. Why are you being so horrible to her?' I didn't want to get into a discussion about what I might have said to anyone."

"What did Elaine say to that? I assume she's one of the girls who posted this picture?"

"Yeah, I think she's probably the one who did it, cos she's the real leader of the two. Karen just does what she's told. Elaine turned really nasty when I stood up for Dan. There was no one around. She'd cornered me outside, and the bell had gone for the next lesson. She spat in my face, and said, 'You'll be next. I don't give a…' – she swore at that point; I don't want to repeat it – 'who you tell. You can sneak to the… er… queen of England for all I care. My dad's a barrister, and he'll make mincemeat of you in court. He'll prove that you and Fat Danni planned it all to get us into trouble."

"And no one saw this and interfered?" Matt's face is scarlet. I can see he's working himself into a state. I agree in principle, but it's so recently that he was in hospital, I need to defuse the situation.

"I assume you got away from her?"

"Yeah, I stamped on her foot, moved away, and ran inside. I popped into the loos and cleaned my face and then went back to class."

"Didn't the teacher say anything?" Matt still sounds angry. I glance at him, but he seems otherwise fine.

"I slipped in when she was busy with one of the other girls. I don't know how, but she didn't see me come in late. The other pupils in my class kept quiet. Karen and Elaine aren't in my stream, and the rest of the girls are okay when they're away from them."

"So what are you going to do about those girls? Do you want me or your mum to go up to school and get this sorted?"

"No way! I'm already terrified about what they might be preparing to send round."

"How about a counter-attack? Are you friendly with any of the other girls who are perhaps in that crowd, but not so under the leader's thumb?" I have an idea forming, but need to hear that my daughter has some backup first.

"Yeah, a few. But some were giving me dirty looks on the tram home today."

"What about the ones in your stream? And how about the boys?"

"There are three or four girls in my stream who are on the edge of that gang, but gave me kind of friendly smiles when I got back to class. The boys are in my stream are mostly okay. A bit geeky some of them."

"Perfect. I think there might be a way out of this."

An hour later, the seeds are sown. Several of Cheryl's classmates have agreed to back her up, and are now in a WhatsApp group, and we've got several parents involved, who are furious at the attempts to draw their offspring into criminal activities, and eager to wipe out the impending evil. With the scene set, and a large tub of Ben & Jerry's ice cream devoured, we all head upstairs for an early night. It's not quite ten, but I'm sure I'm not the only one who's exhausted.

On Tuesday morning I borrow Matt's car to drive Cheryl into school. We're both insured on both cars, but as Matt's not driving at the moment, it will be good for the engine for me to give his a run. Mine is still outside Joanna's.

As agreed the previous evening, I park the car after dropping Cheryl at the side of the road, and walk back to see her meet a few of her classmates at the school gates. They walk in together. Danielle is amongst them. One of the mums stops me as I turn and head back to the car. She's sitting in a 4x4 watching her son join Cheryl's crowd.

"Becky White, isn't it?" She puts her hand out through the wound-down window. "I'm Lesley Goldstein, Joel's mum. We liaised last night."

"Hi Lesley," I shake the proffered hand. "Lovely to meet you. Thanks for offering to help. Cheryl says Joel's a nice lad."

"You're welcome. And thanks. I think I recognise you, and I'm not sure it's from school."

Damn. I think I recognise her too, although I'm not used to seeing her without a wig.

"You're a barrister, aren't you? I think I've seen you in court." There shouldn't be any harm in admitting my past to her, although I'm still trying to keep a low profile. "I was in the police force until last year. I do private detective work now."

Out of habit, I survey the area, but there's no one within earshot now. Most of the cars have cleared, and the kids have gone into school.

"Of course. And your name came up, at least I think it was you, in connection with a recent case. Didn't one of your colleagues get killed? I think you were Becky Wiseman previously?"

"Yes. One problem with my line of work is that it's impossible not to make enemies. When I left the force, I decided it would be better to change my name. Cheryl's stayed as she was for the sake of school and to reduce questions."

"It's fine; you don't need to justify anything to me. I've got a late start today. Do you fancy a coffee? We can get a quiet one at M&S in the Fort."

"That sounds good. I'll follow you down there."

We agree to meet there as soon the traffic permits, as we both know the Manchester Fort shopping precinct well. I text Matt to let him know what's going on, as far as I can, but I'm very curious to hear what Lesley has to say.

Fifteen minutes later, we're seated with a large cappuccino each, in the corner of M&S café, as far away from the checkout as possible. It's quiet, and there's no one around us. Lesley looks around with a satisfied grin.

"This is perfect. Thanks Becky. So we're going to bring down those bitches Elaine and Karen? They used to pick on Joel so badly in primary school, and they still make nasty comments when they see him. So I've got a slight grudge, you could say."

"They're both in a lower stream, I believe."

"Yes, they couldn't get into Solomon, although I believe Elaine is clever enough if she applied herself. Her dad works in Chambers – not in my firm, I'm relieved to say – but he's a vicious bastard, and not above taking bribes in certain areas." She seems to notice my raised eyebrows. "Obviously nothing I can prove, otherwise I'd bring him down too, but it would be my great pleasure getting his daughter charged, or at the very least expelled. And I think we can do this between us."

I appear to have made a powerful and useful ally. Further conversation enables me to understand a bit more about the background. For a talented high-flying professional, Lesley has a surprising love of gossip. Couple that with an engaging grin and a wicked sense of humour, and I find myself liking her more and more as the coffee cups empty.

She's a single mum, widowed when Joel's dad died from bowel cancer three years earlier. She shakes her head as she tells me.

"Poor Joel didn't have the bar mitzvah that all his friends had. He lost his dad two months before, and to be quite honest, we'd spent the previous six months so busy with chemo that no one had any time to think about celebrations. When we knew it was nearing the end, the rabbi allowed Joel to say his bar mitzvah portion at Barry's bedside, and gave Joel a blessing, even though it was too early. When he turned thirteen, he didn't want to go through the fuss. He repeated his portion in shul in front of a small but select congregation, but we were all too upset for a party."

I make sympathetic murmurings. It's so hard to know what to say in these circumstances.

"So anyway, I owe it to Joel to get those girls sorted out. You made a brilliant start last night, getting the nice kids on board, and also their parents. So much easier for bullies to pick on one or two kids by themselves, than to attack a crowd. But I think we can expand on it and turn the tables."

"Sounds interesting. I'm all ears."

She outlines a proposal that involves getting the weaker members of Karen and Elaine's crowd to switch to 'Cheryl's new gang'. Once that's done, and the girls are left friendless, Cheryl and Joel are to give them two options. Either they take down all fake photos and issue a public apology on Facebook and in Assembly confirming that the photos were fake, or they'll get shopped to the police and they'll never have any friends again, throughout the whole of their school careers. In the latter case, they'll also be reported to the school authorities, in which case they might get expelled.

I like it. It's thorough, conclusive, and gets Danielle her friends back. Although it could be argued that she now knows who her real friends are. I mention this to Lesley.

"Agreed, but it's still nice at that age to be part of a crowd. I'm sure she'll be much happier if these cows publicly apologise and confess to faking the photo."

The idea of faking a photo jars me. It seems connected with the case I'm working on, but I'm not sure how or why. I shelve the thought for the moment.

With a plan of action agreed, and time waiting for no one, we say our goodbyes and arrange to meet at her house tomorrow night – with Cheryl, Danielle and Joel in attendance – to discuss the next steps. Meanwhile, Lesley promises to set up a secret Facebook group with all the parents and kids on Cheryl's side, so that key aspects can be discussed and we can keep everyone informed.

Back in the car, I check my phone. There's a message from Finn.

"Joanna says you've been busy. It would be good to catch up and compare notes. Are you free for lunch?"

Chapter Twenty-Seven

It's only been four days since I last struck, but the message does not seem to have got through. Time to deliver another.

I wait for nightfall again. It would be stupid to attack in daylight. I choose dark clothes. A trip to Primark at the weekend replenished my stocks. In case of multiple actions being required, I may need to destroy outer layers again. Cheap, dark items are expendable.

When the time is right, I don a dark hoody and jeans, with black trainers. This time I might need to run. The black rucksack blends right in.

I get a bus to reach my destination. It's not very full, and I'm able to choose a seat by myself, upstairs at the front. A good observation post, and one where I'm unlikely to be disturbed. Just a quick journey, and then I get off the bus, taking the precaution of alighting a couple of stops early. It's only a ten-minute walk from there to the house.

The property is in darkness, shielded from the street lamps by trees. From my rucksack I withdraw the tools: a lock-pick and my trusty knife. It may be a risk to use the same weapon as last time, but it's sharp, light and effective.

A roll of masking tape slides easily and conveniently on to my wrist. A strip of tape over each mouth while they sleep will reduce the chance of them waking the neighbours. Recent surveillance has confirmed they go to bed early, and with no lights on in the house, I'm confident they should be asleep by now.

There's no alarm, and I emerge from the house a short time later, with the job completed. I was more accurate this time, and there's less blood spatter – certainly nothing that shows up on the black clothing. I walk the short distance back to the bus stop and catch the next bus home for my shower.

Chapter Twenty-Eight

Finn and I agreed to have lunch at the Village in Bury again. It's convenient for both of us, as he's a member of the gym there. Joanna and Will declined to join us, so we are alone in a booth. We order salads and diet cokes and sit down to wait for the food to arrive.

"Good to see you, Becks. Are we good now?"

"Of course. How's the case?"

"Not progressing as fast as I'd like. The autopsy was done yesterday and confirmed what we already suspected."

"You mean that she died from multiple stab wounds?" I raise an eyebrow. It's difficult to imagine that the autopsy would come back with anything interesting.

"Yeah, pretty much." His mouth twists into a wry grin. "There was one thing though."

"Oh?"

"There was significant recent bruising, around the ribs and legs, that didn't appear to be connected to the stab wounds."

I take a minute to process this, as a waiter brings our food. When he's gone, I look at Finn.

"You think maybe Troy, for all his protestations of love, might have been beating her?"

"I'm sorry, Becks, but that's the obvious answer."

"It doesn't feel right. It might tie in a bit with the story of one of his fans, but to be honest, we had her down as an over-imaginative liar." I tell him about Sarah, and her apparent conviction that Troy wanted to have an affair with her.

I'm about to add in the details of the visits to Dean and Gemma, when Finn's phone rings. He takes the call, going instantly into the professional mode that I remember so well.

"What's happened?" I ask as he puts the phone down on the table and shakes his head.

"Troy's parents have been found dead in their home. Sorry, I need to sort this out. I'll call you later to fill you in. Sorry about lunch." He leans across and gives me a quick peck on the cheek before grabbing his phone and his jacket and leaving me with two plates of salad.

Rather than eating alone and wasting food, I call Joanna and invite her and Will to join me. They agree and arrive ten minute later to polish off Finn's untouched salad, and to join me in demolishing coffee and sundry desserts. It feels naughty ending lunch with sticky toffee pudding and custard, but my disappointment at being abandoned by Finn is greater than it should be. Serious carbs are required to compensate. Seeing Joanna devour tiramisu and Will eat a huge chocolate fudge sundae helps to relieve some of the guilt. While we indulge, I update them on the latest developments, both with Cheryl and Troy.

We're leaving the restaurant when I spot a familiar figure in the corner. We seem to have been under observation.

"Guys, meet me back outside my house in about twenty minutes, will you? That way I can drop this car off and pick mine up. I just need to deal with something first."

I see Joanna glance across to our observer, and she looks back at me with raised eyebrows. I nod.

"Sure. We'll pop home and pick you up. Make it half an hour."

I wait for a few minutes until they've gone, then walk up to Roger, who's pretending to read the newspaper.

"May I join you for a moment?"

"Please do." He waits while I sit on the chair opposite him. "You've been busy."

"How long have you been watching me?"

"Since we parted, I've kept an eye on your activities. You've got a finger in a lot of pies right now, haven't you?"

"There are a couple of things going on. Have you been hiding in bushes near my house? Or if not you, maybe one of your underlings?"

"That's a lovely word – underlings." He savours it for a long pause. "No. We've got more comfortable ways to observe people of interest."

"Like sitting behind newspapers in foodie pubs?"

"I wanted to speak to you. I thought you'd notice me eventually." He folds up his paper and folds his arms. "Can you go to London? We have a proposition for you, but it involves one of my colleagues who's unable to travel just now. She wants to interview you in her flat tomorrow afternoon."

"What sort of interview?" I rub my nose. "I've not had an interview for about five years. I'm out of practice."

"No need to worry. It's not the sort of interview you can prepare for. Sylvia just wants to meet you. She'll know if you're the right person for the task."

"Okay. Will she also tell me what this is all about?"

"If it's appropriate." He reaches into his wallet and hands me an envelope containing a rail ticket for tomorrow at 10:15 – Manchester Piccadilly to London Euston. Standard class. Off-peak. There's also a slip of paper with a printed address in

Kensington, a travel card for the Underground, and two twenty-pound notes. "That's to cover expenses: lunch, a taxi from the tube station if the weather's awful, that sort of thing."

"What time am I expected?"

"Half past two. Your ticket is flexible, so you can do some shopping afterwards if you like. Theoretically, you could stay down there if you have friends or family, but we would prefer you to return the same day."

"That's fine. I have friends in London, but they would be happy meeting me for dinner. Then they'll see me on to the train. If I park at Piccadilly, in the proximity car park, could I claim back the cost?"

"Of course. Particularly as it appears that someone has been lurking in bushes watching you. Perhaps one of your old enemies. You must have made a few in your line of your work."

"Thank you. Do I need to take anything?"

"Just whatever paraphernalia you'd normally take on a day trip to London. It would be sensible for you to find a good reason to visit the capital. We don't want to publicise this more than needed."

"I could visit Troy's record company. That could be useful."

"Absolutely. Excellent idea. Would you like us to make the arrangements? I could ensure an appointment with his producer if that would help?"

I thank him and get my thoughts together, while he taps messages into his phone. These people seem capable of everything. A moment later…

"Perfect. That's all sorted. You'll be meeting Troy's producer at half past four. I'll text you his name and address. That will give you time for some shopping and lunch when you arrive in London, then you can meet your friends for dinner afterwards. A very productive day."

I tuck the envelope into my bag and thank him. I'm about to leave when a thought occurs to me.

"Am I allowed to tell Matt?"

"Yes. As he's one of us, you're welcome to share information with him. However, be careful in case anyone is listening. All such discussions must take place indoors with the windows closed, and out of earshot of visitors or your offspring."

By the time I get back to my house, Will's outside in the car waiting for me.

"Are you okay, Becky? I left Mum at home – she's got a bit of a stomach-ache."

"In that case, I'll just come and pick up my car. Maybe we can catch up later this afternoon, after I've heard back from Finn."

He agrees, and twenty minutes later, I'm in my house, with my car on the drive, ready to ask Matt what the hell I've got myself involved with.

Matt is out when I get indoors. There's a message on the kitchen table. *Gone for a walk. Back soon.* A bit frustrating, but at least he's finally taking doctor's orders. I make myself a coffee and turn on my laptop to check out the details of tomorrow's journey. When I'm sure it's practical, I search the contacts on my phone and make a call.

"Dan?"

"Oh my God! Becks! How are you doing, love?"

As always, he's very free with his 'loves'. His husband is American, and he's picked up a few questionable phrases, but it's easier these days for me to suppress the pangs of my first love. I'm just delighted to see him so happy.

We exchange pleasantries for a few moments, then I

explain that I'm coming to London the next day and ask him if he's free to meet up for dinner.

"Sure. It'll be adorable to see you again, love. We've not seen you since the wedding. Are you inviting Gray along too, or just me?"

"Whichever. I don't mind. Obviously I want to see you most, but he's a lovely guy; I'm always happy to see him."

"What day is it? I lose track of time. I've been writing a paper, so working from home this week. So much easier to concentrate."

"It'll be Wednesday tomorrow." I smile into the phone. I know he can't see me, but it's so lovely just to hear his voice again.

"Perfect. It's Gray's bridge night. He tried so hard to get me into bridge, but I just don't get it. This is my reward. I get you all to myself for a few hours. What time do you have to head back?"

"I should probably aim to get the train back at eight or thereabouts. I don't want to be getting into Piccadilly much after ten."

"Of course not, love. Very dodgy. I'll book us a decent restaurant near Euston, so we can get you on that train in time. I'll text you the details. What time are you available?"

I explain that I have a meeting at the record company at half past four, and we arrange that Dan will meet me in the Starbucks next door at four o'clock. We can have a quick coffee first, then he'll work on his laptop until I'm finished.

"I've got a meeting with a client at half past two, but I'll be with you as soon as I can. I'm not sure how long my meeting will be, but I'll message you if I'm going to be late."

With my day in London completely arranged, I get my handbag ready. Train ticket, purse (with Roger's forty pounds, twenty of my own, a couple of credit cards, and some coins),

Sylvia's address, hairbrush, lipstick, ibuprofen and Rennies. I put a note on the fridge for me to remember my phone and keys, but it's unnecessary really. I would never go anywhere these days without my phone, and I need my keys to drive to the station.

I'm just attaching the note with a fridge magnet, amongst the mess of information about school concerts, reminders to take the cat to the vet, and hospital appointments for Matt, when he arrives home.

"Becky, are you back?"

"I hope so. Both the cars are outside."

"Hilarious. I was just checking. Are you okay? How was Cheryl this morning?"

I dig back through my memories. It's been a hectic day, and it's only just gone three o'clock.

"Fine." I put the kettle on and tell him about Lesley and the plan for revolution within the school student hierarchy. He seems impressed, but I really want to talk about my trip for tomorrow. I make us both a cup of tea first and persuade him to settle in the lounge with me.

"Do you know someone called Sylvia? One of Roger's connections?"

Matt's eyes widen. "Wow. How did she come up in the conversation?"

"I met Roger today. He was watching me while I was having lunch at the Village." I don't bother explaining who I was having lunch with. It's too complicated, and I don't want to derail the current discussion.

"What was he doing there?"

"Waiting to speak to me, apparently. Although I saw him and made the first approach."

"He does that a lot. It's his MO. He hangs around somewhere visible but inconspicuous and somehow indicates that he wants you to make contact with him. I'm used to it now, but the first few times I wasn't sure whether I should go up to him."

"Useful to know, thanks."

"So where did Sylvia come in? I heard she's a bit incapacitated right now. Just between us of course."

"I believe so. I have to go to London tomorrow. Apparently she wants to interview me about something."

"Very interesting." Matt has a swig of his drink, then puts his mug decisively on the coffee table. "She's Roger's boss. I've not actually met her, but we've been in contact via video call. All highly encrypted of course."

"What's she like? And why do you think she wants to meet me?"

"She's highly efficient. A great people-manager. She seems very sweet, but there's an iron core in there. People put themselves into highly dangerous positions just to please her. It's crazy, but she's reached a fairly high-up position I believe. I think you'll like her. As to why she wants to meet you, she vets most of the operatives. And Roger called me on Sunday and asked me a few questions about your school record and abilities."

"Do you know anything about my time at school?"

"I knew where your school report was. I hope you don't mind, but I photographed a couple of bits and sent them over."

"Okay. I'm quite intrigued. I guess they don't want me for cooking or sewing skills then."

"You were a girly swot, weren't you? Good at all the academic stuff."

"Yeah, mostly. Better at languages than science, but I could hold my own there too."

"I don't think we ever discussed it. What O-Levels did you do?"

"English Language, English Lit, French, German, Spanish,

Maths, Biology, History, and General Studies in Lower Sixth. Then English, French and History at A-Level. What about you?"

"Science all the way. As you know, I'm rubbish at languages. Maths, English – Language only; my teacher chickened out of putting me in for Literature – Physics, Chemistry, Biology and Music. I failed French, but got a Grade 2 CSE in it. It would probably have counted a couple of years later, as a GCSE."

"And your A-Levels?"

"Three sciences. Chemistry was always a must, and then to get in to do Pharmacy, it was two out of Maths, Physics and Biology. I ditched the maths. It's a shame really. Stats would have been useful. I get by though."

"So back to the point: did Roger give any clues about why he wanted to know?"

"He just said... I can't remember exactly... something about wanting to know where your latent talents might lie. He knows about your career with the police, but there are many things you can do for them."

"Do you think it's a good idea for me to get involved? I still have a lot of nightmares and freak out about certain things."

"This might be a good way for you to get back out there, but in a less conspicuous environment. And you've got your work with Joanna as a legitimate cover for any questions."

"Why don't they want her to go down to London?"

"I reckon Roger's keeping her in reserve for now. She... I probably shouldn't tell you this, but she messed up a bit on our last assignment. That's why I freaked out so much when she turned up here that first day. I thought the shit had finally hit the fan. But I reckon they know, and they're a bit reluctant to use her just now."

"The poor woman's been struggling with cancer, and lots of crap at home."

"I never said it was her fault."

"You implied it."

"I didn't mean to. She's great, and very competent, and loyal, and she'll always have your back. I'm delighted that the two of you are in business together. I think Roger will put some legitimate work your way too, but yes, she had a lot going on at that point. Someone got injured because of some information going in the wrong direction. It was an accident, but I knew that it had to have been her mistake. Anyway, I reckon Roger suspects, and that's why you're going to London, and she's not to know about it, except that you've been summoned to go to meet Troy's record producer."

"How am I supposed to justify going without her?"

"I don't know. Maybe say that Finn sorted it out, and…"

"Hang on. She saw Roger in the Village."

"Well, maybe you can say he sorted it out for you to visit the record people."

"He did, actually, but it still looks unfair."

"He's trying to cut costs. He only bought one ticket. You stopped to speak to him, and she didn't."

"I guess that works." I'm interrupted from further comments by the sound of the front door opening, followed by Cheryl coming in.

"Hi Mum and Dad. Guess what? You're invited to a meeting on Thursday night at Joel's house. His mum is organising it. Then on Friday, I think all hell is going to break loose at school."

Chapter Twenty-Nine

I don't get much sleep on Tuesday night, and the little I get is filled with strange and frightening dreams; like scenes from a James Bond movie, with guns, car chases and enemies appearing from the roof of intercity trains. Consequently, when my alarm goes off at half past seven on Wednesday morning, I'm bleary-eyed and more anxious than I should be.

By arrangement, Will arrives at 8:45 to take me to Piccadilly station. Bless him, he's been via Costa Coffee, and picked up a couple of lattes.

"Morning, Becky. I figured you'd need coffee. Have you got anything to read on the train?" Will asks as I put my seatbelt on.

"Damn, no. Have I got time to pop back in for my Kindle?"

"Sure. You've got two minutes."

A few minutes later, I'm back in the car with my Kindle, and also my phone charger and power bank I'd forgotten to pack yesterday.

Will switches on his satnav and sets it to take the traffic in consideration and take us via the quickest route. So we draw up at the station with twenty minutes to spare. I'm marginally more relaxed after the journey. My companion has kept me chatting about literature and movies the entire journey. We've avoided any discussion of the day ahead. I told Joanna and Will yesterday that I'd be visiting Troy's record company and doing some shopping, then seeing Dan. I don't know convincing I was. I could see that Joanna suspected something, but they refrained from pressuring me for answers. Will still insisted on driving me to and from the station.

"I reckon you'll be tired by the time you get back, Becky. You won't want to bother with driving home, but I don't think you'll want to get a taxi either. This is the best solution, and I'm happy to oblige anyway. Making the most of this little beauty." He'd patted the bonnet as he saw me out to my car yesterday evening.

The convenience of being driven by someone I like and trust, and being dropped off right outside the station, is a huge relief. I'm on the station concourse by ten, with another coffee, and a paper bag containing a smoked salmon and cream cheese bagel and a muffin. I need sustenance for this journey. As I put the ticket into the machine at the barrier to the platform, I notice my hand is trembling. I take a few deep breaths and try to calm down. I go to my assigned seat on the train. It's facing the direction of travel, and I'm pleased to see there's no reservation on the seat next to me. The carriage is less than a third reserved, according to an electronic display on the platform. I'm in an airline-style seat, which is also good, meaning I don't have to sit opposite a stranger. I always hate those table seats – there's a choice between uncomfortable silences and making polite conversation, not to mention the difficulty about where to place feet. This is much better. I glance around the carriage. There are a few businesspeople with laptops already open, and several older people who look as though they're heading to the capital for a day out. A family with kids of primary-school age occupy the table seats across the aisle from me. They look very ordinary and pleasant. The children settle down without argument, and immediately start watching films or programmes on their iPads.

I open my Kindle and settle down to read an old favourite from Georgette Heyer; nice relaxing material to calm me down. It's working great until a smartly-dressed, strapping guy in his forties boards the train at Stockport, walks past all the empty seats and plonks himself on the seat next to me. He gets out his laptop and spreads out, forcing me to back into my little corner. After fifteen minutes of this, I'm suffering from severe claustrophobia, and my anxiety is getting the better of me. I find enough elbow space to put my Kindle in my handbag, and I gather up my fleeing courage.

"Excuse me, I need to get out."

The man-sprawler looks at me in surprise. "The train doesn't stop for another quarter of an hour," he says, looking at his watch. Otherwise, he makes no movement to let me through.

"I feel sick. I need some air." If I didn't feel so rubbish, I could have laughed at the speed he picked up his laptop and stood up. He clearly didn't fancy someone throwing up over him.

I move past, muttering thanks, grab my coat from the rack above, and move through the train to the end of the carriage, where there are a couple of seats opposite the toilets. Sitting on one of them, I take some gulps of the fresh air that's blowing in through the small gap between the coaches. I allow myself to calm down again, before standing up and heading to the next carriage along. It's a quiet coach, but that suits me fine. I have no intention of phoning anyone or of playing music. There are more empty seats in here, including several doubles. This time, I take the precaution of sitting in the aisle seat and placing my coat and bag on the window seat next to me. I'm not going through that again. There are plenty of spare places for other passengers to sit.

After a while, I return to my Kindle and eat my brunch, and all remains calm until it's time to get off the train at Euston. I deliberately get off at the other end of the carriage to avoid the man who'd sat next to me, but he catches up with me on the platform.

"Are you feeling better now?" he asks. The words are kind, but the tone is sarcastic, and he tops it off with, "I thought you were coming back. I was on edge the whole journey."

"I'm sorry. I thought I'd made it clear that I wouldn't be returning when I took my coat." I give a half-smile and pick up speed to move away from him. My heart's thumping in case he catches up with me again, and as soon as I reach the concourse, I dive for the Ladies, which is fortunately nearby. Once there, I take some deep breaths and splash water on my face from the sink. There's a touch on my shoulder, and I jump. It's a lady in the uniform of the train company.

"Are you all right, love? Was that man harassing you? I noticed you on the platform."

"He stressed me out a bit." I explained what had happened on the train.

"Poor pet! I hate men like that. They think they can take up a seat and a half, and God help the poor soul sitting next to them. Obnoxious gits they are, if you'll pardon my French."

"Of course, thank you." Her sympathy is very welcome. "I'm probably being really paranoid, but would you mind checking that he's not outside waiting for me? I've got really on edge."

"Sure, love." She puts her hand on my shoulder briefly, before going to the exit and disappearing. She's gone for several minutes, and I'm wondering what's going on, when she returns with a WPC.

"Blighter's still out there. I asked him to stop loitering and move on, and the cheeky swine said 'You can't make me. I'm waiting for someone.' I said, 'Maybe she doesn't want to be waited for.' He was very rude, so I went and fetched the Transport Police who were just heading our way on the concourse. This kind lady came in with me. She'll escort you to wherever you need to go next, while her partner detains that awful man."

"Thank you so much. You're really kind." I smile at her, and then at the WPC who's hovering, looking concerned.

"You're welcome, love. I suggest, if you can afford it, you take a taxi to your destination, rather than messing about with the Tube or the bus."

"Great idea, thanks. I will."

The WPC accompanies me to the taxi rank, and shields me from the man who's being questioned by a handsome Sergeant in his early thirties. The Sergeant is facing our direction and is forcing the other man to face away from me and his colleague. Clever.

Once past them, the WPC becomes friendly and chatty, and we've built up quite a rapport by the time I get to the front of the taxi queue. She gives me a card just before I get in the taxi.

"Lovely to meet you, Becky, although not the best circumstances. Call me if you need any help when you return here later, or if there's anything I can do for you."

"Thanks, Amy. You've been really kind. Look me up next time you're in Manchester."

Once in the taxi, I direct the driver to a shopping centre in Kensington. I've done my research, and this was the location of the Tube station where I was planning to get out and start my walk. A shopping centre is also an innocuous destination for a passenger from Euston. All the same, I don't calm down much during the journey. I'm very on edge after my experience at the station, and keep looking back to make sure we're not being followed. I know

I'm doing a terrible job of looking like an innocent shopper, and eventually the driver asks me through the intercom if I'm okay.

"I had an unpleasant experience on the train and was accosted again when we got to Euston. I just want to make sure he's not following me."

"Poor wee lassie," says the driver, in deepest Glaswegian. Then he fills my ears with tales of taxi chases, and crimes that he's been involved in solving. It turns out that he's a private detective when he's not being a cabbie, and we have a lovely chat, exchanging business cards at the end of the journey when he drops me off. I put the card into my purse and thank the driver before getting out at the shopping centre.

Glancing round, I can't see anybody suspicious. Everyone just appears to be going about their business of shopping, chatting with friends, walking (or in one case, running) towards the Tube station or the nearby Overground. I check my watch. I have half an hour before I'm due to meet Sylvia. There's enough time to pop into Waitrose and grab something to eat along the way. I'm suddenly hungry. Settling for a banana and a Twix, as they're easy to munch on the move, I pay, and return to the street. I've memorised the route, but it takes a minute to get my bearings. My watch tells me I now have only twenty minutes. How on earth can it take ten whole minutes to buy fruit and chocolate? There's no point dwelling on it. I take a deep breath and hurry toward the designated meeting place.

I'm a little out of breath when I arrive outside the flats with just one minute to spare. I do a quick survey of the surroundings. This is a pleasant residential road, with lots of big houses, well-kept gardens, and mostly well-dressed but otherwise ordinary people walking dogs, jogging, and doing normal activities that would be expected in this sort of area. There's a bell on the door against the flat number, but the name tag next to the number is blank. I press the bell. An intercom vibrates, and a female, cultured voice says, "Who is it?"

"Becky. I have an appointment."

"Come in, dear. First floor. It's the flat on the left."

The door buzzes, and I push it open. In the hallway is a mirror, and a quick glance at it shows me how flustered I look. I have a rummage in my bag and extract a hairbrush and lipstick. Twenty seconds later, I'm on my way upstairs. I notice a lift, but choose to take the stairs as I'm in a hurry.

The door to the flat on the left is open, and in the doorway is a smart lady in a wheelchair.

"Come on in." She smiles at me, a welcoming expression that makes me feel more at ease. I realise I've been on edge all day.

I follow her into a lounge – a beautifully-proportioned living room that looks strangely plain and unlived-in. Blue velvet curtains adorn the windows, which are darkened by Venetian blinds, slanted to allow a view of the street. There is a TV in one corner, and sofa opposite, in a fabric to match the curtains. The single armchair is arranged so that the sofa, chair and TV enclose a small coffee table. It's a fairly classic arrangement, so why does it feel so odd?

Sylvia, who I presume is my host, answers my unspoken question.

"I don't live here, dear. No one does. This is a convenient meeting spot. The lift makes it accessible to me, and I live a short distance away. The TV allows for more pleasant passing of time. It is occasionally useful to stay overnight, so the flat is furnished, but not excessively so."

"Surely if you want it to look more normal, wouldn't it be… er… sensible to have some pictures, or pot plants, or something in here?"

"We only acquired it recently. It could do with some work, I grant you." She beckons for me to sit on the sofa. "How was your journey?"

I'm not sure why, but there's something in her voice; an expectation, perhaps, that my trip here was not uneventful. My suspicion grows as I describe my day so far, and she nods, looking totally unsurprised throughout.

"Was the man on the train one of your people?" I ask.

"I sincerely hope not, dear. I'd be appalled if one of ours was as clumsy and uncouth as that." She smiles again. "No, I can think of two reasons your journey was as challenging as it was."

"What would they be?"

"Well, the first is that people like you attract trouble. I don't mean that in a nasty way, but there are certain people to whom certain situations will gravitate. Agatha Christie had that in mind when she wrote Miss Marple – an elderly lady around whom a ridiculous number of murders occurred. Obviously she was a fictional character, but there are people like that, and I believe you're one of them."

"All the murders I've been involved with have been related to work, at least in some capacity or another."

"I know, dear. But even at University, you had some interesting experiences, didn't you?"

I don't bother asking how she knows. I presume these people do their research.

"You mentioned two reasons. What was the other?"

"Anxiety, dear. You were expecting trouble. It made it twice as likely to descend upon you. Yes, I'm sure that man was just an example of an unpleasant traveller, but perhaps because of the purpose of your journey, you magnified it into a melodrama." She must notice the mortified look on my face, as she continues, "Don't worry about it. I know you've had a tough year. It won't jeopardise what we have in mind for you.

Indeed, your anxiety and observational skills make you an excellent candidate."

Despite her protestations, I'm still unconvinced that the man on the train was not planted there, to elicit some kind of response. But I don't argue. There are more important questions.

"So what do you want me to do?"

"Just some training for the moment, dear. I know you've had a decent training in the police force, which will of course be useful. However, there are a few skills that you should learn in addition. Your friend's son, Will: I understand he's an experienced hacker?"

"Yes, I believe so. All legal, as far as I'm aware."

"Of course. He's a nice young man. We have vetted him. Obviously with his father being the unsavoury character that he is, Will could have gone either way. However, he seems to have followed in his mother's footsteps in terms of integrity and intelligence."

"Why don't you bring him in, if he's someone you could trust?"

"Oh, my dear, we are doing. Roger is interviewing both Joanna and Will today, and will fill them in on what they need to know – including the need for Will to share his knowledge with you both." She pauses. "There is another skill I would like you to acquire for me, which I would prefer you not to discuss with anyone other than your husband, who is of course one of our trusted operators. I understand you're good at languages?"

"I was at school."

"Excellent. It's a flair that rarely disappears. The languages themselves fade, but the ability to learn does not." She fishes in a handbag that was on the floor nearby, and hands me an envelope. "No need to open it just now. It contains access codes for you to learn a certain language for free. You have six months, in which I need you to become fluent in Russian."

Chapter Thirty

Leaving the flat some ten minutes later, I'm bemused. I travelled all the way to London to be asked to learn hacking skills from Will, and to learn Russian from a computer program. They gave no explanations. No questions were really asked. I don't think 'How was your journey?' and 'I understand you're good at languages' count as a rigorous interview. Sylvia reimbursed me for the taxi from Euston. She totally understood my reasons and respected my urge to safety. I forgot to mention the cash that Roger gave me, and now have a few moments of guilt until I resolve to return it to him next time we meet.

"One must always do what's necessary to get the job done, and that involves staying safe. Most agents do not need to put their lives at risk, but all would do so if required to complete a mission." She'd looked at me keenly, and must have seen something to reassure her, for she then seemed to relax.

As I walk the distance back to the Tube station I keep my eyes wide open, but spot nothing suspicious. I'm not keen to take risks just yet, and still have another appointment to get to.

Time is getting a bit tight, and I'm relieved that the Tube is regular, and not too overcrowded. It's now quarter to four.

Dan is already in Starbucks when I arrive, a fashionable but slightly stressful five minutes late. There are two coffee cups in front of him. He stands up to greet me, and pulls me into a huge and very welcome hug.

"Becks! How are you? I got you a cappuccino. I know you're in a rush."

"Thanks Dan. You're a lifesaver. I probably need to go in fifteen minutes. You know I hate being late."

We spend a pleasant quarter of an hour catching up on the usual sort of news that old friends discuss, focussed mainly on him. It's relaxing to listen to him chatter about new furniture, and his and Gray's new chocolate-brown Labrador puppy. We'll save the important stuff for later.

He promises to wait in Starbucks for me. He's going to take me back to his house afterwards. Gray's cooked dinner and left it in the oven for us both. Far better than a busy restaurant for a private chat.

The record company is accessed through a smart building near King's Cross station. I report in at a reception desk on the ground floor, and they send me up in a lift to the fifth floor. I'm greeted there by a youngish, harassed-looking man in his early thirties, wearing black jeans and a shirt and tie.

"Becky White?" He looks inquiringly at me, so I smile and nod. He has a good firm handshake, but forgets to introduce himself.

"I'm so sorry, I didn't catch your name."

"I'm Vic, Victor Casey, Troy's producer. Shall we go into my office?"

I follow him into a large, modern, well-lit space with its own coffee machine on the wide window ledge. He offers me a coffee, which I decline (having just finished one), and we sit opposite each other on either side of the oak desk. I fold my coat and place it on the carpeted floor next to me.

"What did you want to know? Your man who rang and arranged this said you needed some background about Troy and the band."

"Yes. How did you meet them? How well do you know them?" That will do for starters.

"I saw them at a gig in London. They were supporting an act I was checking out with a view to a contract. That band was shite, but there was something about Troy Cassidy, and his band were pretty talented too. I approached them at the end of the night and invited them to come along here the next day. We had a chat about terms and stuff. They were supposed to sort themselves out with a manager, but they've not got round to it yet, so I'm sort of managing them as well as producing their album. They could really use a manager right now though. Troy's destroyed about the loss of his wife. He was besotted with her. Refused to do any publicity that involved him with stunning models. Said Linda wouldn't like it, and that's not what he was about."

"Did you believe him?"

"Course. Why else would a bloke turn down the opportunity to photoshoot with a bunch of hot girls? I wasn't asking him to screw them, just to take a few photos, but he said he couldn't do it, so we rounded up some motorbikes and leather instead. He seemed pretty cool with that."

"What can you tell me about the rest of the band?"

"As I said, talented lads. All quite good-looking – got to take that into account really – kerb appeal matters. It sells records if the girls fancy them. Harry Pollard – he's the guitarist – is the one the girls go really gooey about – even more so than Troy. My secretary says it's his floppy hair and dreamy blue eyes. Don't quite get it myself, but I can see he's a draw. Takes the music seriously though. They all do actually. Respect them for that. Not all the kids do – so many these days are just after fame and fortune. You know what it's like – it's all about celebrity. So it's great when we come across a band who can write their own stuff, and who care about the music. Real, proper artists."

"What about the others?" I check my notebook as I'm jotting things down throughout the meeting. "Zach and Gaz? Is that right?"

"Yeah. Zach Finch – he plays keyboards and sax. The dark, quiet, moody type, but he's a nice bloke most of the time."

"Not all the time?"

"Like I say, he's a bit moody. Likes his own way." Vic looks thoughtful for a moment, as if deciding whether or not to tell me something. He glances at me, and I keep my expression interested but otherwise neutral. Experience has shown that it's a good way to get people to reveal more information. "To be honest, I think he had a bit of a thing for Troy's Linda. Some days you'd think he hated Troy, then he'd pull himself together and be fine for a while." He hesitates. "If it had been Troy who'd been killed, I'd stick Zach up there as your number one suspect, but I don't reckon he'd have hurt a hair on her head."

"How about Gaz? Sorry, I don't know surnames."

"Gaz is Gareth Edwards. Tall, skinny, ginger lad with a gleam in his eye and a strong sense of mischief. He's the drummer, prankster and optimist in the band. I'd say he's also the glue that holds them together. You know, talks Zach round from his strops; keeps Harry on the straight and narrow when he looks like being distracted; supports Troy through those low confidence times that all artists go through. Gaz is a good lad. Very level-headed."

"Does Harry often need to be kept on the straight and narrow?"

"Hard to say really. I've only known them a few weeks. We've met a few times, including a five-day stint when they were here in London recording the new album. We got ten tracks laid down – all great. Pretty fast too. Like I said, you know when you're dealing with professionals. They just got on with the recordings. Did as many takes as needed, without throwing wobblers like some kids do. There were just glimpses here and there – mostly towards the end of each day, when people were getting tired. You could see that John would have walked out at four with half a job done, when Troy stopped for a phone call with Linda. And Harry would flirt a bit with the production assistants between takes. Gaz would pull them back together, tell a few jokes, threaten to put frogs between the bedclothes if they didn't sort themselves out. All good-humoured, but you could tell how much this meant to him."

"You don't think it meant the same to the others?"

"Zach cared a lot; you could see he did. They all did. But when the jealousy took hold, he was a friggin' nightmare. Harry – like I said – he was also a pro. You could see music meant the world to him, but he was also excited by the whole process. And I reckon he wanted it to be fun. Not just hard work."

"What about Troy?"

"Focussed, hard-working and energetic. But then, it got to about four every day, and he'd want a break to chat with his wife and kid, and that's when it all went a bit… tits-up."

"Thanks. That's really useful."

"Are we done now?" He looks at his watch, and I check mine too. It's just gone five. "Parents' evening at school tonight. I said I'd be home in time."

We finish with a few pleasantries about the joys or

otherwise of meetings with teachers at school, as I get my coat back on. He passes me a business card.

"Let me know if there's anything else I can help you with. Poor bugger. I hope you catch his wife's killer."

"Thanks. We'll do what we can. I'll call you if I think of any other questions."

Forty-five minutes later I'm sitting with Dan at his kitchen table, looking across at a pleasant park in North London. He and Gray have bought a lovely modern, ground-floor apartment in a convenient area, five minutes' walk from Stanmore station. I make all the right noises about the flat, which (not surprisingly) is immaculate.

"We had to change the carpets last week. I'm sure you can imagine, Becks, bringing Tilly in after a muddy walk – well, we loved our cream carpets, but they had to go. And of course, toilet training is a challenge with a young puppy. We're getting there now – she's nearly four months old – but honestly, it's been a nightmare. You know me well enough to know I can't stand mess."

"How on earth are you managing? It's hard enough to toilet train with a house. I don't know how you'd do it with a flat."

"Gray and I are taking it in turns to work from home. It's fine most of the time." He leaps up from his chair and grabs the dog, just as she's about to squat in the corner. "Open that door, Becks." He nods towards a patio door, which leads on to a decent-sized enclosed terrace with a grassy patch. He puts Tilly on the grass just in time to prevent his suede shoes from getting wet. "Thanks. She's learning. And I don't think we could have managed without this little garden. We're so lucky to be on the ground floor. The upper floor balconies are a bit titchy. The only other alternative is to be on the top floor, with a roof garden, but I hate heights. Even after all this time."

A memory surfaces: a railway bridge, with Dan as a terrified student, clinging on for dear life until I pulled him to safety.

"Trauma leaves its mark. There are a lot of things I'm scared of these days too – all because of things that have happened in the past." I follow him and the puppy back inside.

"Is that why you left the police?" He gives Tilly a doggy treat.

"Kind of. It's complicated. But it's liberating being a private detective. Obviously I still have contacts within the force, but I can leave all the procedure to them, and focus on actual detecting."

Dan gives me a long hard look, then goes to the kitchen and starts washing his hands at the sink. "I'll let you get away with it for now, but one day you're going to have to tell me the full story." He puts on a pair of spotlessly-clean oven gloves and removes two full plates from the oven. He places one in front of me, and the aroma turns my legs to jelly. Gray is a fantastic cook, and the *coq-au-vin* that has landed in front of me looks and smells divine. He opens a bottle of wine – a white that complements the main dish perfectly. I realise that my old friend has become highly educated since our last meeting.

"One day I will, I promise. But at the moment it's still too raw. And life really has got complicated. I'd love the simplicity of a flat, a partner and a puppy."

"Life's never simple, love. You remember my sister, Sharon?"

"Sure. Is she okay?"

"No. She's got leukaemia. Advanced. She's on chemo, including some innovative trial drug. If we're lucky it'll give her another couple of years, but she's unlikely to see fifty."

"Oh God, Dan, that's awful." I do some quick sums in my head. I think she must be about forty-six now, or thereabouts. "Does she live near here? Do you get to see her much?" I think back to Dan and Gray's wedding, a year ago. She'd looked thin, but otherwise well. I know, from my occasional catch-ups with Dan, that Sharon is married with three teenaged kids. My appetite recedes a few notches.

"She lives a couple of miles away. Pretty useful really, and Gray and I take the kids out sometimes if she needs a break."

I'm silent for a moment. I always liked Sharon. I can't imagine how awful it is for Dan, whose remaining family, ie his dad, is a waste of space.

Dan seems to read my mind, as his next comment is, "Dad can't be bothered to come down and see Sharon or the kids. The old sod is still too wrapped up in his business to give a shit. If it was anyone else, I'd give them the benefit of the doubt, and think maybe they can't handle the situation, but as it's him…"

"I wish there was something I could do to help." I take a few mouthfuls of food, and Dan does the same. The fun has gone though. I wish I hadn't mentioned life being simple.

"You could investigate Dad's finances and have him up for fraud. I'm sure it can't all be kosher, what he does."

"You wouldn't, seriously, would you?"

"Only because it would upset Sharon. Anyway, we'll see. Maybe one day he'll be useful for something. God knows what, but stranger things have happened. He's not really spoken to me since the wedding. He had enough trouble accepting that I'm gay. Having a son who's married to a man is more than he could handle. The fact that I'm happy is totally irrelevant to him."

"Are you happy with Gray?"

"Absolutely. I mean, he drives me crackers sometimes, but he's my soulmate. I've never felt this way about anyone before.

Not even Rick, all those years ago." He pours me a second glass of wine.

"I'm pleased you found someone amazing. You deserve to be happy."

"Thanks. But I defy anyone to be miserable living with a man who cooks like this. And you've not seen dessert yet." He dextrously steers the conversation into happier waters, telling me about the cruise they went on for their honeymoon, and the time Gray spent in the galley having cookery lessons.

Dessert is as good as promised, with a light and fluffy sticky toffee pudding, but then we have to hurry to get back to Euston. On the station concourse, while my train is being prepared, Dan holds me tight, as if we were students again.

"I've missed this," I murmur against his shoulder.

"Me too. I don't have as many real friends as I'd like. Stay in touch, Becks. And next time you have to come down to London, stay over. You saw our fabulous spare room – with the purple carpet and king-size bed. You're always welcome."

"Thanks. Give my love and best wishes to Sharon. If there's anything I can do to help, let me know."

"Sure." He glances up at the departure board. "Hey, that's your platform just popped up. Come on, I'll walk you over."

The train journey home is much less eventful than the outgoing trip, but I have such a lot to think about that it's only when I get off the train at Piccadilly, and meet Will outside near the taxi rank, that I realise I've not checked in about Troy's parents.

Will has no news for me, other than that he and his mum met with Roger today, and he's under instruction to teach me hacking. Chatting about how he'll do that takes up most of the journey, and it's only after thanking him and going into my house that I check my phone and realise the battery's dead.

The house is in darkness, and everyone seems to be asleep when I get in. I'm tempted to leave the phone until tomorrow, but a sense of responsibility prompts me to plug it in to the charger and turn it on.

A barrage of beeps greets me as soon as the phone finds its signal. Seven missed calls. Three from Finn, two from Troy, and two from Cheryl. There are also several texts from each of them.

Chapter Thirty-One

Cheryl's texts are fairly straightforward:

'*What time are you home?*' and '*It's all happening tomorrow. Hope you can be around.*'

Being around might be a challenge, but hopefully I can work something out. I type back, just in case she's awake even though it's nearly eleven o'clock. '*We'll sort it. See you at breakfast.*'

Troy's voice messages are barely coherent. His texts progress from '*where r u*', through '*call me*' and '*where the f*** r u*' to '*call me, ffs. U supposed 2 b helping*'. Between the lack of punctuation, the text-speak, and my state of tiredness, I feel disinclined to respond, but force myself to tap out, '*I've been working away today. Just got back, and found my phone battery had…*' I hesitate before typing the word '*died*' – it seems insensitive. I finish the sentence as '*my phone had turned itself off.*' After dithering for a moment, I hit *Send*, then add, '*I'll call you tomorrow. It's late now. Sorry.*'

Finn's messages are more detailed and technical, but generally amounting to the fact that Troy's parents had been stabbed multiple times, they'd died from their stab wounds, no weapon had been found, and the house had been sealed off for forensic examination. So far, there are no obvious clues. It's clear from his texts and voice mails that he knows I've been in London today, and that Joanna had informed him of my meeting with Troy's manager. His final text is, '*Good job, Becky. We'll catch up tomorrow x*'

I take myself off to bed, trying not to feel slightly warm and fuzzy from the rare '*x*' at the end of that last text. It's totally inappropriate, but my head is spinning from everything that's going on.

As I tiptoe past Cheryl's room, she calls out softly. "Mum, is that you?"

I open her door. "It's late. Why aren't you asleep?"

"Nervous about tomorrow."

"What's the plan?" I resign myself to not getting to sleep for a while yet, and curl up on the red sofa-bed that matches the bedding and curtains. It's placed on the other side of the bedside table, so it's easy to chat to her without raising our voices.

"As you know, the meeting was supposed to be tomorrow night, but Joel got a nasty message from Elaine – threatening all sorts of stuff – so his mum said we'd better get started straight away. She picked me and Dad up after dinner, and we were round at her house for an hour and a half bashing everything out."

"Was anyone else there?"

"Just Dan and a few girls from my class, who hate Elaine, plus all their mums. Anyway. We've arranged that after Assembly tomorrow, the six of us are going to the Head, and we'll tell him what's been happening. We've got a letter from Joel's mum saying that if this isn't appropriately dealt with, then she'll be involving the school governors, the council, the press and the police. She showed us the letter, but it's sealed now, so I can't show you. But it lists all Elaine's and Karen's crimes, the evidence, and potential criminal charges that could be imposed."

"That wasn't quite what she was planning though, was it? I seem to recall she had other plans."

"Yes, but the message to Joel made her really angry. He told me afterwards that he's never seen her so furious. I reckon she wanted to stamp it out fully."

"Can't she just provide the letter to the school? Why do you all have to put your heads on the block first?"

"Dan's mum asked the same thing. Apparently, it would come better from us initially. We're reporting being bullied, and we've pooled our resources to help one another. If there's any doubt, then we produce Joel's mum's letter. She's a barrister, so there's no reason to doubt her."

"Elaine's dad's a barrister as well. But then it makes sense to get your side of events in first, before they have time to manufacture anything."

"Exactly. Mum, will you be able to wait outside with Lesley, then we'll contact you afterwards and let you know if we need extra support?"

"Sure. What time are you going to see the Head?"

"It'll be about nine-thirty. You should be free for ten. I know you get busy with work." There's nothing in her tone to suggest she's annoyed about this, so I take the comment at face value.

"That should be fine. I can make calls while I wait, and be available if you need me to come in." I stand up. "And now, Chezz, it's bedtime. We've got a big day tomorrow, so let's try to get some sleep, okay?"

With all the thoughts spinning around my head, it was never going to be a restful night, and I wake from an uneasy doze at half past four, and fail to get any sleep from then onwards. I turn my alarm off before it gets into its stride, and head into the bathroom for a cool shower to try to wake myself up properly.

Cheryl looks slightly more awake than I do, but neither of us says much until two large mugs of coffee have been consumed – each. By the time the caffeine kicks in, it's time to go. Matt arrives in the kitchen as we're about to leave, and wishes our daughter good luck.

"You look knackered, Becks. You'd better come home after Cheryl's finished and get some sleep."

"Thanks. I will if I can, but I've got a lot to do. I'll come round. I might grab another coffee from Costa or Starbucks if I can't get back here for a while."

Cheryl's quiet in the car. The half-hour battle through the traffic is spent listening to the radio to avoid the silence.

I pull up at the kerb to drop her off. "Good luck. Let me know as soon as you can how it goes. I'll be waiting at the end of the road. You know it's impossible to park here for more than thirty seconds."

"Sure. Thanks, Mum."

I drive about a hundred yards, and pull in behind Lesley's big car. She gets out and comes to my window.

"Hi Becky. Sorry for bring everything forward. Did Cheryl fill you in?"

"Yes. It's fine." I smile, and inwardly resign myself to not getting any work done just yet.

"Come and sit in my car. I've brought cookies and I really don't want to scoff the lot. Please, help me!"

I laugh, but my conscience tears at me. "Can you just give me five minutes, Lesley? I got back late last night, and there are a couple of calls I need to make to reduce some stress levels. If I make appointments with people later today, they're less likely to bombard me with frantic calls in the next hour."

"Sure. Totally get it. Make your calls, but don't take too long, or all the cookies will be gone." She chuckles, and heads back to her own car.

I breathe a sigh of relief, mixed with some trepidation, and get my phone out of my handbag. Who to call first? I flick back through my messages. Finn seems pretty chilled, so I send him a quick message.

'*All okay? Delayed at school. Can I call you about 11?*'

Two blue ticks appear within seconds, then the app tells me someone's typing – hopefully Finn.

'*No probs. Make it 12. And I'll call you when I pop out for a butty. You know what it's like here.*'

I send back a quick *Okay*, and turn my attention to Troy. Only a phone call will do here. I look around me and the streets are pretty empty, apart from the odd late drop-off further back along the road. No one seems to be paying me any attention. In the car in front, I can just see Lesley looking at her own phone. I locate Troy's number, and hit the green *Connect* button.

"Becky?"

"Hi. So sorry about last night."

"Not your fault; these things happen. Sorry for my stroppy texts. I got into a bit of state."

"I'm not surprised, Troy. Is anyone looking after you?"

"Yeah, Gaz invited me to stay at his flat. Otherwise…" He doesn't fill in the gaps. It's not really necessary. This poor guy has just lost his wife and his parents.

"Where's your daughter?"

"She's still with… Linda's parents. They're great with her. I'm a fucking wreck. I don't want her to see me like this. I managed to hold it together for ten minutes yesterday to speak to her and ask her about school."

"Is the family liaison lady helping at all?"

"She tries." There's a brittle laugh. "I just don't get it. Why would someone want to kill Linda, let alone Mum and Dad? You know, they've always been so great with me. Supporting me when school was shit, and when the careers people were saying music wasn't a real job." He breaks off.

"Do you want me to come round? I've got some things to do this morning, but I could come to you for about two-thirty if that would work?"

"Yeah, I guess. Maybe you can help more than the police. They're all very official, but I don't think they give a shit about me. You and your friend have a better... I dunno, maybe a better bedside manner."

"I've got to check Joanna's free, but assuming she is, we'll see you this afternoon. Please just drop me a message with Gaz's address."

He agrees, and a minute after ringing off, the phone pings as the address is sent through.

I finish with a quick message to Joanna to say I'll call her later this morning, and to check she's free this afternoon.

'Sure. Come round here when you're free. Maybe we can get some lunch and fill each other in.'

With that sorted, I turn my phone to vibrate, go out in the now torrential rain, and knock on Lesley's window. She directs me to the passenger side, and I rush round and open the passenger door.

"Get in, sweetie. You're just in time. Four cookies left. Two each." She offers the luxury triple-chocolate-chip treats from M&S, and I take one. They look delicious, but I don't want to seem greedy. I'm also exhausted, as the caffeine rush is beginning to ease off. I nibble at the biscuit, wanting to make it last. "You're looking a bit tired, Becky. What time did you get back yesterday? Your husband said you were in London."

I'm a bit surprised Matt gave away my location, but as I'd made it a multi-purpose visit, I don't suppose it matters.

"Yes, I had some work meetings, and took the opportunity to meet up with an old friend from uni."

She picks up on this, and we have a chat about the challenges of keeping up with old friends, even in these days of social media.

"Strangely, it was easier in the past, where you made the effort to correspond by email or phone at least a couple of times a year, but nowadays... I don't know, even New Year greetings are sent over Facebook," Lesley says.

"Facebook has a lot to answer for. If it weren't for that, we wouldn't be in this situation."

"True, but there are some advantages. I've met you, for one thing, and I rather think your Cheryl and my Joel are getting on well."

I smile, but she might be right. He was waiting for her on the pavement when I dropped her off, and she went to greet him with more enthusiasm than she'd shown all morning.

I glance at my watch. It's nine-thirty. "I guess they'll be going in to see the Head about now."

"Yes. I told them to speak to him first, and then use my letter if he seems to be reluctant to act. We need to strike pre-emptively before that bastard gets a chance." Lesley grimaces, and I spend a few seconds working out who 'that bastard' might be.

"Elaine's dad, you mean?"

"Yes. He's a sneaky sod, and he'd do anything to protect his darling daughter. That's why we had to get this done today. Did Cheryl tell you about the message Joel received?"

"She just mentioned that there were some nasty threats."

Lesley picks up her phone and shows me the message: '*Tell your mum to back off, prick, or u'll be next.*'

"Charming. What do you think they had in mind?"

"The kids all figured it meant photos, although Joel swore he hadn't given them any ammunition."

"It doesn't take much. They can Photoshop anything these days, and if they say it belongs to a certain person, it's difficult to disprove. I saw plenty of instances of that when I was in the police."

"Well, quite. So obviously, we couldn't let that get out. Time to nip it in the bud."

As if on cue, my phone rings. I glance at the screen before answering.

"Hi love, how's it going?"

"He only believed us when he saw Joel's mum's letter."

"She's here now. I'm sitting in her car." This is discreet code for *Be careful what you say*.

"Oh, okay. I'm not on speaker, am I?"

I reassure her, but then ask the key question. "So what happens now?"

"I think the Head is going to phone Joel's mum, then hopefully he'll kick ass, and Karen and Elaine will get... sorry, Mum. Got to go. I'll call you later." She disconnects before I've had time to say 'Bye'.

Lesley is tapping away on her phone. She looks up. "Joel prefers texting rather than actually having a conversation. He said my letter worked and the Head will be calling me shortly."

"That's pretty much what Cheryl said too. I'm going to have to get going, now I know they don't need us to go in. Please will you let me know what the Head says?"

"Of course. Thanks for your company during the wait." She grins.

"Thank you! For the company and the cookies." I beam at her. "Definitely what I needed this morning. The carbs are kicking in now."

Back in my car, I message Cheryl quickly to say I'm on my way home, and set off. But I'm still ridiculously tired, and have to focus on the drive. I'm even beyond auto-pilot. By the time I get home it's just after ten, and I go inside and go straight upstairs.

Matt's in the bath, and I call out to him. "I'm going to sleep. I'll see you in an hour."

It's really rare for me to sleep during the day, but I'm out within a minute. When my alarm goes off at quarter past eleven, I feel a bit groggy, but this is rectified by another quick shower and more coffee. By the time it's midday and I'm waiting for Finn to call, I feel properly awake and alert.

I message Joanna and let her know I'll be round after I've spoken to Finn. I've just sent the message when he calls.

"Hey, how are you doing?"

"Okay thanks. How are you?" It's nice that he's being all friendly and concerned, but I need to cut to the chase now. "And how's the investigation coming along?"

"I'm fine. Investigation is going fine on one side, but struggling on the personal side."

"How do you mean?"

"It's difficult to speak here, but you know what my team's like now. They've not got all your people-skills. Troy won't talk to them. He just clams up and says he can't bring himself to even think about it."

"Funny that. Joanna and I are due to meet with him at two-thirty this afternoon. He wants to talk to us."

"Bloody hell, Becky. How do you do it? You've always had this knack of getting people to open up – even the friggin' criminals want you to listen to their confessions."

"Don't know. I just like listening to people I guess. But let's be practical for a minute. What do you want from Troy? I'm sure I can cover the basics, like where he was that day, and about the relationships, but are you after anything specific?"

"You know the drill. Deaths were between 10pm and midnight. Neighbours heard nothing. Killer wore gloves. No footprints or anything useful to aid identification."

"There must be something from forensics. Are they still on-site?"

"Yeah, likely to be there all day, and possibly for another day or two after that. They'll keep plugging away. They're a diligent bunch."

"Okay, I'll go for the human angle, and see what I can get from Troy."

"Great. How about we meet up at Joanna's again for a takeaway? Eight-ish?"

"I'll eat with my family. Cheryl's got stuff going on and she needs me. But I'll come afterwards and drink hot chocolate or something. See you later. Message me if you think of anything else."

It's time to go and see what Joanna has been up to. I can't believe it's so busy that I've not had time to speak to her yet. I'm about to leave the house when Joanna calls me.

"I've just had a call from Penny. She's in a right state. Three of her friends have been killed. She couldn't say anything else on the phone, but she wants to see us straight away. She's getting a taxi and she'll be here in twenty minutes."

Chapter Thirty-Two

Three more people are dead. All because of me. So why have I not achieved my goal?

The target is distraught. What do I need to do to make myself indispensable?

I need to get closer. I have to be available.

No more death – for a while at least. There are still cards to play...

Chapter Thirty-Three

I'm at Joanna's within ten minutes. She's got sandwiches on a plate and crisps in a bowl.

"Help yourself. Better to eat now, rather than in the face of tragedy."

"What exactly did Penny say?"

"It was hard to make head or tail of it to be honest. She sounded pretty incoherent. I got that three of her friends are dead, and there was a suggestion of foul play, but don't ask me exactly why she thinks that."

I help myself to a tuna sandwich. "Lovely chunky bread. Did you have this in already?"

"No. I got Will to nip up the road to the bakery as soon as Penny had called. Nice, isn't it?"

"Where is Will?"

"Shaving. He'll be down in a minute. He wants to observe the meeting. We decided it would be better not to introduce him at this stage."

I've just got time to finish the sandwich when the doorbell rings. I adjourn to the lounge while Joanna gets the door.

Penny half-stumbles into the room. Her eyes are red-rimmed and she's devoid of any make-up. She's even paler than usual.

"Come in and sit down." I put my hand on her arm and guide her to the armchair.

"Thanks." She sniffs and I pass her a box of tissues that Joanna has thoughtfully placed on the coffee table.

"When you're ready, why don't you tell us what's happened?" I sit in the other armchair, within touching distance so I can comfort her easily.

Joanna brings her a glass of water from the kitchen. She gives me a brief tilt of her head and a wink. I assume she means that Will is watching the CCTV from his laptop upstairs. He got the audio sorted very easily within a day of his arrival. He's a useful addition to the team, but I don't know if he'll be able to stay. That's another conversation for another day.

I return my attention to Penny, who's sipping the water, but hasn't starting talking yet.

"Come on, lass," says Joanna, becoming more Scottish with suppressed irritation. "We can't help you if you don't talk to us."

"Okay." Penny gives another snivel, blows her nose on the tissue, then sits up straight. "When I was at uni, I had three really close friends. I found out last night that they'd all been killed in a burglary a few days ago. They still lived together."

"Where did this happen?" I ask.

"In Huddersfield."

"Can you give me their names?" I take out a notepad and pen.

"I already wrote them down for you." She fishes out a piece of paper from her handbag and hands it to me. There are three names listed: Kim Parker, Jennifer Russell and Leigh Brooks.

"Thanks. Do you know exactly what happened?" I have a slight niggling feeling, but I can't yet pinpoint why.

"I'm not sure of the details. I think they were home asleep when the burglars broke in. They were found dead by the police next day after a neighbour was alerted by the broken window."

Although she's upset, I can't get rid of the suspicion that this is not the cause. I must do some digging here.

"How well did you know the girls?"

She looks at me in disgust. "I already told you, they were my best friends at uni. We lived together for three years, first in a flat, then we moved out of uni accommodation and found that house in Huddersfield. But after graduation, I got a job here, and had to move to Manchester. They got jobs that paid well enough for them to cover the rent of the extra room. It gave them some living space, which was good." She puts her head down and covers her face with her hands. "Oh God, I can't believe they're gone."

I pat her shoulder repeatedly for a moment. If she is acting, she's doing a pretty good job of it, but my niggles haven't completely gone away. I let them lie for now though. I glance at my watch, and then at Joanna. It's ten to two, and we need to leave in ten minutes to get to our meeting with Troy.

"Why don't you have some more water?" Joanna passes her the glass, and she takes a sip. "I don't think today is the day for any more questions. You need to go home and get some rest. Is there anyone who can come and look after you?"

"My mum lives in London and all my friends are now dead, so no."

"What about a neighbour?" Joanna's persistence is admirable. I'm fighting an inexplicable urge to give Penny a slap. Shocking really – I'm not usually so unsympathetic.

"I'll be okay by myself. Everyone in my block keeps themselves to themselves. I like it that way." She takes another tissue and blows her nose. "I'd better be going. You've got a lot to do if you're going to trace the burglar that killed them. Because I was wondering if it had anything to do with the fact that I should have been staying there that night. I cancelled last minute because of a migraine, but what if my stalker thought I would be there, and instigated the break-in?"

"That's important information, Penny. Thanks for telling us. We'll look into it and liaise with the Huddersfield police. I have a few contacts over there." I watch her stow the used tissues into her handbag. "Do you need us to get you a taxi?"

"I've got an Uber coming in a minute. I arranged it for two o'clock when I got here, before I knocked on the door. I figured it would be long enough. Anyway, I've got a work meeting at three, so I'll go straight there. It will help me take my mind off things." She seems to have pulled herself together and is now quite calm and business-like. Her phone buzzes. "That's my Uber. It says it's outside."

Joanna looks out of the window. "Yes, there's a taxi parked up."

Two minutes later, she's gone. We wait another minute for the cab to get off the estate, but we're both keen to leave. Will's going to drive us again. He'll be heartbroken when he hands that car back on Monday.

Joanna sits in the front this time and handles the satnav. I settle myself comfortably in the back. I'm tired still, but adrenaline is keeping me alert.

"So what did you think of that?" Will asks, as he releases the handbrake and sets off.

"I'm not sure. She was obviously upset, but some of it didn't sound right." Joanna echoes what I've been thinking.

"Good. I thought it was just me thinking that. When we get back, I want to look closely at her story, find out about this burglary and dig into the relationships. As I said, I've got a contact in Huddersfield – one of my pals from training moved over there a couple of years later when she met and married a Yorkshireman. We've stayed in touch. Ellie is totally trustworthy and will do me a favour if I ask her nicely."

"Great. You've got some useful friends, Becky." Will turns his head and grins.

"Keep your eyes on the road. Yes, over the years, I made a lot of friends in the police, and lots of them moved around the country. A few even moved abroad, so I've got contacts all over the place."

Now that we've got a plan for Penny, there doesn't seem much point bashing it over in the car, and the conversation drifts. Will puts the radio on.

We arrive at our destination at just after half past two. I'd already messaged Troy to warn him we were running a bit late. I didn't want him freaking out. Gaz lives in a smart apartment block in Didsbury. The three of us get out of the car this time.

Joanna presses the buzzer, after checking with me which is the correct flat number.

"Come up," says an unfamiliar but friendly voice. "First floor on the right."

The door is open when we get upstairs, and the man in the doorway is recognisable as Gaz from Vic's description. Tall, gangly, ginger-haired and freckly. He reminds me of the guy who played Gregory in *Gregory's Girl*. Attractive in a geeky way. He beckons to come into the flat.

"Hi, I'm Gaz, or Gareth if you prefer, but most people call me Gaz."

We each introduce ourselves, and then I add, "We're from the White Knight Agency. We're helping Troy." Internally I add 'or trying to', but some thoughts are better not voiced.

He ushers us into a pleasant living room, with a black leather sofa and gaming chair, and blue carpet and curtains. The magnolia walls are covered with framed photos and certificates. In each corner of the room is a pile of books, post, magazines and CDs respectively. I stifle a smile, but Gaz must have been following my gaze.

"Sorry – last-minute attempt at tidying up." He grins. "Troy will be along in a minute. I sent him for a shower."

"It's good of you to look after him." I lead the conversation. Perhaps I feel more as though I know him after my conversation with the record producer.

"Someone had to do it. Zach had a few personal issues with Troy, and Harry is… Well, he's Harry."

"How do you mean?"

"He's still a lad. We're all the same age, but some people grow up and others not so much. Don't get me wrong, I love him like a brother, but I feel ten years older most of the time."

"I met your producer in London yesterday."

"Vic?" Gaz looks interested. "What did he have to say?"

"He said that you're the prankster of the band, but that you're also the glue."

"Perceptive of him. Yeah, probably. Anyway, I guess you can understand why it's me that's looking after Troy."

"Of course I can, but it's still good of you." I take a deep breath. "If you don't mind me asking, how well did you know Linda?"

His expression softens, and for a moment, I think maybe more than one of the band members were in love with her.

"She was a like a sister to me and the other guys. Well, not all the other guys. Zach was besotted with her. So I guess it was just me and Harry that loved her like a sister. We saw her several times a week, and she was part of our lives. So we're all grieving in our different ways."

"How about Troy's mum and dad? Did you know them at all?"

"Yeah. When we were at college, we used to go to Troy's house in the evenings and weekends for rehearsals and song-writing. Pat – Troy's mum – would bring us freshly-baked chocolate brownies or treacle toffee. She was a lovely woman. I didn't know his dad so well. Just enough to say hi to if he opened the door to us. He seemed like a nice bloke, but reserved."

"Thanks. That's really helpful." I glance at my watch. It's nearly three and Troy's not come in yet. "Is it worth checking on him?" I glance towards a door that looks to lead to the rest of the apartment.

"Yeah, maybe. Give me a minute."

We sit in companionable silence while Gaz goes to check on his friend. He comes back a couple of minutes later, frowning.

"I don't suppose any of you are medical?"

"I don't know if a qualified first aider counts? What's the matter? Is he okay?" He's obviously not, or Gaz wouldn't be asking, but sometimes we say the most inane things.

"He's lying on his bed with his eyes closed, but he doesn't look as though he's sleeping naturally. Can you come and have a look?"

I follow Gaz into his spare room, where Troy is slumped on the bed. He's pale and still. I move closer and listen for his breathing. It's there, thankfully, but shallow and quick, and I'm concerned enough to suggest that an ambulance might be a good idea.

"What should I tell them?"

"I would say that your friend is unconscious, and his breathing is shallow. That should get them moving. They won't expect a diagnosis, but call from here. They might ask questions that are more easily answered while you're here. Meanwhile, I'm going to put him in the recovery position." It takes a bit of effort because of the way he's positioned. Gaz leaves the room with his phone clamped to his ear, and returns a moment later with Will. I mouth 'Thanks' and let Will help me manoeuvre Troy into the safer position.

"Yes, he's still unconscious, but another friend has just put him on his side… Okay, thanks… how long do you think it'll be? Oh great, thanks." He looks at me and moves the phone away from his mouth and ear. "They're going to stay on the phone in case there are any changes."

I give him a thumbs-up and he returns his attention to the ambulance controller. I glance at my watch out of curiosity.

"Where's your mum?" I whisper to Will, not wanting to distract Gaz.

"Sussing out the lounge." He grins. "I can get her if you want?"

"No – let her carry on sussing."

The ambulance is only ten minutes. I'm taken back for a horrible moment to Matt's heart attack, but push the thought away. It's not the time to fall apart, and anyway, he's doing really well now.

Gaz lets the paramedics into the flat, and we move aside to allow them access to the patient. I watch as they check his pulse, oxygen levels and blood pressure.

"Has he taken anything?" The pretty blonde looks gentle, but must have a core of iron to be doing this job.

"He doesn't normally take drugs, if that's what you're asking." Gaz sounds faintly defensive.

"I'm not suggesting he does. Has he been depressed or not sleeping?"

"His wife and parents have just been murdered, so yeah, he's depressed and not sleeping."

"Oh gosh. I'm so sorry. I didn't know." She glances at Troy again, then at her phone which I assume has information from the call centre. "Of course. Troy Cassidy. Sorry, I should have realised, but we don't usually get calls out to famous people, so I don't pay much attention to the names other than as a mode of address."

"We'll have to get him to the hospital and run some tests."

The other paramedic, a tall, broad chap in his forties, stands up and goes to the door. "I'll get the stretcher. We need to get him downstairs."

Gaz goes in the ambulance with Troy to the hospital, after getting our phone numbers, and promises to keep in touch.

Back in the car, we discuss the situation and possible next steps.

"Do you think he's deliberately overdosed?" I settle into the back seat.

"With a young kid? I doubt it," says Will. "Most likely he took something to help him sleep, forgot he'd taken it, and then took a second dose. A friend of mine at uni did that once. He had to have his stomach pumped. There were no lasting effects though. I guess it will depend on what he's taken."

"Absolutely. They'll do a tox screen when they admit him, and hopefully Gaz will keep us posted. Joanna, do you think we should interview Dean and Sarah again? Find out if they knew Troy's parents?"

"It's worth a try, but I think just a quick phone call to each of them should be enough. Maybe we should include Gemma too. It depends on whether you want to suss them out beyond that quick question."

"I don't know. They're all suspects, although I'm less sure about Gemma. I just think we ought to keep closer tabs on them."

"I reckon we need to discuss all this with Finn later. He might be better-placed to 'keep tabs' as you suggest." Joanna checks her watch. "It's nearly four. Why don't we head home and reconvene later?"

"Shit! Yes, I need to speak to Cheryl. Yes, please, let's get back." I give them a brief rundown of what's been happening at school.

"Bloody hell! I think you should give her a call and let her know you'll be back soon. Otherwise she's going to get seriously fed up with you." Will glances around at me as he turns the key in the ignition. "You call her. Me and Mum will sort out navigating us back."

Cheryl doesn't answer, but messages me a moment later.

'*Hi Mum. I'm hanging out with Joel. All went okay. Talk to you at dinner. I'll be back for 6. x*'

'*Great. See you then. x*'

"She seems to have made a new friend out of this anyway. She's out with the lad whose mum sorted everything out. I'll get all the details later."

"Sounds good." Joanna smirks at me. "Boyfriend?"

"Who knows? Possibly. I shall gently extract information from her over dinner. If I pick up chocolate pudding from the shops on my way home, she'll tell me everything."

"I'm liking your techniques, Becky. Whenever Mum wanted me to tell her anything, she'd sit in my room until I revealed all. It was painful. The first time she did it, she sat there for six hours on a Saturday, without cooking or anything, and I don't think she even went to the loo. After that, if she was still there after fifteen minutes, I gave in. It wasn't worth the hassle."

"You should be thankful if wasn't your father asking." Joanna looks straight ahead; her tone is grim.

"Yeah, well, his method was to ask once, and if I didn't answer within five seconds, he's start removing his belt. I didn't let him get beyond the first belt loop. It was far less painful to just tell him what he wanted to know." Will sounds remarkably calm about it.

Joanna is still rigid in her seat. I put my hand on her shoulder and squeeze gently. "It must have been awful. We'll keep you safe from him now."

"That reminds me, Mum. I was going to ask if I could stay a bit longer. At least, I need to go back on Monday. Unfortunately, I have to return this little beauty," Will pats the steering wheel lovingly, "and I've got a few things to collect from home. But if you'll have me, I can work from your house as easily as from my flat, and I like it in Manchester. What do you think?"

Joanna's shoulders appear to relax. "You can stay as long as you like. I feel safer with you around, and you're good company for your old mum."

"You're not that old." He flashes a quick grin at me, while we're stopped at a red light. "You've still got a couple of years before we pension you off."

———

Back at home (after a brief stop at the shops for the chocolate pudding), I check in on Matt. He's been making steady progress, and is now walking every day, building up his strength. He's watching darts on the telly when I get in.

I raise an eyebrow at him and then go into the kitchen to get dinner ready. He follows me.

"What's up?"

"Darts isn't your usual spectator sport. I don't recall seeing you watch it in the past."

"I'm obeying instructions." He grins.

"Who from? Your doctor?"

"Roger. You're supposed to be learning Russian and hacking; I need to learn all about darts."

"Seriously?" Cynicism filters into my tones. There's no point keeping secrets from Matt. Not about this anyway.

"Yep. He's given me a couple of other things to focus on too."

"Like what?"

"Getting fitter again. And watching over my family. When I'm able to drive again, he wants me to take an advanced driving course."

"That all sounds very pleasant and safe." I check the time and put a casserole in the oven (prepared by Matt earlier in the day and put in the fridge – he seems to have developed some skills whilst he's been off).

"Yeah – I don't quite get the darts request, but he's clearly got something in mind. The driving makes sense. I've got another couple of weeks before I can start driving again, but I've checked out a few courses, and I think I'll do the IAM Roadsmart test. That was the one Roger suggested."

"So he didn't give you a lot of choice then?"

"He said it was my decision, but you're right. When he gives a suggestion, it usually means he expects it to be followed." He watches me as I sink onto a kitchen chair. "You still look knackered. I hope you're planning an early night after Cheryl's told us her news."

"I wish I could. Finn's coming over to Joanna's to compare notes on the Troy case. It's all got really complicated. Troy's in hospital. We found him unconscious at his friend's flat this afternoon, and we don't yet know why. And Penny showed up earlier having a wobble because three of her friends have been killed in a burglary, and she's gone all paranoid thinking it's linked to her. But it doesn't quite add up. Which reminds me, I need to call Ellie." I reach out to him across the table and grab his hand. "Be a sweetie and make me a coffee?"

"Sure. You sound like you need caffeine to get through this evening."

Chapter Thirty-Four

Our meeting with Finn is cancelled. I'm less disappointed than I expected. My weary brain is past being able to absorb any more information, and a migraine is threatening by the time he texts me at seven to say he won't make it. He reschedules for tomorrow, and I go to bed. I don't remember resting my head on the pillow, and wake up fourteen hours later, at 9am, refreshed and alert.

I check my phone before going for a shower. There's a message from Gaz. '*Troy's ok. OD'd on sleeping pills. Not too many. He'll be out of hospital tomorrow.*'

I check the time of the message. Ten last night, so Troy will be back at Gaz's today. That's good. I message back. '*Sounds good. I'll call later and see how he is. Are you happy to have him back at yours?*'

'*Sure. But I'm locking the medicine cabinet and hiding the key! Speak later.*'

Another message is from Joanna:

'*Matt tells me you've gone to bed poorly. Hope you're feeling better soon. Speak tomorrow.*'

'*Sorry. Probably should have called you. Assumed that as Finn cancelled, that was me free to go to bed!*'

The phone pings within seconds. '*Hey, don't worry. You needed to sleep. How are you?*'

'*Lots better. I'll be better still after coffee ;-). Speak soon. I'll call you after breakfast.*'

Showered and dressed, I wander downstairs to find Matt in the kitchen cutting bagels.

"Morning. Where did you get those from?"

"Dad dropped them off on his way to the golf club. He was worried about you. Said you'd been running around like an out-of-control golf buggy for days. He reckons smoked salmon bagels are medicinal."

I'm inclined to agree with my delightful, and slightly scatty, father-in-law. By the time I've eaten my first bagel, loaded with cream cheese, smoked salmon, lemon and a little black pepper, I'm feeling a lot better. The coffee is helping too.

Matt's sitting opposite me, eating slightly healthier options – with just a scraping of cream cheese and thin slivers of salmon on bagel halves.

"You've got some colour in your cheeks now, Becks. Dad was right."

"Yes." Time to focus on the essentials now, though. "How was Cheryl this morning?"

"Fine. When you went to bed early, she arranged for Joel's mum to give her a lift to school this morning."

"Are they going out?"

"I think it's imminent. They obviously really like each other."

"Can we go through again what happened yesterday? My head was spinning by the time she got home yesterday. I gathered everything was okay, but apart from that, I've not a clue. The details completely escaped me."

"There's not a lot more than that really. From what I

gathered, the Head was a bit sceptical until he read the letter from Lesley. Then he did a bit of an about-turn and released Cheryl and her friends. Apparently he called them back in later to say that he'd suspended the girls involved pending a full investigation. He'd been in touch with Wendy as well, and she'd filled him in on their criminal activities, and said they had sufficient evidence to prosecute if Danielle wanted to press charges. That bit I got from Wendy herself. She phoned the landline last night, after failing to get through to you on your mobile. She wanted to fill me in from her side."

"That was nice of her. I'd better call her as well later." I finish my coffee. "So it sounds as though Cheryl's crowd will be fine. No repercussions."

"The school is working with the police to find out if the girls' social media accounts can be deleted, together with all content they've posted. It should be possible. That will clear any residual problems. Hopefully, the suspension will become expulsion. The school can't afford to have kids like that." Matt looks angry – not a normal condition for him.

"How would you feel if one of our girls had been a bully?"

"It wouldn't have happened. They've got lovely parents, and a stable background. Statistically, it's unlikely."

"I don't think I've given them a lot of stability this year. They've had a lot of worry thanks to their parents."

The conversation is interrupted by my phone.

"Becky, is that you?" Gaz sounds anxious.

"Yes. Is Troy okay? Is he home?"

"I just picked him up from the hospital, and we went via his house to check for mail and for him to pick up some more clothes. The police have finished there. We picked up his post and brought it back to mine. He's just opened an anonymous letter threatening to kill his daughter."

My thoughts scramble for a moment. The problem with

having children is that every threat to a child feels personal. I take a deep breath and try to get my emotions under control.

"Okay. Is he there? Can I speak to him?"

There's a slight pause, then jagged breathing in to the phone.

"Troy, it's Becky. Take some deep breaths." I pause and listen to him try to control his breathing. "Where's your daughter now? Have you checked on her?"

"She's with Linda's mum and dad. I've told them she's been threatened. They won't let her outdoors alone. They're very sensible, but, shit, this killer is something else. He's killed my wife and my parents. How can he threaten my baby?"

"You need to tell the police."

"I can't. The letter said I'd regret it if I breathed a word to the authorities."

"Can you send me a photo of the letter? Handle it with gloves. It might be evidence later when we catch the killer. There might be fingerprints on it. No point adding extra prints to it."

"Okay. But can you and Joanna come over? And is her son helping you out? Gaz said there was a young man with you both yesterday; said Joanna was his mum."

"Yes, Will. He's a nice chap. About your age probably. And how are you feeling? Were they okay at the hospital?"

"Yeah, I was lucky, supposedly." He sounds bitter. I guess 'lucky' doesn't quite describe him currently. I promise to bring Joanna and Will to see him later this morning, and disconnect to make the arrangements.

***

Back at Gaz's flat an hour later, Troy is pacing the living room, running his hand through his hair, which is sticking up at all angles.

I introduce Will, then say, "Shouldn't you be resting? At least sit down. Gaz, is there any chance of a cup of tea please?"

"Sure. I'll put the kettle on."

With everyone's refreshment needs met, and Troy sitting on the sofa sipping his drink, I get out a pen and paper. I've got the photo of the letter which I received by text about ten minutes after the call this morning, but I ask to examine the original. Gaz puts on a pair of leather gloves and brings it over to the dining table where I've settled myself. I extract a paper of latex gloves from my handbag and take it from him.

It's a sheet of white A4 paper, perhaps 80 grams per square metre, with folds to show that it was in a standard DL size envelope.

"Do you have the envelope still?" I ask. Gaz produces it, still with his gloves on. My supposition about the size was correct, and the only other thing to note was that it's a white envelope with a printed address label, and a self-seal adhesive. This is not surprising, but I always hope a criminal will be stupid enough to lick the envelope. I produce a plastic zip-lock bag from my handbag and deposit the envelope inside before turning my attention to the actual letter. Like the address label, it's printed, in standard Arial 12-point font.

Mr Cassidy,

Matters are not progressing as they should. The next step is your little girl. Reconsider your behaviour, or she will be in mortal danger. Do not tell the police. If there is any increase in activity because of this letter, you will never see your daughter alive again.

Regards.

"It's very vague, isn't it?" Will has been reading it over my shoulder. He turns to Troy. "If I was the killer, I would be a lot more explicit in my instructions. I mean, what the hell does *'Reconsider your behaviour'* mean?"

"I dunno. I don't even know what I've done to bring this

on. I'm nice to everyone. Who would do this? And, shit, does this mean I'm the reason Linda, Mum and Dad are dead?"

Everyone in the room says, "No," emphatically, at the same time.

Gaz goes moves along the sofa and puts his hand on his friend's shoulder. "Seriously, mate. This is some mad psycho. You can't be responsible for what's happened. Only a crazy person would kill and hold you to blame."

"This clearly is someone with a grudge against you though, Troy. Whilst Gaz is quite right, and that you can't be blamed for the deaths of your wife and parents, we need to take this opportunity to look at who you could have upset. Remember, something that seems trivial to you, could be interpreted by someone else as a major insult." I place the letter into a second zip-lock bag as I finish speaking and put it on the table next to the envelope.

"What? You mean I might have taken the piss out of someone for a laugh, and they've been so offended they've killed my family?"

"Yes. Anyone you've made fun of, for whatever reason – I need their names, the situation and what you said."

"Bloody hell. I suppose the first one to mention should be Zach, but he adored Linda. He'd never have harmed her." He turns to Gaz. "Did I ever take the piss out of you or Harry? This is crazy. I can't bloody remember."

"You took the piss out of everyone, mate. It was just you. We were all used to it, and gave back as good as we got. No; it's more likely to be an outsider. Someone who didn't know us so well."

"Gaz, can you think of any specific instances where people might have been upset by something Troy did or said?" I turn my chair properly so I'm facing them all. Will and Joanna are now sitting on the armchairs. I'm the only one left at the table, but I don't want this to feel like an inquisition.

"Okay, yeah. There was that tall girl who fancies the pants of him. Like a super-fan. What's her name?" Gaz looks at Troy for confirmation.

"Sarah?"

"Yeah, her." He gives Troy a suspicious look, perhaps wondering why his friend should remember the name so easily. Gaz shakes his head slightly and turns back to me. "Sarah was pretty obsessed with Troy, and got a bit stalker-ish. I reckon she's a prime suspect."

"Thanks. She's on our list. Who else?"

"Dean is a wannabe rock star with no talent, and less sense. Troy's been a bit harsh with him at times as well. Other than that, the only ones that really stick out are those two photographers that follow us around Manchester. Come on, Troy mate, you're better with names than I am."

"Nigel and Penny you mean? Or Gemma?"

"Gemma's that student, isn't she? Sweet girl. I don't think you were ever horrible to her. I can't imagine anyone being nasty to her." Gaz looks at me. "You can take her off your list. No, I'm talking about the newspaper people – Nigel is a complete prick – even I've been rude to him. Penny is okay, but she seems a bit obsessive. I think Troy's been a bit impatient with her occasionally."

"We've met all the people you mentioned. I wouldn't argue with any of those comments." Joanna is looking fascinated by Gaz's observations. "Is there anyone else, or should we be focussing our attention on those four?"

"Dean, Sarah, Nigel and Penny?" Troy sounds incredulous. "They're all a bit odd, but surely none of them would kill. It's ridiculous. We're looking for a psychopath, not just some sad normal person. Although I remembered where I knew Nigel from. He used to work in the hospital when I met Linda, and he'd make excuses to see her. Like so many blokes, he was besotted with her. She got a bit freaked out by him – she used to say he was dead creepy, but when she went back to work after maternity leave, he'd left, and I didn't see him again until he showed up with Penny at our gigs."

I give this some thought, but it seems a bit odd that someone who adored Linda would stab her so many times.

Nothing of any further significance is discussed, and shortly afterwards, Joanna, Will and I leave the flat.

Back at the car, we discuss tactics.

"Becky, how would you deal with this if you were still in the police?" asks Will.

"I'd set up a noticeboard and put on all the evidence and information so far. Then we can work out what should get done next and by whom."

"Brilliant," says Joanna. "Will, drive us to the nearest B&Q. We need to buy a noticeboard."

An hour later, we're sitting in Joanna's kitchen. The new whiteboard is now adorning the wall above the kitchen table, and the said table is laden with sandwiches, coffee and markers. I help myself to a sandwich and a swig of coffee, then pick up a black marker pen and start writing.

I'm a spider-gram person, so I start with a central bubble labelled *TROY*, and add branches out to his family, the band, and to the various suspects. I've got this far, when Joanna reaches over, takes the pen out of my hands, and cleans the board with a dish-cloth.

"What are you doing? What's wrong with what I wrote?"

"You can't organise it like that, it's too messy." She opens a drawer and grabs a ruler. A neat table appears on the whiteboard within a couple of minutes, showing columns for *SUSPECTS, MOTIVE, OPPORTUNITY, EVIDENCE* and *SUPPOSITIONS*. "There. That's better."

I shake my head. "I led over a hundred cases using my diagrams. All my teams seemed to like them."

"They probably got used to them over the years. I agree with Mum. I prefer columns and lists. Sorry, Becky. You're outnumbered."

I glare at Will. Who does he think he is? I'm about to argue, when I'm stopped in my tracks by a vivid recollection of Finn's comments on my presentation style. "Fine. You two will have to do the writing then. I can't do anything that neat."

A short while later, Joanna has completed the table with logic, neatness and accuracy, but we've still got remarkably little information. We have four suspects (although they all seem unlikely) and very little physical evidence (only the letter and envelope). Opportunity is currently blank, as we don't know enough yet, and motive... we seem to be down to jealousy for Sarah, and possibly revenge for all of them, based on Troy's own confession of making fun of them. It all feels very vague.

We need to speak to Finn.

Chapter Thirty-Five

I am finally getting closer — manoeuvring into a position where all can be claimed.

There are just a few finishing touches required for my plan to work…

Chapter Thirty-Six

Finn's call comes through when I'm back at home, catching up on the hated but much-needed ironing.

"Hi, how are you doing?" I turn the iron off at the socket and hit my head on the ironing board as I resurface. The iron falls on to Cheryl's blouse, and I rescue it without further mishap.

"You okay, Becks?"

"Yeah. Good thanks. How's it going?"

"Er, fine. Erm, are you sure you're okay?"

"Just wrestling with the iron." I feel the lump forming on my forehead where I banged it. "Anyway, when are you going to come and see us? I think it's time for us to compare notes."

"Are you free this evening? I've told the team I've got a family commitment and I need to finish at five. I can be with you and Joanna for six-thirty if that works for you both. Takeaway is on me."

"I'll check with her and Will and get back to you."

Joanna and Will agree to meet up then. Meanwhile, it's time for me to do some work. I need to contact my friend in

Huddersfield. With all arrangements in place, and confirmed with Finn, I put the iron away and turn on my laptop.

I start by checking emails. Most of it is junk, but there's a message from Sylvia with a link to the Russian course she wants me to take. I fire off a quick email to say thanks, and open my contacts to find Ellie. I dither for a moment between phone and email, but it's fairly urgent, as before we meet up with Finn I need to know if Penny is lying. But before I call, I search for the newspaper article reporting the burglary and murder of the three girls. All their names are mentioned, so it would be perfectly possible for Penny to have used the article for her own purposes – even if I don't understand why she would do that.

Ellie answers my call on the fourth ring. "Howdy stranger! Not heard from you for yonks. What have you been up to?"

"Hi, Ells. I'm fine, thanks. You remember I wrote to tell you I'd resigned."

"Yeah, you're going to have to tell me what happened."

"Not today. It's still a bit raw – even after all these months. But I've started up a detective agency now, and we've got a couple of cases. I could do with your help, actually, if you've got a few minutes?"

"Sure, fire away. I'm armed with coffee and hobnobs."

I smile, even though she can't see me. We had many a case discussion with those same refreshments all those years ago. I explain the situation with Penny and the news article about the burglary.

"Actually, Becks, I'm working on that case. The girls were murdered horribly. Stabbed with a kitchen knife or something similar, according to the post-mortems. Obviously that information is not freely available."

"Is it possible to find out the girls' history, and discover if they were really at university with Penny, and if she ever lived with them?"

"Yes, that should be straightforward enough. I'll get my Sergeant on to it. I'll get back to you. I'm not sure why your client would lie to you about that, but I trust your nose for a fib."

Ellie calls me back an hour later. "Your nose might have failed you this time, Becky. Penny did live with those girls. At least in the first year, according to university records."

"Hmm. Something still doesn't feel right though. Okay, thanks Ellie. I'll see if I can find out a bit more. Have your team questioned the neighbours?"

"Yes. One side, Number 17, were there, and heard some noise, but thought the girls might have been having a party. Apparently they could be a bit wild. The occupants at 17 were devastated when they found out what happened. The people at Number 21 were on holiday. They got back yesterday to find a crime scene on their doorstep. They're not happy."

"Is there any chance I could go to speak to them? On both sides?"

"I can sort something out. They might be a bit more open with you. Number 17 holds a family of sorts. Mum is in her early thirties. Michelle Turner. She has a son of six years old, but there have been occasional episodes of shop-lifting. She doesn't really like the police. Step-dad, Barry, is a bit older – nearly forty. Also, a bit of a history of burglary and petty theft. Obviously we're looking closely at them because of the history, but neither of them have a record of violence."

"What about the holiday crew on the other side?"

"More traditional family. Husband, wife and three kids. He's a teacher."

"Hang on, why was he on holiday? It's not half-term yet." I check my mental calendar for Cheryl's holidays and realise she'll be off next week. "Or are the holidays different here?"

"Yes. It was half-term last week, and that school had an inset day on Monday, so they returned on Sunday night, with a day to recover, supposedly." Ellie follows up with the names of the parents – Frederick and Carly Granger. "I'll send you over their contact details when I've cleared it with them that you're coming to visit."

"Great, thanks so much. Please let them know that I'm just going to be asking for information about the girls, and their habits and that sort of thing. Hopefully, they'll be able to tell me what I want to know."

It takes a little while to sort out arrangements, by which time I've been able to have a coffee, and update Joanna and Will on the latest developments. They agree I should go into the interviews with the neighbours by myself, but Will is happy to drive me there for support. If it looks dodgy, he can come in with me. Joanna is feeling headachey and wants to have a sleep this afternoon.

Will picks me up at half past three.

"Hi Becky. Chauffeur at your service." He grins at me as I get in to the posh hire car.

"Thanks. I appreciate this. I could drive myself, but it's good not having to. How much longer have you got this beauty for?"

"I'm driving back up to Edinburgh tomorrow. There are a few things I need to sort out, like giving notice on my flat, taking the car back on Sunday, and I'll have to get myself a car for the future. I've already spoken to work. They're happy for me to work from home permanently, so they don't care where I live. I reckon by the time I've sorted everything out, I can be back here again by the end of next week. It doesn't matter if my flat's empty for a few weeks."

"You've got a daughter, haven't you?" I ask tentatively. I don't want to upset him, but I think we know each other well enough now for me to ask.

"Yes. My ex-wife has just moved in with her new partner, who lives in Preston, so it works out much better for me to live down here, then I can see my little girl at weekends much more easily."

"Have you met the new partner?"

"Yeah. He seems okay. A nice bloke. A bit boring, but that's her lookout. I guess she sees something good in him."

By the time we draw up in the required street in Huddersfield, I know all about his daughter, his ex, and the history of the relationship. He turns to me a little sheepishly as he turns the engine off.

"Sorry. I've not stopped talking for the last half an hour."

"It's fine. It's interesting to hear about your family. I'm pleased you'll be close enough to see Chloë when you move in with your mum."

"I don't think I'll be living with Mum for long – probably just while Dad's a threat, and then I'll find myself somewhere to live around here." He looks out of the passenger side window. "There's someone at the door. He looks like he's waiting for you. Do you want me to come in?"

I'm about to decline when I glance over at the man on the doorstep to Number 17. "Yes, please. He looks like he could eat me for breakfast."

Will nods, and we get out and approach the large man, who's wearing a dirty white vest. His bare arms are covered in tattoos, and his expression is less than welcoming.

"You that detective?" he calls to us before we're halfway up the garden path.

"Yes. I'm Rebecca. This is my associate, Will." I very rarely use my full name, but it seems sensible when faced with a probable ex-con, who looks as though he might know all my enemies. I vaguely recall Ellie saying this guy had no history of violence, but I'm reluctant to push him too far.

"You better come in. Least you don't look like cops."

I glance at Will, and then down at myself as we follow Barry into the house. Will's wearing black jeans and a plain bottle-green hoody. I'm dressed in my current standard work clothes – black trousers, a flowery blouse, and a black woolly cardigan. We both look safe and innocuous. We could be collecting for charity.

The house is untidy and smells of weed. The poor kid is not growing up in the healthiest environment, but that's not why we're here. Although, apparently it gives us cover, as Barry's next comment shows.

"Yer look like the bleeding social services. I'm sure you and her could be sisters." He leads us into a sitting room with a grubby blue sofa, covered in dog hairs. "Wife and kid are out taking the dog for a walk, so you can say what you like. We won't be over'eard."

His grin gives me the creeps, but I take a calming breath, and perch cautiously on the cleanest part of the sofa. I can't be accurately described as fastidious, but I have my limits. Will is a much more particular person than I am, and almost squats against the sofa. After a moment his legs give, and he succumbs to sitting properly. He grimaces at me though when our host's back is turned, and I send a sympathetic grin back.

When Barry finishes piling up papers and pushing the toys into a corner, he slumps in the armchair and looks expectantly at me.

"I expect my friend told you when she arranged this visit, but we're trying to find out some more about your next-door neighbours – those girls that were killed a few days ago?"

"Yeah. What d'you wanna know?"

"What were they like?" It's best to start with the basics, but I won't take it too slowly. I'm having to breathe shallowly as it is.

"Pretty girls – least, two of them were. Leigh, the ginger one, was a bit mingin', but can't have everything. They were all happy to spread their legs for a bit of cash when they got short.

Sometimes they'd do it in return for drugs, but they weren't addicts or nowt."

"How often did you sleep with them?" I understand now why he's pleased his wife is out.

"Varied. One or two times a week with one or other. Went through phases. Kim was pretty keen for a while, and we'd be at it a few times a week for no other reason than she fancied me. Then she got herself a thug of a bloke. Easier to stick it in one of t'other girls after that. I'll miss 'em to be honest."

I avoid glancing at Will. A sudden urge to giggle is threatening, and I need to stay focussed.

"Did you ever meet one of their friends? A blonde girl called Penny?"

"Yeah. She wouldn't let me near 'er though. Bit stuck-up, that one. But a few weeks gone, she had one 'eck of a row with them. Was calling 'em slags and all sorts."

"Did you hear this?" Will interjects.

"A bit. Least, I 'eard shouting. Jen told me everything later, after a quick shag that evening while the wife was at bingo, and kid was with his gran." He wipes his nose on his already grubby vest.

"What did Jen say?" The urge to laugh has been replaced by nausea, but I need to know what happened.

"They'd fallen out over something stupid. Jen wasn't even sure what started it, but then this stuck-up cow started calling 'em all sorts of names, and saying 'You'll be sorry', and that kind of shit. Jen didn't believe her, but kicked her out."

"Did Penny come back at all?"

"Not sodding likely. Jen told me a couple of days before the burglary that she never wanted to see Penny again. Even though they'd been friends for years. Said the cow had been slagging 'em off on Facebook and stuff."

"Thanks Barry, that's really helpful." I glance at Will, and he nods. He'll be able to drill through the social media channels and show us the side of Penny that she's never revealed to us.

I feel vindicated. I was right. If Jen had previously told Barry that they'd fallen out, Penny couldn't have been due to spend the weekend with them.

We say our goodbyes to Barry, giving him ten pounds for his trouble. Maybe he'll get fish and chips for his family instead of blowing it all on girls, drink and drugs. You never know.

Two doors away, on the other side of the crime scene, is Number 21 – the residence of the Granger family. Unlike Barry, they wait until I ring the doorbell before opening the door. Carly lets us in. She's a pretty, athletic-looking redhead.

I show her our business card. "I'm Rebecca. This is Will. He's only joined us recently. We're still waiting for the new cards to be printed. May we come in?"

"Of course. Sorry. I was just busy with some work. I run my own accountancy business from home. It makes sense with three kids and works well when they're all at school." She leads the way into a living room that couldn't be more different from Barry's if it tried. The proportions were the same, but everything else is unrecognisable. The wallpaper and carpets are complemented by spotlessly-clean furnishings of crimson and gold. There is no clutter at all, and after instructing us to sit down, Carly offers us a cup of tea. Moments later, we're served with tea in china cups and slices of carrot cake.

"Thanks. This cake is gorgeous," I say once I've swallowed my first mouthful. "Did you make it yourself?"

"Sort of. I like to pretend I'm a domestic goddess, but my baking skills are enhanced by packets of premixed ingredients. It saves a lot of time and effort, especially as we only got back from holiday yesterday." She grins at me, and as I grin back I refrain from commenting that buying one from the shop saves even more time and effort. I also wonder at her ability to bake when her friend has just been murdered, but maybe she finds it therapeutic.

"It's lovely, anyway. And it's good of you to talk to us. We just want to find out a bit more about your late next-door neighbours."

"Sure. There were three of them. All girls. Graduates. Jen did her degree in Accountancy, like I did, although I'd graduated a few years before she started. There were four of them at first. They moved in next door in their second year."

"How long ago was that?"

"That would have been a bit over seven years ago now. Jen, Kim, and Leigh stayed. Kim is a teacher now at the same school where Frederick teaches. He'd often give her a lift to school. If I remember correctly, she did Biology, but she teaches General Science as well to the Year 7s and 8s. Leigh studied History, and works – sorry, worked – I can't get my head around this – she worked as one of those heir hunters. She loved her job so much." Carly gets out a tissue from her pocket and blows her nose loudly.

"I'm so sorry. It sounds as though you knew the girls really well."

"Yes. I didn't know Penny as well, as she left shortly after her degree, to do an internship with a newspaper. She'd done a photography course and wanted to do journalistic photography. I would hear all the news from Jen. I'd tutored her through her accountancy exams and we became close friends as well as neighbours." She shakes her head. "It probably seems weird that I'm not in tears, but I go through phases. At present, I just feel numb, then suddenly it hits me, and I'm in bits. It doesn't feel real talking to a detective about them. I just wish I'd been here that night. Maybe I'd have heard something and called the police."

"It's not impossible that the intruder waited until you were on holiday. He or she may have trusted to drink or drugs to keep the residents of Number 17 asleep, but you were a bigger threat."

"Maybe. I still feel guilty for being away though." She gulps some tea, and I can see that the intermittent tears are threatening.

"Sorry, do you mind if I just ask another question about Penny?"

She sniffs and straightens up. "Sure, go ahead."

"How often did Penny visit the other girls?"

"Until recently, she'd come over and stay for the weekend every couple of months, and would pop in there for the odd evening in between. We're only a ten-minute walk from the station, so it was easy enough for her to get here, even though she doesn't drive."

"You said 'until recently'. Why?"

"The girls had a big row. I didn't hear it myself, I was out that day, but Jen told me all about it afterwards. She was in bits. She was the closest of all the girls to Penny, and they'd apparently said some awful things to each other."

"Did Jen say what it was about or when it occurred?" Will picks up the questioning. He's stayed pretty quiet until now, but has been jotting in a spiral-bound notebook.

"No. Well. It wasn't that she wouldn't say, it was that she didn't know. She said it just exploded out of nothing. Penny could be a bit volatile. Dead quiet and polite and reserved, then suddenly it would all erupt, and you'd find out she'd been heading towards a meltdown for ages. So this wasn't the first time she'd done this sort of thing, but according to Jen, she hadn't previously directed at all three of the girls before. It was usually either Leigh or Kim, but never Jen until now. I don't think Jen mentioned the exact day, just asked if I'd heard. I hadn't, so I assumed I must have been out."

"How did the girls get on with the neighbours on the other side?" Will looks up from scribbling.

"They're scum, specially him. Barry!" Her voice is full of contempt. "He's been trying it on with those girls ever since he moved in. Won't take no for an answer. Jen says just after the row with Penny, he was round on the pretence of borrowing some milk, and digging for the dirt. He'd obviously heard the noise. Then when he realised that Jen was alone that evening, he jumped her, and raped her."

"What did she do? Did she report it to the police?" The stories are differing quite a bit here, and although it could be down to perspective, I want to understand if Barry's version can be trusted, or if Jen's making excuses to her mentor. I'm inclined to believe Jen, but years in the police have taught me that not everything is straightforward.

"She was terrified. He threatened to do worse than that if he suspected she'd told on him."

"Do you think he might have been the burglar?" As soon as the words are out of my mouth, I can see it wasn't the wisest thing to say. Her face blanches.

"Oh God, I hadn't thought of that! I hope the police are checking him out."

"We'll discuss this with them and find out. We'll keep you informed as far as we can. I'm sure it would be good for you to know your neighbourhood is safe." I reassure her as well as I can, but I can see she's still quite alarmed. "He's never attacked or threatened any member of your family, has he?"

"Not my immediate family, but Jen's like a younger sister to me. How could he have done this?"

"We don't know if it was him. It might have been a random burglary that went wrong. Will and I are working with the police. We'll find out who did this." I probably shouldn't be wondering just now how the hell we're going to get paid for any of these investigations. Our best bet is Troy, but he's only going to pay us if we find out who killed his family. Currently, the link between this and Troy's case is tenuous. And Penny, the link, is also one of our clients. We're no closer to finding her stalker either, although… "Actually, can I just ask a slightly odd question?"

"Ask what you like if it will help."

I check my notebook, and ask Carly if, to the best of her knowledge, Barry was home on the dates Penny had told us she was followed.

"I can't vouch for all those dates, but he usually plays darts in the local pub on Fridays. Frederick's in his darts team. I can let you know about those specific dates when he gets home. If you give me a number or an email?"

We exchange numbers, so I can also let her know how the burglary case is going.

We pop into the station afterwards to see Ellie. The officer on duty at the front desk asks our names.

"I'm an old friend. Please can you just tell her Becky's here to see her?"

He looks a bit doubtful, but picks up the phone. I suppose I could have texted her, but I have a gut feeling that this is the right thing to do. She emerges a couple of minutes later, wearing a black trouser suit and cream blouse. She's lost a few pounds since I last saw her, and looks thinner than she should, and tired. Despite the professional attire, she greets me with a hug, before turning to Will.

"Who's your friend?" There's an admiring twinkle in her eye. She always did go for the geeky type, and Will's quite attractive.

"He's my business-partner's son, and will probably join us as an associate in the next few weeks. He's been helping us out and is very good." I inject a repressive tone into my voice. "Will, meet Ellie."

He grins at me, then at her. "Nice to meet you, Ellie." He offers her his hand for shaking, but she gives him a peck on the cheek instead, blushing slightly.

"Great. Now we're all friends, how about we find somewhere to chat?" I'm conscious of the looks we're getting from the front desk officer. Fortunately, the waiting room is empty.

She leads us into an interview room a short distance from the entrance, and after a few minutes catching up on news, gets to the point.

"So were you right, Becky?"

"Yes. Penny had a huge row with the residents of Number 19 a few weeks before the burglary. Awful things were said, and it seems the rift was permanent. Both Barry at 17, and Carly at 21, confirmed the argument. Jennifer, or Jen, seems to have been the informant for both, although…" I hesitate.

"What?"

After a quick glance at me, Will picks up the tale. "Barry conveyed the idea that the girls would sleep with him in return for cash or drugs, and that he had consensual sex with Jen on the occasion that she told him about the row. Meanwhile, Jen told Carly, who seems to be a kind of mentor, that Barry had raped her."

"So it's not impossible that Barry staged the burglary to cover up the rape." I rub my nose, and Ellie immediately picks up on the action.

"You don't think he did though?"

"Firstly, if he raped her, why would she tell him about the row?"

"Perhaps she told him over a cup of tea, then he raped her?" suggests Will.

"Okay, let's go with that for a minute. Becky, what else is bothering you?"

"I suppose I just felt that Barry, coarse though he is, didn't seem like a rapist. And I can't help thinking Penny fits in somewhere. Otherwise, why would she lie about an intended visit to the girls, when she didn't have to bring them into it at all?"

"Yes," says Will, "but Penny came to us because she was 'feeling more threatened' after her friends were killed. Perhaps Barry has been following her?"

"Carly is going to let us know if Barry was at the pub with her husband on the nights when Penny said she was being followed. It's darts night on Fridays, apparently. It seems probable that he'll have an alibi for those nights."

Ellie is looking thoughtful. "So if Penny lied about the intended visit to the girls, perhaps she was also lying about being stalked."

"It doesn't make sense though. She's no motive for doing that." Will frowns. "Why pay money to a detective agency to track a non-existent stalker?"

"You're both right." I say. "Something definitely doesn't add up."

A call comes through at that moment for Ellie, so we take our leave, thanking her for her help, and promising to liaise. We head back to Joanna's for our meeting with Finn.

Chapter Thirty-Seven

It's easy to take the child. Even with the precautions they've put in place following my letter.

A forged letter to her school paves the way, introducing the relative that might pick her up as her family is so indisposed at this troublesome time.

So when I turn up, a bit before 'home time', to collect the child ("Yes, we must leave now. So sorry, but I'm in a rush. I'll be dropping her off with her grandparents shortly, but they can't make it here today.") they release her with minimal fuss.

Her resemblance to Troy freaks me out, but if I have to kill her, so be it. Just a means to a necessary end…

Chapter Thirty-Eight

It's nearly six when we get back, and we've just got inside when my phone rings. Troy's name is on the screen.

"Hi," I start greeting him, but I'm immediately interrupted.

"Becky. You've got to help. She's gone."

"Who? Your daughter?"

"Yes, my little Emma. Taken out of school. The bloody idiots at school let her go because they'd had a letter supposedly from me. A friggin' typed thing. They didn't even sodding think to check with me."

"What time was she collected?" I ask, keeping my voice deliberately calm.

"Quarter past three. How soon can you get here? I'm still at Gaz's. I've only just found out she wasn't with Linda's parents. They were supposed to pick her up, but when they arrived, school said she'd already been collected. They assumed I'd picked her up, until I phoned to talk to her just a few minutes ago."

I promise to be with him as soon as traffic allows, and the three of us set off. Joanna is feeling better now, although she still looks a bit peaky. Will drives again, and I drop Finn a message to inform him of what's happened.

'*Don't come roaring up with all lights flashing. They'll be looking for evidence of police involvement, and you might put the girl in danger.*'

'*Sure. I'm not stupid, Becks. And we don't even know where she is yet. I'm going to have to wait for you to let me know.*'

A few incidences of when he's been dangerously gung-ho cross my mind, but I suppress them, and send back a reassuring message that I don't doubt him.

Will puts his foot down on the journey, dodging cars on the motorway and nipping through traffic lights on amber on the ordinary roads. Consequently, we're with Troy 23 minutes after his call, although Joanna is looking even paler than she did when we left.

"Are you okay, Mum?"

"Just a bit queasy after that manic journey. If Gaz can make me a cup of tea, I'll be fine."

But once inside Gaz's flat, all thoughts of tea are forgotten. Troy's phone rings the second we get inside. He holds it up to show that it says '*No Caller ID*', and presses the green *Answer* button, followed by the speaker icon.

"Hello?" He answers cautiously. At this stage it could be British Gas!

It's not.

"We've got your little girl. You need to come and get her. Come alone. No police." It's a man's voice. It sounds vaguely familiar, but I can't pinpoint it.

"I can't drive at the moment. I'm on meds."

"You can bring a driver. Just you and the driver though." He gives an address. One that makes my body go into overdrive. It's the location of a warehouse. I've been there before. My mind blanks for a moment, and I miss the rest of the instructions, although the call ends just a few seconds later.

"Becky?" Will crouches down near the chair I don't remember sinking into. "Are you okay?"

I take some deep breaths and grit my teeth. Troy's daughter has been kidnapped. The cogs in my brain resume their usual motion, and a lightbulb comes on. I now know why Lesley's comment about fake photos jarred. It wasn't exactly the photos that were fake in this case, but the whole set-up. And I'm fairly sure I know who the killer is.

"Yes, I'll be fine. That caller – it sounded like Nigel. That annoying guy from Band On The Wall, who works with Penny." And who used to fancy Linda. It makes sense after all for him to be involved.

Joanna nods slowly.

So does Troy. "Bloody hell. Yeah, I thought I recognised the bastard. Right, who's coming with me?"

"All of us." I suppress the gut reaction to my statement. I need a clear head, not clammy palms, nausea and a racing pulse. "I know that warehouse. There's a road a bit further down, and out of sight." That had been my downfall previously. This time I would make it work for us. "Gaz, can you drive Troy? Will can take me and Joanna, and we'll stay out of sight until the time comes for action."

"Sure. Troy, I'll drive you, mate. Becky's right. It's a sound plan."

"Why didn't they ask for a ransom?" asks Will. "It's a strange set-up. It sounds like a trap."

"That warehouse usually is. That's why we're staying out of sight. Troy, we just need to fit you up with a listening device. We'll meet you there." I suggest a route for them to go. It should take them about twenty minutes. The route I have planned for us should take about fifteen, and will allow us to get discreetly in place before they arrive.

As I kit Troy out with the equipment, I can feel him shaking. It's not surprising. He's clearly terrified about his daughter. He's just lost everyone else he loved. Despite my own fears, I can't let him lose his little girl as well. I have to conquer my own demons.

In the car, away from Troy and Gaz, we go over the plan, but also take a few minutes to review what we know. Joanna is on her phone while Will and I re-hash our knowledge.

"Did you know Penny knew Troy at school?" she suddenly pipes up.

"No – how did you find that out?" My pulse speeds up another notch. This feels important.

"When you'd gone to Huddersfield earlier, after the paracetamol kicked in, I started thinking, and emailed a few questions over to Troy. One of them was about his school. I checked back against the questionnaire from Penny, when we first took her on as a client. It looked as though she was a couple of years below Troy at the same secondary school."

"That doesn't necessarily mean she knew him though, or vice versa." Will's voice of caution fails to have an effect. Joanna has more information for us.

"No, but I contacted the school, and spoke to the Head. She's new there, but said she'd ask around amongst some of her more longstanding staff. This is the email she just sent me." Joanna passes her phone to me. I start reading to myself.

"Read it aloud, Becky. I can listen and drive at the same time, and frankly the suspense is killing me."

I grin at Will, but relent.

"*My Head of Science remembers them both well. She said Penny had an obvious crush on Troy from the time she was about thirteen. When Mrs Dixon was teaching Troy, she'd often notice Penny outside the door before or after the lesson. There was a stronger and more lasting obsession than is usually seen in girls of that age. Natalie Dixon took an interest in the emotional welfare of the pupils, and tried to persuade Penny to open up about her feelings, but without success. After Troy left, Penny had a couple of short-lived relationships with boys, but always seemed discontented. Natalie suspected she was still hankering after Troy.'*

"So does that affect our case?" I ask. "I'm trying to get my head around the implications. Also, that call was from Nigel. Would he have assisted Penny to that extent?"

"I don't know. But it makes more sense that he'd help Penny, rather than kill Linda. If she roped him in because he has a grudge against Troy for 'stealing his girl', he'd probably be only too keen to help. Maybe he doesn't know that Penny murdered Linda?"

"Possibly. But more likely his grudge against Troy outweighs his horror at what Penny has done. Or he just hasn't thought about it."

"Either way, we've just arrived at the address you gave me, Becky. I assume the warehouse is near here?"

I nod. My stomach has suddenly gone into hyper-drive, and I suppress a wave of nausea.

"Okay. I'll let Finn know where we are and ask for discreet and careful back-up. Please God that Nigel – and Penny, if she's involved in this – won't be armed."

"Whoever killed Troy's family is capable of further murder, don't forget." Joanna puts her hand on my shoulder. I don't know if she means to be reassuring, but it doesn't work. "They might not have guns, but they're pretty adept with knives. We need a stronger plan before we go barging in there."

"Stronger than the one I proposed earlier?" I hand Joanna back her phone.

"Yes. You were going to go in, negotiate with Nigel, and get Emma back for Troy. It's a bit weak."

"Obviously, we're going to be listening to Troy, and when it's appropriate we'll go in and help." I hear my phone ping and check the message that's just arrived from Finn.

'Bloody hell, Becks. Are you okay going in there?'

'No choice. Can you back us up?'

'I'll be there in 15.'

"Finn will be here with back-up in fifteen minutes." I show them on the map where the warehouse is. My instincts are shouting at me. *Go home. Get out of here. This place is a death trap.* I ignore the voice in my head, and turn on the receiver for the bug that Troy has hidden on his person.

"Are we nearly there, Gaz?" Troy's voice comes through loud and clear. I turn the volume down a notch.

"Just a couple of minutes, mate." The car falls silent for a moment. "Right this is it. I guess that's where they're holding Emma. Do you want me to come in with you?"

"Nah, you'd better not. Keep an eye out for Becky and that lot though."

"They know what they're doing, mate. It'll be fine." Gaz sounds as though he might be reassuring himself as much as his friend, but Troy buys it.

"Cheers."

We hear the car door shut a few seconds later, and Troy's heavy boots on the tarmac. The sound of the back door into the warehouse brings on another wave of sickness for me. I frown and grit my teeth. This is not the time for memories.

"Hello, Troy." Penny's voice comes through clearly on the receiver.

"Where's my Emma?"

"Nigel's got her safe, just a little way from here."

Panic seizes me for a moment, and I glance round swiftly. We're on a residential road, on a drive concealed by bushes. The owner of the house and drive is Wendy's youngest son, and I've already messaged him with a warning not to come out and ask questions. He knows me of old, and can be trusted to do as he's asked. This is as safe a location as it could be in the circumstances.

Will reaches over and opens the glove box. He extracts a woolly hat and a false beard. half a minute later, he looks totally different.

"I'm just going to wander out on the road and have a recce. I won't do anything else, I promise," he whispers.

Meanwhile, the conversation in the warehouse is continuing.

"Why would you do this?" Troy sounds horrified; shocked and sick that the sweet, pretty photographer has been involved in abducting his daughter. "Did you kill Linda?"

"Of course I did. Got in a few kicks first, too. And I killed your stupid parents. Did you know they told me off for walking past your house when we were growing up?"

"How did you know me then? I didn't think we'd met until you started photographing me and the band a few months back."

"Same school, Troy. I was two years below you. I loved you then, you know. I'd have done anything for you. But you were too stupid to see it. Then when you went to college, I'd skive school and come to see you. You never even noticed me."

"I'm sorry. Why didn't you say something?"

"I waited for you to see me. Then you met that bloody bitch and married her. I tried to get over you, but something changed inside me. When I started working at the paper, and got to see you doing gigs, it felt like a second chance. But you still ignored me."

"There were a lot of photographers. How was I to know you were any different? I didn't recognise you from school."

There's a click and a crackle. "You'd better bring her in here, Nigel." A moment's silence follows.

Will returns to the car and pulls off the beard and hat. "No sign of any man with a little kid in a car. They must be waiting somewhere else."

"Okay. I'm going to get closer to the warehouse. I'll do up

my coat, and no one will pay any attention to me." I have a dark blue parka that looks the same as hundreds of thousands up and down the country. Completely undistinctive, but with usefully big pockets. "Joanna, you'd better take this." I hand her the receiver. "If things get really sticky, call Finn. Do not come and rescue anyone yourselves. Penny is clearly an obsessed lunatic. That makes her dangerous. She's just admitted to killing three people who got in her way."

It's early twilight, so I can still see my way clearly, but it's harder to see distinct features of other pedestrians. There are a few people around – innocent commuters or residents taking a shortcut through the area, or walking to the shops. I walk through the alleyway that leads to the industrial street housing the warehouse. My legs are shaking and I have to take some deep breaths to ease the palpitations in my chest. I pause at the end of the alleyway.

The warehouse is actually the building on my right, separated from me by a fence and a lot of greenery, but there's no way in from here. I will need to walk across in front of it, in full view, or dodge between the fence and corrugated metal wall, fighting my way through the undergrowth. That seems to be the best option. I feel in my coat pocket for the sharp scissors that I brought with me. Going into a situation completely unarmed is always foolish, but this time my armoury will have a practical benefit too. I creep round to my right, and immediately dive into the gap. There's space to squeeze through for about fifteen feet. The twilight is definitely helpful now, as no one would think to look for me here. A cut here, and a snip there, allows me to get to the end of the building, parallel to the alley. Then a slight gap opens up. I know there's a back door just along from here. It was my undoing last time I was here. Hopefully, this time it will be my saviour.

I try the doorknob, but to no avail. From my other pocket, I extract a wire, and cautiously and silently insert it into the lock. The lock clicks, and I tentatively open the door. It leads me into an empty corridor, but I can hear voices emerging from an area beyond an internal door. My palms are sweaty as I edge closer.

Chapter Thirty-Nine

I am finally here, in front of him, and he's in my power. I have his child. She's on the way here with my accomplice.

How much can I make him suffer? Should I make him suffer any further? I want him to be mine. Even now, after all this, I am still in love with him. My heart beats faster because he's near, and my edges soften a little as I see his distress. I am weakening.

But memories flood in. The times I was near him and he ignored me. When I saw him with HER, and his besotted behaviour made me sick. That should have been me.

I need to decide what I want.

Chapter Forty

A door opens in the distance. I hear crying. Then Troy's voice.

"Emma love, it's going to be fine. Daddy's here."

"Why should it be fine? I have some demands you haven't heard yet. You need to obey me, or she'll die." Penny's voice is harsh. Maybe a little anxious. I can work with that if I must.

I'm able to suppress my reaction to being back here by focusing on the case in hand. That is, until there's a sound like a gun firing outside. It's most likely a car backfiring, but its effect is dramatic. With my heart beating out of my chest, a thundering in my ears, an inability to swallow and legs that won't support me, I sink to the floor and wrap my arms around my knees. Penny and Troy are still speaking, but my brain won't process the sounds. My ability to do my job has deserted me.

I don't know how long I've been like this, but suddenly the back door opens softly. I'm exposed here, so I look up. I'm unable to do much more, but relief floods through me when I see Joanna and Will walk in. She rushes to my side, while he goes to the door and listens through the crack.

"What happened out there?" I try to whisper but my mouth is so dry, only a hoarse croak emerges.

"There's some drugs thing going on down the road. We heard the gunfire just as we were emerging from the alley. Will saw a body on the ground, but we didn't linger. We came straight here." Joanna whispers directly into my ear. The voices from the other room are testament to the thinness of the walls.

I'm still unable to take much in. The trauma from my previous horrific experience in this place is now vivid, and taking over my whole body. Joanna is still crouching down next to me, and rests a hand on my shoulder.

"They've got the little girl in there. Will is going in. He'll try to diffuse the situation. If he fails, I'll join him, but I think we need to play it by ear now." What she means is that I'm now useless, so our previous planning has fallen apart, but I'm too distraught to argue with her.

"Sure. Will, be careful. Penny at least is likely to have a knife of some sort. She admitted to having killed Linda, and Troy's parents." Pulling myself together enough to whisper this information to my friends takes immense effort, but it focusses my mind slightly, and I feel the panic recede just a notch. So when Will opens the door into the main area, I'm alert enough to listen again. Joanna squeezes my hand, but I sense her anxiety now that her son is in there.

"What the hell are you doing here?" Penny's voice from the other side of the wall is sharp and angry. "You're part of White Knight, aren't you? Why aren't you investigating my stalker?" She laughs, but it chills me more than her anger.

"Which stalker is that, Penny? Is that the one from your imagination, or were you the one doing the stalking?"

"Aren't you the clever-clogs! I needed to find out more about Troy's whereabouts. I figured you'd be less likely to suspect me if I was a victim too. I got quite a bit of useful information from you lot."

"Maybe you're less clever than you think you are." Will sounds cool and calculating. "If you hadn't raised your profile, we might never have thought of you. The unobtrusive photographer of bands. The paparazzi. Why should we suspect? But no. You thought a double-bluff would work. So here we all are."

"You're only here because I gave Troy instructions on where to find me. You didn't work it out for yourself."

"No? So how did we find out that you'd murdered your ex-housemates in Huddersfield? A neat mixture of revenge against them and another 'blind' so we wouldn't suspect you."

The momentary silence suggests Will's hit a nerve. There's a slight scuffle, then…

"No, you don't, you bastard. You're not spoiling my plans. We're evenly matched, but I bet me and Nigel could take out you and Troy easily enough. Nigel's been desperate for years to get his own back on Troy. Stupid git told me all about it over drinks last year; how Troy pinched his girl out from under his nose. I knew then that Nigel would help me."

I glance at Joanna. My courage has been slowly returning to me throughout this conversation, and it's time for us to go in and destroy Penny's misconception.

Joanna opens the door and enters first. I send up a quick prayer for my weakness to not return, then follow her in.

"Seriously? What the hell are you lot doing here?" Penny looks disgusted at first glance, but I see a glint of fear in her eyes.

"We're here to make sure justice is done." I'm pleased with how calm my voice sounds. Inside, I'm quivering like a jellyfish. "Nigel, let go of Emma and let her go to her dad."

Nigel looks over at Penny, but before he has a chance to argue Will is behind him, wrests the knife from his grip, and has him in a headlock.

Troy seems suddenly released from stasis as the immediate

danger to his daughter is removed, and he runs to her and lifts her into his arms. I signal to him to take her out of here and back to Gaz's car, and press a few buttons on my phone.

Will doesn't release Nigel even when Troy is gone.

"Drop your knife if you don't want your friend to suffer, Penny," Joanna says calmly. "I don't suppose I've mentioned it before, but my son is a master of martial arts. All those trips out on Saturday mornings and school nights appear to have been worth it."

"I don't give a shit about Nigel. He was a convenient means to an end." She dives at me with the knife, but my own judo skills have significantly improved since my student days, and I'm able to dodge the lethal weapon, duck under her guard, and have her arm twisted up behind her back before she takes another breath. The knife falls to the floor, and I kick it away from her.

"You bloody bitch. Now what? You can't arrest me. You're not police any more."

"No, but we are." Finn enters the room with a posse of armed and uniformed officers. "Well done, you three. I saw Troy and his little girl coming out and figured this was the time to come in. Then I saw your message, Becky. Thanks."

Arrests are swift and neat, and Penny and Nigel are taken into custody. One of Finn's officers bags up the knives as evidence.

I'm just calming down when a memory returns. *Finn's face in the aftermath half a year ago. His expression of relief is overlaid with fear.* I didn't make sense of it then, but there's a click as pieces slot into place.

Chapter Forty-One

Finn betrayed me. As he approaches me now in that warehouse, I can see the shock in his eyes as he notices the shock in mine. He glances round. I follow his gaze and see Joanna talking quietly to Will in the corner as the police do their work. We have a moment or two of privacy. We really need hours, or maybe no time at all. What is there to say to a friend who puts your life in danger? Only one word.

"Why?"

His shoulders slump.

"I'm so sorry, Becks. I was in such trouble. Gambling debts had got me into deep shit. They offered me a way out: to get you into that warehouse at that particular moment. Someone wanted you out of the way. I never found out why. Without them knowing it, though, I put precautions in place. I can't describe how relieved I was when they worked, and you were still alive. I was gutted about Rachel; she wasn't supposed to be involved, but at least it wasn't you." His voice shakes, and despite my horror at his revelations, I'm inclined to believe him.

"Who made you that offer?" Perhaps there is more than one question I need to ask.

"I don't know. The letters came by post, with instructions on what to do, and what the consequences would be if I didn't."

"So you were blackmailed, and you didn't pursue the criminal who was threatening you?"

"I wasn't in my right mind. That whole period, from about a year earlier, I got caught up in addiction. I had problems with alcohol as well as gambling. And there was a bit of coke too. Seriously, I was a mess. After what happened to you, I took some time off. I said it was shock, but I went into rehab. I badly let you down. I'm so sorry."

"I need time to think about this. I'll get back to you. Are you clean and dry now?"

"Yeah. Sober, clean and gamble-free for fourteen weeks, three days and eight hours." He puts a hand on my shoulder.

There are none of the usual flutterings. In contrast, my stomach clenches in something akin to hatred. I vow to myself to get past it somehow. But for now, there's business to attend to. I grit my teeth. I don't know if he senses my reaction, but he quickly drops his hand to his side.

"So, I assume Penny and Nigel will be charged with the abduction of Troy's daughter and possession of lethal weapons. What about the murder charges?"

"I had a call from Ellie over in Huddersfield. She said you'd been to see her, and that you suspected Penny was more involved than she should be in the recent murder of her ex-housemates."

"Given the evidence, I think it's a serious possibility."

"I agree. Same MO as Troy's wife and parents," Finn seems more relaxed now we're back on neutral conversation, and my antipathy eases. "Anyway, well done for all your work on it. I have to admit, the forensics and our team hadn't even considered Penny as a suspect." His uneasiness returns slightly. "I hope we can continue to work together, Becks, despite what's happened. I hope you can forgive me."

Forgiveness or otherwise needs to be shelved for the moment, as there are things to be done. The evening is progressing quickly, and I take to my phone for a minute to tell Matt and Cheryl that I'll be back late, but that this case is almost over now.

"Just loose ends to tie up now, but you know what that's like, Matt."

"Sure. Are you okay? You sound a bit… I don't know… maybe a bit traumatised."

"It's been a tough day. I'll tell you about it later, or depending what time I get home, tomorrow. Finn's invited us to the station to fill him in on our findings, then to observe the interviews with the suspects."

Finn had obviously felt guilty for his previous actions, but I think his invitation sprang more from the need to fill in his knowledge gaps. Despite his shortcomings, he's a practical soul.

Will drives us to the police station. Unusually, we're all quiet. Too much has happened, and too recently for us to celebrate, but after about ten minutes of quiet, I rouse myself to speak.

"Well done, both of you. You're amazing, and I'm proud to work with you."

"Does that mean I can be part of White Knight permanently?"

"I'd be happy for you to be a permanent fixture on the team, as long as your mum agrees. But what about your computing job?"

"I got an email today, offering voluntary redundancy, but

with the option to call on me as a consultant. So I can do some freelance work on the side to keep my hand in, and help with finances, but the redundancy package would help tide us over for a bit anyway."

"Joanna, are you happy with that?" I see no reason she wouldn't want her son working with us, but it seems right to ask.

"Yes, of course. I think Will's shown himself worthy of a place at White Knight, and he's easy to work with. He's even okay to live with, and he's a better cook than I am."

The light-hearted discussion of the future calms me down, and I'm in a better mood by the time Will pulls up outside the station.

Finn has arrived before us and is out of his car already as Will turns off the engine. He comes over and waits as we get out.

"I'll take you all up to my office. We can have a chat, and then you can watch as I interview Penny and Nigel. Does that seem reasonable?"

"Sure. Have you still got that coffee machine in your office?"

"Course I have. There's a whole selection of pods, so you can keep yourselves supplied throughout the interviews. I've even got biscuits. I guess no one's had dinner. This wasn't quite what I had in mind when I suggested exchanging information this evening."

"No problem." Will grins. "Coffee and biscuits sounds great. Thanks."

When we get to Finn's office, I look around. It's moderately tidy, as long as you don't look too closely at the piles on the in-trays – he has three of these, and rarely gets round to going through them. I glance at him and see he's watching me.

"I need you to keep me in order, Becks." He smiles wryly. "None of the team ever challenge me like you did."

I refrain from asking why he betrayed me then. He's already explained. And also, I would prefer to keep it between Finn and me for now. I'll tell Matt later, but that's all.

He must realise that he's not getting a response, because he glances round to check the number of chairs, then leaves to fill the deficit. Joanna gives me a sharp look. I can see she senses that all is not well between me and Finn, and I decide to make an extra effort to be normal with him.

Sitting around his desk with coffee, we keep the conversation focussed on evidence and our recent knowledge and suppositions. Finn takes copious notes.

"I'm going to have to interview Penny. I wish you three could be part of that, but at least I can let you watch."

"Will you have your phone on?" I ask. He always used to turn off his phone before going into a meeting with the suspects.

"You know I don't usually." He pauses. "But I suppose I could make an exception. Are you suggesting that you'll text me if I need prompting or if something comes up that I'm not aware of?"

"It would make sense. I think we've told you everything we know, but it's not impossible that there's some little detail that we didn't know was important. We've been working in this job for long enough to know that it's all in the details."

"Very true, Becks. Okay. That's a plan then." He switches on a screen and fiddles with some buttons, until the screen shows Penny, looking sullen, and an apparently exasperated duty solicitor. "Right. Wish me luck, folks. I'm going in."

Chapter Forty-Two

I have observed many interviews over the years, so this should be quite ordinary, but given the circumstances, I am fascinated to hear this story from Penny's perspective. If she'll talk.

Finn opens the interview in the usual way. He's accompanied by a young Sergeant that I don't recognise, who he introduces as DS Ian Timms. He addresses Penny as Miss Ellsworth whilst reading her rights to her. Then, with the formalities over, Finn starts with the events of today. However angry I am with him, I can't deny that he's a sensible and thorough police detective.

"So tell me about this afternoon. Why did you abduct Emma Cassidy?"

"No comment."

"Do you deny that you abducted Emma?"

"No comment."

"Look, Penny. I want to help you, but I can't do that if you won't talk to me. I need to understand the circumstances from your perspective, because right now, the evidence is extremely damning." Finn is lying, but it's a good tactic. He's also switched to calling Penny by her first name. Another good strategy. The evidence is actually pretty flimsy, although now that we have a suspect, there is a warrant to search Penny's flat. It's hoped that this will turn up further proof of her guilt.

Penny is looking uncertainly at her solicitor, who responds in kind but firm tones. "You don't have to say anything, Penny. But don't forget, if you fail to say something now and you would like to use it later in court, it may be too late."

"Fine! Okay, yes, I abducted his daughter, but he deserved it. He was being stupid."

"Would you like to expand on that, Penny?" Finn's tone is neutral, but I know him well enough to sense his relief.

"I sent him a letter warning him that if he didn't change his behaviour, his daughter would be taken away. He didn't change."

"Was this the letter?" Finn reaches into a black leather bag at his side and extracts the plastic bag holding the letter that Troy received. Penny glances at it, then nods.

"For the purposes of the recording, Penny has just nodded assent. What did you plan to do with Emma once you had taken her?"

"It depended on what Troy said. If he'd agreed to my terms, then I'd have let her go."

I can't see Finn's face from the direction of the camera. He and the Sergeant have their backs to it, but I suspect him of mentally rolling his eyes. He would show a poker face though.

"What were your terms, Penny?"

"He had to agree to be with me. To marry me and be mine for ever."

"After you'd murdered his wife, who he loved, and his parents, who I presume he also loved?"

"He did. He was close to his mum and dad. That's why they had to go. Anyone who got in my way had to go."

"So you admit to killing them?" Finn's tone is neutral, but the solicitor murmurs in Penny's ear.

"I don't admit to anything except for wanting Troy." Penny sounds mutinous, and her tone is childish.

I glance at Joanna. "She's not normal. This is not normal behaviour even for an obsession."

"Killing everyone who gets in the way is also not normal." Will points at the screen. "Let's see what else she says."

"Tell us what happened with your friends in Huddersfield." Finn changes tack.

"We argued. They were being really bitchy to me. Jen said I'd never get married. She said no one would want me. The others laughed and agreed with her. I don't see why not. I'm prettier than they are, so maybe they're jealous. Anyway, I'm pleased they're dead. They didn't deserve to stay alive."

"Did you cause their deaths?"

Penny flushes after her solicitor gives her a discreet nudge. "No comment."

The interview continues. Our suspect continues to withhold answers to direct questions regarding the murders, but gives herself away in so many other ways. She builds a picture of a lonely young girl who developed a crush on an attractive boy. But unlike most crushes, this one didn't go away; it developed into an unhealthy obsession with a man who was not interested in her, and never would be. As a result, six people are now dead.

After the door closes behind Finn and Ian, Penny turns to her solicitor. "How did I do?" she asks. She looks almost triumphant.

"I'm going to have a hard job in court if you want me to plead innocence, but I'll have no problems with getting a plea of insanity, if that's what you're after."

"What do you mean? I'm not crazy. They had to die, and I did it. That doesn't make me mad."

"Penny, you killed six innocent people. That makes you

either insane or evil. The court will find you guilty of one or the other. Would you prefer to be in a hospital or a prison?"

The door opens and Finn comes in. I turn to him with a finger on my lips, then point at the monitor.

"Neither. I want to marry Troy and live happily ever after."

It's impossible to judge whether she believes it can happen, but it's clear to me she's lost her grip on reality.

The solicitor shakes her head in apparent disbelief, or maybe shock, and a heartbeat later the door opens again. A couple of uniformed officers enter and remove Penny.

"They'll take her off to the cells for tonight," says Finn. "Do you guys want to get going, and I'll catch up with you tomorrow?"

Chapter Forty-Three

The days that follow are filled with news coming through. Matt is less shocked than I was to discover Finn's betrayal.

"I always knew something was wrong there. He visited you once in hospital, but then we heard nothing more from him. It smacked to me of a guilty conscience. Obviously it coincided with his rehab, so maybe that's why he didn't come to see you again. All the same, it just didn't feel right."

I accept his explanation. There's no point asking why he said nothing at the time. I had enough to cope with. A betrayal by Finn would have been too much for my fragile mental state. I'm not able to shrug it off, but work is taking priority, and I speak to Finn almost daily as news comes through.

An initial examination of Penny's flat reveals only her fingerprints, but the bins have not yet been emptied, and yield many items of bloodstained clothes that link the wearer to the murder scenes of the girls in Huddersfield and of Troy's parents. The clothes are found in black bin-liners.

"How did she get them from the crime scenes?" I ask Finn by phone. "She had no car as far as I can tell. And her moped was in the garage the entire time being fixed. I kept ringing up to make an appointment to check it out, and had to cancel each time, but I don't think it left the garage the whole time. Surely she didn't travel on the bus in bloodstained clothes?"

He comes back to me the next day.

"They found a rucksack under a loose floorboard of her flat. Inside were bloodstained black trainers, and next to the backpack was a black t-shirt, hoody and leggings. They match an outfit that someone of her height and build was seen wearing as they got off the bus from Huddersfield in Manchester on Thursday night last week. The complete kit has gone off to forensics to check for DNA matches to tie her to that crime scene, and possibly the others."

Another day, he calls again.

"We've found the knife." He sounds triumphant.

"Well done. How and where?" I put the mobile on speakerphone so that Joanna and Will can hear. Will has just returned from Edinburgh in a clapped-out Ford Focus, which he quickly leads us to understand won't be a fixture for long.

"Well, after we found that loose floorboard, it seemed sensible to check for others. We couldn't find any, but one of our SOCOs stubbed her toe on the kitchen plinth, and it moved – the plinth, not her toe."

"And?"

"Behind the plinth, there was a flattish black case, containing house-breaking tools, and a lethal-looking knife. There were signs of blood on the blade, although it had been rinsed. It's gone to forensics for a detailed examination, and they're taking apart the sink to check for blood in the plumbing, if that's where she's been washing her tools."

"That's impressive detecting. I hope your team will get a lot of kudos for this."

"Sure. Someone took a photo of the bruise on Katy's big toe, and it's got pride of place on the case noticeboard – with the headline *BIG TOE SOLVES CRIME*. Not strictly accurate, but it seems to cause a lot of amusement."

After ending the call, I search my phone for Katy (who I remember fondly from previous cases). I locate her quite easily from an archived contacts list, and send her a message congratulating her on her excellent detection skills, and wishing her toe a speedy recovery.

With the case wrapping up well, I devote a few days to my family. Matt is much better now, and is looking forward to being able to drive again next week.

Finding our client guilty of murder is a bit of a worry on the financial front, but then, Joanna rings me.

"Guess what's arrived in the post?" She sounds as giddy as a teenager.

"No idea." I reckon she wants to tell me herself, and who am I to spoil her fun?

"A cheque from Troy. A reward for finding the killer." She pauses, and I give her a few seconds to build up to telling me the amount. "Becks, it's for ten thousand pounds!"

"Wow. That should keep the wolf from the door for a bit." I make a mental note to drop him a thank-you message as soon as the call ends.

Cheryl and Joel are definitely going out now, and she seems happier than she has been for many months.

I spend today typing up notes from the case. We have some lessons to learn, and we'll be discussing them over a takeaway this evening. It's now a week to the day since Emma's abduction. I followed up with Troy this morning. Gaz and the boys, and Linda's parents, are rallying round and supporting him and Emma. It will take a long time for him to get over this, but he has family, and he has good friends to help.

I return from my takeaway at 10pm. It's been a good session, discussing the case with Joanna and Will, but as I drive into my path, my skin prickles. Something is not right. I glance around the street. The neighbours' cars are parked as usual, but a black Audi is there too. It's familiar, but I can't think for a moment. I turn the engine off, brace myself, and get out of the car as swiftly as I can. I rush into my house to be greeted in the hall.

"Well done, Becky. You did a good job on that case." Roger is standing in the doorway of my lounge, leaning against the doorframe. "You have work to do though. There's no time to relax. I know you haven't yet started those Russian lessons, and your hacking skills are still awaiting their existence. Get on with it. You will need them very soon."

When Roger has gone, Matt turns to me.

"This arrived while you were out." He hands me a brown envelope.

I open it and extract a sheet of white paper containing a few lines of print.

Fascinated to see you have reunited with your friends in the police force, ex-DI Wiseman. Your new name is far less formal – I like it.

I was however sorry to see the ease with which you escaped my friend on the train. We will be better prepared next time, and you will have no way out.

Looking forward to seeing you again soon, Becky White. Remember, you are being watched.

TO BE CONTINUED

Also by Jo Fenton

THE BECKY WHITE THRILLERS

Revelation

Fabergé

THE ABBEY SERIES

The Brotherhood

The Refuge

Acknowledgements

Thank you to everyone who has made this book possible.

Firstly, as always, I'd like to thank my amazing friend and incredibly talented editor, Sue Barnard. We've worked together on four books now, and it's always a huge pleasure.

Sue is also one of the Manchester Scribes, who have helped with monthly critiques of the earlier chapters, and made sure I was on the right track, despite the difficulties of moving to critiquing via zoom! The other awesome Scribes are Pauline Barnett, Louise Jones, Karen Moore, Claire Tansey, Awen Thornber, Helen Sea and Grant Silk.

Another critical step in the writing process is Beta Reading. My fantastic beta readers were hugely important in making sure the story worked on all levels and ensuring there were no plot holes. Massive thanks to Sue Barnard (again), Pauline, Barnett, Ray Fenton, Katy Johnson and Karen Moore.

As always, my family are essential in supporting me through writing my novels. I could not do without my fabulous husband, Ray, for all his help and advice, reading, sharing ideas, and continuing to do far more than his share of housework so I could have valuable writing time. My lovely boys, Michael and Andrew also listened to me bounce ideas around and were very honest with their feedback.

Thanks also go to my mum, Rhoda Myers, who helped again with my final proofread despite treatment induced fatigue.

Finally, a humungous thank you to both my first publisher,

Darkstroke, and to my new publisher Bloodhound for all the hard work needed to launch this novel and for all the fabulous support along the way.

About the Author

Jo Fenton grew up in Hertfordshire. She devoured books from an early age and, at eleven, discovered Agatha Christie and Georgette Heyer. She now has an eclectic and much loved book collection cluttering her home office.

Jo combines an exciting career in Clinical Research with an equally exciting but very different career as a writer of psychological thrillers.

When not working, she runs (very slowly), and chats to lots of people. She lives in Manchester with her family and is an active and enthusiastic member of two writing groups and three reading groups.

A note from the publisher

Thank you for reading this book. If you enjoyed it please do consider leaving a review on Amazon to help others find it too.

We hate typos. All of our books have been rigorously edited and proofread, but sometimes mistakes do slip through. If you have spotted a typo, please do let us know and we can get it amended within hours.

info@bloodhoundbooks.com